The
Double Life
of
Incorporate
Things

Cover and interior design by Stephen H. Segal
Cover photo by Nik Merkulov/Fotolia

Published by Deus Ex Victoriana
For more information and contact details:
leannareneehieber.com
twitter.com/leannarenee
facebook.com/lrhieber

The Double Life
of
Incorporate Things

by
LEANNA RENEE HIEBER

"There are some qualities—some incorporate things,
That have a double life, which thus is made
A type of that twin entity which springs
From matter and light, evinced in solid and shade."

—Edgar Allan Poe

Chapter One

OCTOBER, 1880

The New York Herald:

MADISON MADNESS—"MOURNING" HOOLIGANS
WAGE RAMPAGE ON CITY

Saturday night, a horde of black-clad youths, men and women in an altered state, recklessly endangered themselves and others in a sprawling public fit following a "wake" at the home of the British Emissary's daughter Lavinia Kent. The Kents have lived in New York City for nearly six years. While her family was out of town, it seems Miss Kent threw a soiree that Poe in all his ridiculous dark abandon would have envied for one of his tall tales. Even Miss Kent's poor chaperone was persuaded to partake in "The Cure": a chemical concoction promised to obliterate melancholy and despair.

Miss Kent chairs the group known as "Her Majesty's Association for Melancholy Bastards," a group affiliated with British actor Nathaniel Veil. When asked why they were all dressed in funereal attire, one girl known only as Raven—presumably in honor of Mr. Poe—said she'd come not only to partake of The Cure but for a wake. (Though no one had died.) They were, it was said, in "mourning for their life."

Those who took the substance, which could be inhaled as a powder or mixed into a fluid and consumed, were then purportedly changed mentally and physically. An hour after imbibing the concoction, the party charged up Madison Avenue, howling and tossing aside anything or anyone in their paths. Witnesses described superhuman strength, mesmerism, and suggestion. Those who encountered the mob said the youths held onlookers in thrall, even as they were roughhoused and bullied.

After a while, horrified onlookers said the crowd simply collapsed, silk frocks and coattails ruined, mourning veils shredded. Strewn on lawns and street corners, the youth had to be roused by various officers of the peace. Most, once roused, fainted dead away again or began weeping. "We're not animals," Raven insisted. "We don't lose our heads like this. Nathaniel will be so angry with us." Miss Kent herself declined to comment.

Whether Nathaniel Veil had any hand in this mess is unclear save for the association with his Association. The fact that this could be a mere publicity stunt has escaped no one. Veil recently returned to England to continue his run of ACROSS THE VEIL, a show on Gothic themes, musings on life, death, and dramatic explorations of the paranormal. (A show, this newspaper might add, that did not receive a favorable review within these pages.) After this little interlude he may want to be wary of his welcome back as he is slated to return for another run at the Astor by the end of next month.

Participants in the incident were charged with disrupting the peace and public drunkenness. A search for the provider of said "cure" is being launched by police, albeit with skepticism. Is there really a drug at work here or was this an excuse to lash out? Surely its merely sheer, overdramatic hooliganism at its morbidly dressed worst.

I set the paper down slowly enough to see the thin edges shake as the full, personal impact of the newspaper article hit me.

"Natalie, what is it?" Jonathon asked, staring at me with those eviscerating blue eyes of his. I opened my mouth but no sound came out. Damn my unpredictable, inconstant voice.

For the past many months now, I'd been pummeled by one strange event after another, pulled into the center of a paranormal whirlpool. At least in this case, we had an inkling, some sense of the next onslaught. Still, a foreshadow was hardly a comfort. We couldn't have guessed the scope.

Now it wasn't just myself or Jonathon Whitby, Lord Denbury, in danger, with the occasional collateral victim. Now it was a crowd. I knew the Association. I adored them. They weren't hooligans or criminals, they were gentle souls, artistic and individual. Overdramatic, yes, but a threat? Hardly. This maligning was the work of The Master's Society, turning lambs into lions in ungodly experiments, leaving them for fodder in sensational, indelicate journalism. It could only get worse. Exponentially worse.

"It's begun," I finally managed to reply quietly, sliding the paper across the lacquered console table behind the sofa toward Jonathon's reach. "Another phase. They've gone after the Association. And the papers will vilify those poor dears, every last one of them. Jonathon, the demons won't give up..."

I rose nervously, going to the lace-covered window of Mrs. Evelyn Northe's fine parlor so I might watch New York City's richest and finest parade about Fifth Avenue, Central Park their magnificent backdrop, while Jonathon read the article that had so upset me.

Once he finished he looked up, tossing the paper onto a nearby writing desk. "Indeed. The demons seem hell-bent on making everyone else as miserable as they must be. Well then, let's find that laboratory where that damnable concoction was brewed." His upper-class British accent made his words crisp and biting, his tone laced with a bitter undercurrent; he was a man ready to go to war. "Shall we?"

I turned to him as a trolley car rumbled downtown, the rattle of the long cab matching my nerves. Jonathon was across the room, sitting tall and composed in a blue armchair upholstered in a fabric as expensive as his black suit. The blue of the chair magnified the shocking ice blue of his eyes. Waves of onyx locks framed his handsome face and completed the elegant symphony of blue and black. I wondered if there would ever come a time when he wouldn't take my breath away when I turned to look at him. Or if I'd ever stop being terrified of losing him.

"Jonathon, no, we can't go," I finally replied. "You've been compromised. You can't play the demon. Remember the note?"

"Ah yes." He smiled, a bit too confidently. "This note?"

He dipped a hand to an interior pocket and pulled out two items, a folded paper and an envelope. He opened the first folded paper, showcasing one line of neat black script that had chilled me to the bone. Even from across the room the words hissed:

"They're coming for you."

The phrase had become a recent feature in my nightmares. "Yes, that note," I said through clenched teeth.

He smiled again. "But I received *this* in yesterday's mail. A new development. Have a look."

He slid the small, neat envelope across the console as I'd done with the newspaper. We had to sit across the room from one another, being unmarried. It was the moral thing to do. The fact that no chaperone was present was a testament to the fact that any who knew us had given up on the idea that Lord Denbury and I could ever have a *normal* courtship. Still, we *tried* to be proper.

The envelope was addressed to Lord Denbury in the same neat, flourished script as the warning note had been, the paper of a finer weave than had ever passed over my gloved fingertips. There was a small black seal on the back, with a crest that looked important. But I suppose all crests look like they carry weight. If our family had a crest, I'd no idea; I was descended of middle-class academics.

I opened the note Jonathon had already unsealed and read:

My dear Lord Denbury,

Your situation has made itself known to me. First, let me say I am very glad to learn you're not dead. Secondly, I'm glad you're no longer a demon. Thirdly, I'm terribly sorry about all your wretched luck.

I followed the course of your portrait with some interest and have been in contact with a friend, a solicitor who I understand assisted you. Mr. Knowles informs me you made contact with the "Majesty," one of three heads of a group known as the Master's Society. Ears we have employed inside that very office in Earl's Court you visited tell us a lackey could be en route to look in on you. I doubt kindly, so don't prepare tea. Take care.

But know you are not alone.

I was assigned to New York City five years ago, employed in most secret investigation, by orders from the highest and most precious in the land. I wish to meet with you. To do so, please hire a southbound carriage at the intersection of 75th and Lexington this coming Friday at 1:25 in the afternoon. Instruct the carriage to turn right at 74th, continue south down Madison, right on 72nd, and then westward; we shall meet at the park entrance. Don't worry, I'll find you. Keep your faith and your head, you'll need them both.

Your friend,

Sir G. Brinkman,
Secret Investigator
Employed by Her Majesty, and Empress, Queen Victoria
PS Please burn after reading

I looked up at him, frowning. Secret investigator? "You've spies? Here? Spying on us? Why?"

"British spies span the world, my dear. We've an Empire, remember."

I wrinkled my nose. "Last time I checked, this country fought a revolution and threw you out."

"All the more reason for spies." Jonathon grinned. He glanced around to see if we might be seen, jumped to his feet, and rushed to lock one strong arm about my waist. "We must keep a watchful eye on our wayward cousins here in our former colony." He pressed his forehead to mine. "Who knows what they might get up to? We have to make sure they're on their...best behavior..." He trailed a hand down my body.

I giggled as I gasped. His ability to set me afire remained overwhelming. Leaning in to him I murmured with my lips so very near his. "Are *we* really the ones who need watching? I'd beware all those entitled lords thinking they can just come over here and have their way with any American girl..."

Jonathon blinked. He slid his hands down my waist and clapped about my bustle. "Can't we?" He grinned as I laughed, diving in to kiss my neck. It was true. He could have his way with me if I wasn't careful. But before that happened... There was a little business of engagement. One could not play loosely with virtue. Not a woman with any pride or decency. Not a *lady.* "Ah, but you're not just *any* American girl," he murmured, his breath hot upon the hollow of my throat. "You were the inimitable girl heaven sent to save me. The *only* girl to see my plight. The only one brave enough risk your life for mine." He pulled back to gaze into my eyes, his playful seduction transformed into deathly earnest. "And I'll not lose sight for one moment of the fact I'll never be able to repay the debt."

I kissed him softly on the lips, wanting to indulge more, but painfully aware that at any moment meant Father or Mrs. Northe could come around the hall and in through the open pocket doors. "You mustn't live in debt to me," I murmured.

"Then I'll live a life in love with you," he replied.

There he went again, with words to make me weak in the knees. Such words meant I threw myself at him for another kiss, this one longer. We heard a step on the stair. He broke away with a moan and stepped back a few paces. We looked, but no one approached the pocket doors of the parlor so he didn't cross the room entirely.

"I must meet Brinkman. Straightaway. Just as he's said," Jonathon said brightly, fishing in another pocket for a box of matches. He'd been enjoying Mr. Northe's den of fine cigars a bit too often, it would seem, to have matches so easily on hand.

I raised an eyebrow. "You seem rather cheerful about it."

"Help, Natalie, my love. We finally have *help*."

"We've always had Mrs. Northe."

"And bless her for all that she's done. But remember, we've not always had her. She ran off to Chicago in the hour of our need—"

"And in doing so saved your friend, and who knows what else she got up to out there, she was up to something—"

"Natalie, we'll need all the help we can get. And if it's from Her Majesty herself? Well then, color me a bit patriotic and proud!" Jonathon cried, and if I wasn't mistaken, he almost puffed out his chest a bit. He struck a match and suddenly the note from Brinkman was in flames per the agent's request.

"How will you know Brinkman, Jonathon? An elaborate path to the park hardly helps you identify him. How do you know he's not one of *theirs*?"

Jonathon tapped between his eyes. "If nothing else, the curse gave me second sight. It has proven true that I see auras of brimstone, like hellfire, upon sight of a Society operative. But around Knowles there is a faint pale light. Mrs. Northe too. And you? Simply angelic. I'll get one look at Brinkman, and friend or foe will be immediately evident."

"Just... take your pistol." I folded my arms. "And I'm going with you. I hope you memorized those instructions because I don't remember the details of what you just burned."

Jonathon sighed. "I copied them down, Natalie. Will it do me any good to say that I don't want you to come with me or be placed in any possible danger—"

"Teams work together and that's final."

"I supposed as much—"

"But what do I tell Father?" I asked earnestly. The ongoing question that would plague us until we could make our relationship more permanent was what to tell my father. The truth? Or a pleasant lie that would harm no one and keep him from worrying? But considering we were unable to shield Father from the horrors that had befallen me on Denbury's account, I didn't know what he'd accept or reject. Before I could wonder further, Jonathon answered.

"That it's a lovely day for a walk," Jonathon said with even brighter cheer, this time forced, moving to stand a further pace apart from me and looking toward the open pocket doors.

"Indeed," my father said, startling me with his entrance behind me. "It's a lovely day for you, Natalie, to show your lord here your precious Central Park!"

I had wanted to celebrate our recent victory over the demon by spending days luxuriating in my beloved park, sharing my favorite place on earth with the incredible man who had fought with me, through hell and back, to be by my side. But fear of "they're coming for you" had us keeping more indoors, with Mrs. Northe's private guards on the watch. We hadn't told my father about that note. We were scared he'd forbid me from seeing Jonathon again, as he'd done just before I nearly died. My throat still bore the faint traces of the demons' bruises.

"Don't you think so, Lord Denbury?" my father said, his eyes bright. "A beautiful day in the park to set things on the *proper* course?"

"Yes, Mr. Stewart," Jonathon said. I could have sworn a nervous shudder rippled through him.

I had grown intimately accustomed to body language during my many years suffering from Selective Mutism due to the trauma of my mother's death. Years of silence meant I could read physical cues like a book, and I read Jonathon uncannily well. And while I had only perused a part of that particular library and I wanted to pore over every page, something about his nervousness had butterflies launching into flight within me too. Something about my father's phrase and tone kindled a little spark of hope...

Jonathon fidgeted with his coat sleeves. He never fidgeted. I bit my lip.

Father at long last broke the tense silence. "Evelyn has excused herself I know not where," he said mournfully. "I was hoping to promenade with her, alas, I must leave it to the young." He wagged his finger. "Though I shan't be *too* far behind..."

"Ah. Yes." Jonathon said, patted his breast pocket, moved crisply into the entrance hall, checked his reflection in the tall wardrobe mirror, and turned to me with his most winning smile. "Miss Stewart?" He held out his arm.

"My lord." I smiled, my heart hammering, and we set off, Jonathon suddenly acting as though he'd seen a ghost...

Chapter Two

There is nothing so beautiful in all the world as Central Park in autumn. I've been known to make bold and declarative statements that I will later temper if I'm in less dramatic of a mood. But this is a statement I can put my full weight behind no matter my state of mind.

Central Park is heaven. And even more so if you're in love.

I had been nearly killed several times in the past few months. There's nothing that gives a person perspective as much as facing death, and nothing that gives as much liberty to speak dramatically as having survived. I had not known Jonathon Whitby, Lord Denbury, for long. And yet, we had saved each other's lives several times now. Nothing shows truth of character or purity of heart more than saving another soul. I daresay Jonathon and I knew more of one another in a mere few months than those who have spent untroubled years side by side. We had seen death side by side, and our mere survival had shed a deal of light on love.

Descending the stoop and drawing onward toward the grand expanse of the park ahead of us, I had hopes in my heart, as any young romantic might. My father had his pressures and concerns. Denbury's lineage had still further strictures. I was a nervous wreck, wondering if this might be the day that he would ask for my hand or if some heretofore unknown obstacle would yet keep us apart. He was eighteen, as I would be within a few months, and we were no longer children. Society placed demands upon a man and woman who enjoyed each other's company in the way that we did.

My preoccupation was overtaken, as it always was, by the charm of the park. My racing thoughts calmed once surrounded by lush green, over eight hundred acres worth, in winding vistas and charming expanses. The park has been over thirty years in its construction, with improvements yearly. It is a man-made Eden sculpted and curated to present myriad poetic compositions and countless breathtaking views, built to be like a living salon of landscape portraits. A thousand different parks live within one long central rectangle. Eden lives at the heart of Metropolitan chaos. In any and all directions, the view is beautiful. And the park brings out the beauty in people, wanting to wear their Sunday best even on a Tuesday. The park remains an event in and of itself. Not barred or gated like royal gardens of old, this was built as, and will remain, a park of the people. And the people are devoted to that which is theirs.

We entered the park from one of the transverse open gates; many of them had begun to have names etched in stone, but this open mouth had yet to be named. Jonathon and I strolled arm in arm, my light yellow lace parasol cocked at an angle to block as much of the hazy autumn sun as possible. My father hung back many paces, pretending not to be looking at us, a newspaper tucked under his elbow. I felt strained and scrutinized, and my natural urge to relax against Jonathon's hand that so often liked to wander freely over my back was held in check. My muscles were rigid against my corset boning, Jonathon's hand stiff upon the stays; all the effortless ease of our relationship felt stifled by all that was expected of us.

Once we were inside the park Jonathon looked to me to guide him, and I gestured forward, curving slightly downtown along a winding path, one I knew well.

Jonathon took in the surroundings. "Lovely place. It looks like the English countryside."

"I believe that was rather the point," I replied.

Jonathon shook his head. "Americans. You child imitators."

I scowled. "Don't tease my favorite place. You just wait until you see her..."

Ahead of us lay my patron saint, my angel, the crux of the park's magic.

The Bethesda Terrace was the park's new crown jewel, an enormous arched stone terrace with finely hewn stairs and elaborate stone carvings on vast rails leading in a grand descent to a brick courtyard below, stretching generously out toward a still pool of water where gentlemen rowed parasol-bedecked ladies in rowboats about a curving inlet, a more thickly forested patch of the park beyond.

At the center of this grand plaza was the Angel of the Waters, tall and gloriously presiding atop her fountain; a vast circular basin and uplifting cherubim lay below her. She represented that biblical story of fresh spring bubbling up from the rock she touched, her step bringing forth life and renewal, her wings outstretched, the folds of her skirt billowing, her form of powerful grace serving as a memorial for the Union dead. The fountain poured water from a basin at the angel's feet toward a larger basin below, and then dropped further unto a vast wide circular pool, its basin at knee level.

"This is admittedly spectacular," Jonathon murmured.

This got a smile out of me, and I squeezed his hand before breaking away. Bending to touch my fingers into the water, I instinctively brought my wet finger to my forehead and made the sign of the cross as if in renewal of baptism. The angel had become, from the moment I first laid eyes upon her, my patron saint. I brought all my troubles and joys unto her. Today I had brought her my greatest joy, this man at my side. Despite all the troubles he'd inadvertently laid at my feet. I begged the angel's blessing as if she were my mother, and I hoped that my mother indeed was watching now, as she'd been present in my last battle. I could only hope she was with me now when life was so gloriously alive, not only when death was so perilously close.

"We've been through so much, you and I," Jonathon began hesitantly, taking a seat upon the rounded basin ledge of the fountain. "I don't know where to begin. How could I capture the last few months?" He spoke as if he weren't sure he were in the right tense or even language. A decisive conversationalist in normal circumstances, this was an odd departure.

"My diary helped frame my thoughts. At first. But then, in gaining my voice, I no longer needed a diary in the same way. Then I had you to talk to... So just...talk to me," I offered with a little smile. Jonathon stared into the water, his handsome reflection looking up at him with wide eyes. He didn't seem able to look at me so I looked at all the glory around him.

Behind Jonathon marched the beautiful Romanesque arches of the terrace platform where painted tiles graced the ceiling and led couples promenading, children running, contemplative souls wandering on their own, underneath the transverse road and toward another grand staircase beyond that led up unto the Great Mall where trees arched in one long avenue toward Manhattan's bustle once more. The clop of horse hooves atop the terrace, beyond its grand balcony, was a gentle, lulling rhythm as fine carriages, open calashes, and carts rolled past in steady streams.

Jonathon was oddly still, but the park around him burst with life and activity. Boys ran about in clusters on the grass, couples reclined upon blankets in the shade of the rolling hills that sloped up beyond the terrace walls, the occasional bird fluttered about from tree to tree, a few notes of music were carried on the breeze from a balladeer or from a boat passengers serenading on the water.

"There is so much expected of me," he murmured. "So much I'm afraid I've failed at because of everything that's happened to me. I don't know if I can fix it, Natalie. Can I be the lord I'm meant to be in this lifetime anymore?" He pierced me with a wide, panicked stare that unsettled me. I wasn't sure what answer he wanted out of me, and his nerves were affecting my own confidence.

"I believe," I said, trying to keep my voice calm. This was not helped by the sight of my father. He stood far beyond on the terrace balcony and looked away when I looked up. "That you, Jonathon Whitby, can do and be anything you wish."

"All that's been taken from me, Natalie. It's maddening. Every day the anger and injustice of what's been done builds. I've had no resolution. No justice. I don't want to be driven by revenge." He looked up at the beautiful surroundings, and I kept hoping he would take comfort in them as I did, but he looked back into the water again, and I could see the expression of his reflection darken. "I hate when hate consumes me... That's not who I want to be."

These were hardly the words of affection, promises, or question I was hoping he'd ask.

"No, hateful isn't who you are," I said, trying to be soothing. I understood his pain, his loss, never allowed to grieve his parents, his estate, all that had been stolen for no comprehensible reason. But I couldn't change what had been done to him. "Look around you, at this beautiful space, none of what happened to you matters here—"

"But it's here, in me, and I can't just ignore it," he hissed, hitting his chest with a fist and standing suddenly. He began to walk away. I followed, forward, toward the inlet of the reservoir beyond, where a path veered off along thick bushes. "I don't want to rise to all the challenges I'm being put to. Right now, I'm not sure I want to be the better person, not toward my enemies." He whirled to me, grabbing me by the arms then dragging me farther into a copse of underbrush. "But you, I do want to be better to you..." he murmured, a desperate edge to his voice that I hadn't heard since his soul's trapped days in the painting. "And your father insists I do what's right. Of course. But I just... I'm forced to do so much..."

I blushed, feeling awkward. "I don't want to be the reason you're forced into anything."

I couldn't be sure about where my father had shifted to; for the moment the foliage blocked us from the above road. I'm sure our disappearance had him wondering too.

"Well, like it or not, Natalie, you are," Jonathon responded. His clipped words were not comforting. "I have to do many things that defy convention. My life has seen to that now. You're not of my class, not of my world, but I must do right by you."

I stared at him, wondering if I'd just been insulted while he was trying to be "noble."

"I know I'm not of your station," I murmured, kicking at a pebble on the uneven path with my boot that, next to his, was hardly as fine. "Not of your world. I already feel awkward about that, Jonathon, you don't need to make it worse—"

"Natalie, I don't mean—"

"I don't see how else that could be interpreted, it's true..."

This path wasn't as kempt or populated, and perhaps it was this that emboldened Jonathon. Clumsily, he dived in to kiss me, which I allowed for a moment because I was too disoriented to stop him, though an inelegant pawing wasn't his usual method and I was debating on whether or not to be insulted. The upper class often dismissed the rest of the world with ease. I could not tolerate that for myself; it would hurt too much to be thought "lesser" when I didn't believe that to be true. I drew back and stared at him. He stared back with wide eyes, a flash of panic in those ice-blue spheres.

And then, suddenly, he dropped to his knee, one hand fumbling in his pocket for something, a branch whacking me in the leg as he did so. My eyes went wide. No, no. After that troubled outburst? And here? In the shrubbery?

"Marry me—" he began but was stopped by my fingertips as they pressed fully upon his mouth.

"No, Jonathon, you're doing it wrong."

He blinked up at me for a long moment before ducking to the side of my hasty, shushing fingers, abandoning whatever had been in his pocket. "Beg your pardon?"

"Jonathon, the way you're talking? No. You're unsure, sweating and stammering—"

"Proposals make men nervous—"

"And vaguely rude. You need to be absolutely sure about this, pressured by nothing else but your own heart." I looked around at the unkempt underbrush we were surrounded by, frustrated. Did I not deserve some grand place where if his noble offer was seen by others, it would merely be applauded? Was I some secret to be kept? Hidden? Yet another of his burdens, rushed into legitimacy? "And we're in the middle of the *bushes*, Jonathon," I added, hurt in my tone. "Try again with a...better vista. Darling."

He stared up at me from his knee, baffled, speaking as if he could not believe his own words. "You, Miss Natalie Stewart, just turned down a British Lord."

I blushed, partly in embarrassment, partly in frustration. "I did not turn you down, though considered your entitled position, I bet you aren't used to that."

"All that's happened to me of late hasn't felt very *entitled*, Natalie," he said, deep pain in his voice.

I stared up at him with wide eyes, willing him to see both the overwhelming love in my heart and my fear that he wasn't ready. "I want to marry you," I exclaimed and said his title achingly, "*Lord Denbury*, and be a lady to you, like none other could ever be. But only if you sound like you really mean it." I stared at the ground. "Ask me because you don't think class matters. As if my father doesn't matter. You ask because you *want* to—"

"For the love of God, Natalie, I *want* to marry you!" he exclaimed, exasperated.

I looked into his eyes a moment, my stomach churning. "Here? In a tangle of briars? Here it's like I'm some rushed secret you're afraid to share, like you're hiding me—"

"That isn't true, and that isn't fair," he muttered, standing finally, brushing off his slightly mud-besmirched knee.

"Maybe it isn't. But this isn't the place. And you're not in a state of mind that should make this promise. Not right now."

"You are something else, Miss Natalie Stewart," Jonathon said with a chuckle, shaking his head. His chuckle lightened the admittedly awkward moment, and I dived in to kiss him softly upon the cheek.

"My father often uses the word 'particular,'" I offered.

"I may add 'difficult,'" Jonathon muttered, stalking away and back to the path. I followed after him. It wasn't as though I could argue that point. But I wouldn't apologize, either. Facing death, it would seem, only solidified my stubborn self. I had to believe there would be a better moment ahead for a proposal.

At the head of the path, I could see my father pretending to be engrossed in a newspaper he wasn't holding right side up. I could see his gaze zero in on my hand. He wasn't the best with subtlety. When he did not see a ring there, he frowned and tried to wipe the disappointed expression off his face when he saw us looking at him, but it was too late. He knew there had been no progress toward propriety today, and I'm sure he assumed it was somehow my fault. There was an exchange between my father and Jonathon—perhaps an eye roll or an exasperate shrug—but I missed it, needing to focus on lifting my skirts enough to not trip up the walk. I caught the swing of my father's head as if he'd been shaking it wearily.

We all walked in silence to Mrs. Northe's home where we had planned on eating dinner together. As Mary let us in the front door, I noticed extra top hats on the pegs beside the great foyer armoire and heard voices in the parlor beyond.

The widowed Mrs. Northe appeared to greet us, statuesque and stately as ever, blonde hair with streaks of silver swept up in artful, stunning filigree clasps that were nothing compared to the finery of her plum gown and the elegant jewels glittering about her smiling face.

She approached us with a fond chuckle, kissing my father on both cheeks first, a different fondness in her blue eyes for him than the affection she had for me, something I was still getting used to, but thankfully their courtship was unfolding far slower than mine, as was likely the case with a widower and a widow. I couldn't say I entirely understood the draw. I adored my father, but he just didn't seem nearly as interesting as Evelyn Northe. I knew that was very unfair of me to think. It would seem Mother and Evelyn were very similar. Maybe my quiet father's gentle, steady hand and sensitive heart were just the sort of thing for inimitable, imperious women.

Taking up my hands in hers, she glanced at them briefly. She was dressed to the nines, finer than a mere dinner with friends required. A subtle exchange of expressions between her and Lord Denbury, her raised brow and his shrug told me something was a bit off. It then hit me like a swift punch to my gut. There had likely been a celebration planned for the evening. To celebrate our engagement. My stomach dropped even further as I looked up into Mrs. Northe's eyes and watched as she masked any presumption and beamed implacably, utterly unruffled.

"I've quite the dinner party lined up tonight, friends," she said in the sisterly, conspiring tone I was accustomed to, "but we've *very* serious business to discuss, and so it's best that we save our celebratory airs for another day." In this, she absolved me of my mishap. I tried to give Jonathon a look of apology, but he was actively avoiding my gaze.

Maybe I was too particular. But I couldn't have said "yes" being that uneasy. In the shrubbery. What's done was done and I hoped there'd be a picture-perfect opportunity in the future. In the meantime, we had company. Mrs. Northe's tone indicated she had gathered out-of-the-ordinary company. For that respite, in this case, I was grateful.

Chapter Three

I looked up at Mrs. Northe, wide-eyed. "Should I...be in finer dress for dinner?" Suddenly the knee-buckling certainty that I could never suitably fill the role of Lady Denbury nearly caused me to stumble against my mentor and substitute mother. I'd turned the poor man down anyway. I'd be lucky if he had the patience to ask me again. My throat felt dry, and I tried to recover myself.

"If you'd like to dress, I've kept something for you upstairs." She chuckled. "But the company here is hardly the kind for that sort of ceremony."

"Did I ruin everything?" I whispered, seeing that Jonathon was eagerly responding to my father's awkward prompt about something museum related.

"I don't know, did you?" she whispered back, flashing a maddeningly mischievous grin.

"Maybe." I sighed. "I'm so sorry about dinner, I didn't know you planned anything—"

"Oh, this is hardly for you. Toasting your engagement would have been a delightful distraction. But with the papers being the way they are—"

"You saw about the Association, they're being targeted, just like Jonathon was—"

"Of course and I've already taken action, which is why this dinner is more important than when, exactly, you accept that dear boy's hand. Come along, let's make introductions." She gestured me forward down the entrance foyer and into the lavish dining room, and I was reminded of all the reasons why I was eternally grateful for her. Though being indebted to anyone chafed at my "woeful sense of independence," as my father called it.

All the best and finest was laid out, glittering and appetizing. The room was as rich and lush in carpeting and drapery as it was in the spread of food before us in crystal, silver, and gold-trimmed china with peacock feather patterns.

I wondered about the elegant silver-haired man in a fine navy suit near the head of the table, but it was the sight of Reverend Blessing, who had helped lead the charge in our recent battle against demons, that had me beaming a smile. And then I recognized another face at the table, a haunted red-headed woman I'd last seen backstage at Nathaniel Veil's show.

"Many of you are acquainted, save for this fine chap here to my right," Mrs. Northe began, brushing a satin-gloved hand that spoke of great familiarity across the gentleman's shoulder. My father's jaw clenched imperceptibly. No one but me would have seen it, but after spending much of my life mute, I read body language as if it were spoken. "This is Senator Rupert Bishop," Mrs. Northe went on, "nobly representing our state in Washington. Rupert and I were childhood friends and attended our first séance together, when was that..."

"Good God," the silver-haired man exclaimed, the chiseled angles of his face curving into a gamesome expression. "Nearly thirty years ago."

Mrs. Northe made a face and batted a hand. "Why did I *ask*? To be clear, we were *children* when we called our first ghost. Rupert's hair turned to winter at twenty, so let's just not speculate about our ages." Everyone chuckled. Mrs. Northe turned her charming presence to my father, and his jaw eased. "This is Gareth Stewart of the Metropolitan Museum of Art and his daughter Miss Natalie." I offered what felt like a somewhat awkward smile. She did not introduce Jonathon. He hadn't entered the room and was perhaps still lingering in the hall.

My father bowed his head to the assembled company and addressed Mr. Bishop. "Pleasure to meet you, senator. My late wife was grateful for your support of her causes. You may have met her, she was always out and about..." he said with soft fondness that made me ache for the woman I'd never known, save for the fact she saved my life twice, once from the grave. She died for me when I was four, pushing me out of the way of a reckless carriage, and her spirit returned to rescue me yet again, from a demon's grip.

"Helen Stewart, you must mean, what a loss," the senator said quietly. That my mother had made an impact a senator could recall more than a decade after her death caused a lump to rise in my throat. My father nodded briefly, by now steeled to the loss but never unaffected by the mention of her name in public.

"She was the toast of our ASPCA benefits," Reverend Blessing piped in with his sonorous voice, a brilliant smile flashing a white crescent across his brown skin.

"Yes, she was," Senator Bishop added. "As passionate against animal cruelty as she was to cruelty to *any* creature!" Bishop shared in the reverend's warm smile before turning kind, gray-green eyes to my father and then to me. "Mister and Miss Stewart, I'm sorry to say I've been in Washington when your Metropolitan soirees grace the upper echelon of the town. Let's coordinate, as I'd love to attend one in the future."

"We'd be honored to have you, sir," my father replied.

Jonathon entered. I hoped he hadn't been out there pouting. Whatever his mood, he was the picture of calm stoicism as he bowed his head to the assembled company and spoke with crisp softness that could hold a room in thrall. "Reverend Blessing, sir, good to see you, and why, Miss Kent," Jonathon murmured, turning to the redhead who was sitting a seat apart from everyone, dressed all in black as was the custom of Mister Veil's *Association*. "I..."

"Didn't expect to see me here?" Her tone was clipped with a fine London accent made more pointed by her anxiety. She set her pretty lips into a prim line, her eyes glittering with tears that she held back. "Yes. I couldn't have predicted it, either. But as you well know Mrs. Northe is a godsend."

"Miss Lavinia Kent." Mrs. Northe gestured, presenting the poor, haunted girl before shooing us all into our places at the table.

"I'm afraid I still don't entirely understand what occurred, Miss Kent," Senator Bishop began gently, leaning his tall form closer across the table in a way that was engaged but nonthreatening. "Papers never tell the full story, nor an unbiased one. Could I ask you to elaborate?"

Lavinia stared into her soup as she spoke, seasoning the broth with an occasional tear, her British accent lighter for her years in New York. "We had seen the leaflet for a "cure for melancholy" at Nathaniel's show, in the program. I know he"—she looked up guiltily at Jonathon—"and you, Lord Denbury, had asked me to go take them all out. And I did, but I kept one. It haunted me, called to me. I wanted to know what it was about, and I wasn't the only one who had kept one of those papers. Curiosity is such a temptation. I inquired after the address, and a package was simply sent to my home in reply, a few vials and testimonial tracts. We distributed the drug and awaited bliss. For those of us who've attempted suicide, we hoped for salvation. It was instead an invitation to hell. True, the serum had an amazing effect. Opposite what it promised. Intense euphoria became torture. There was nothing to stop us, least of all ourselves."

Her bright eyes were reddened by tears, her mouth twisted with shame and pain as she continued. "And that's the horror of it. See, we've learned to combat our demons; we were just looking for a bit of help. But this hurt instead, the cut direct. What's the worst insult to weary people who valiantly manage to control their demons? Take away their control and make them the demon. There's nothing more cruel."

There was a quiet silence. Not tense, but merely empathetic. Her words paralleled Jonathon's experience eerily. I looked over and saw the same haunted visage I recognized from the days when his soul was trapped in a painting while a demon ran around in his likeness. Mrs. Northe broke the quiet gently by prompting. "Miss Kent's family was going to—"

"Send me off to a histrionic ward," Lavinia finished harshly what Mrs. Northe had begun delicately.

"But the senator and I told them there was no need for that, and I offered to take her in," Mrs. Northe replied.

"We've seen too many delicate souls, gifted souls, ruined by a world that doesn't understand," the elegant Senator Bishop added. "You remind me so much of my ward, Clara, gifted and sensitive. If I hadn't taken her in after her parents' death, I don't know what would've become of her. Some souls simply aren't for this earth. And yet, we are put here for a reason. To help those who *are* here understand that life is so much more than the limited dimensions of a first glance."

Lavinia clung to the senator's words as if they were a rope leading her out of a dark tunnel. I liked this man. I agreed with his words heartily and was compelled by his demeanor, his effortless magnetism, but something ate at me. Something that wasn't the senator's fault at all, but Mrs. Northe's...

What about Margaret Hathorn? Poor, misled, and maddening Maggie, who had stupidly gone and unwittingly cracked open dark matters she had no business in, all because Mrs. Northe didn't seem to want to bother with her. All because Mrs. Northe had ignored Maggie for me. Maggie was Mrs. Northe's niece, family; I'd just been a poor mute girl wrapped up in a magical curse, and I'd swiftly become Mrs. Northe's cause célèbre. Maggie ended up courting evil into her own home, evil that nearly killed us both, because Mrs. Northe hadn't taken her seriously enough to intervene before the girl was too far gone. And yet, Miss Kent was worthy of salvation?

Where *was* Maggie? Had she been left to rot in some histrionic ward instead? Maggie was an idiot, certainly, but all she'd ever wanted was to be included, though she didn't understand the first thing about Spiritualism and what she did know was wrong. Mrs. Northe had no patience for Maggie's constant sensationalism, a trait I'd never allowed myself. I hadn't had the luxury of romanticizing dark magic. It had always been trying to kill me. I wanted to raise this issue, to demand an answer about why Mrs. Northe continued to fail her, but Lavinia continued and so I held my tongue. Though I caught Mrs. Northe's eye, looking at my hand to the side of the fine china where I'd clutched a finely pressed napkin too tightly, my knuckles white. I stared at the fine table setting and tried to remember which silverware setting went with which course and felt sick to my stomach again.

"My family never understood me," Lavinia replied to the senator, "but after this, they have no wish to see me, ever again. They're back to England out of embarrassment, it would seem. I hope they don't try to get Nathaniel arrested—"

"I won't have it," Jonathon exclaimed. "We'll bring the Master's Society to heel—"

"With care," Mrs. Northe cautioned. "With evidence. That is what we need. Evidence. Now more than ever, you mustn't be headstrong but measured." She turned to Lavinia.

"Do you think being in England will cause Mr. Veil more trouble than here?"

"If he returns to New York, I can try to offer some measure of protection. I've...resources," the senator said mysteriously.

Lavinia lit up. "Whatever your advice may be, my friends, I'll take. And however I can help, I am in your debt."

"We'll find a way you can be useful and find ways to put your talents to work," the senator said, with the sort of assurance that made you believe in God, that everything had its time and its season.

"And we'll find those responsible," Jonathon murmured. Lavinia just looked over at him with wide, aquamarine eyes and nodded. Sometimes the idea of a vengeful God was a comfort too.

"The appropriate authorities will," my father added, giving Jonathon a warning glance. There would be no discussion of Mister Brinkman the British spy at the table, clearly.

"I pray daily for resolution of all your affairs, Lord Denbury," Reverend Blessing said, clasping his dark hands together.

"Thank you," Jonathon replied. "I'll have to return to England at some point and settle the last of it, and I'll need all the prayers I can get."

I hadn't thought about his needing to return home again, but of course. What if he went and never came back? I'd given him nothing to tether him here, to me. New York was not his home. He'd been kidnapped here. I suddenly had no appetite whatsoever, feeling whatever I'd gained might truly be lost thanks to nerves, youth, and stubbornness.

The revered led us in a brief and prosaic grace, and we then took to our first course, a golden broth soup. After a moment, the reverend added, "Do let me know, Lord Denbury, if there is anything I can do in the meantime."

"Can I visit those greyhounds of yours?" Jonathon asked with a small smile. "Those two girls could brighten any man's spirit. Good thing about dogs, so loyal, so forgiving, don't really care about any of your particulars, just take to you in good faith," he said gamesomely, but every word was a stab at me. I became fascinated by turning the spoon in the broth so that

I wouldn't look at him or blurt out something pleading, silly, or defensive. I'd been silent for so many years, and in that time, my thoughts had no reins, as there was no danger of them finding voice. I had to be careful I didn't let something fly from my mental stable that would do more damage than good.

The reverend erupted in a low, endearing chuckle as Jonathon referenced his hounds rescued from a coursing run where they'd been mistreated. "Bunny and Blue were just as fond of you, my lord," the reverend replied. "Let's plan a day in the park; they're a sight to see out there. Appreciate them while you can, our rescuer found a permanent home for them. A Bronx farm." Blessing's deep brown eyes misted over. "It'll kill me to see them go, but I watch them strain toward any open door. Every living thing must be allowed to let run in the space that suits them..." His attachment to the veritable zoo of his house was one of the reasons I'd so instantly trusted him with my life. That and he was a damn good exorcist when called to be one. He looked up with a sudden grin. "But Mrs. Dawn has a new commission for me, a smaller pup who needs nothing but care. Little Sallie isn't seeing well these days, so being inside would be a blessing, with someone to dote on her a bit. That I can do."

"On the feast of Saint Francis, reverend, I'm coming to your house. That Assisi fellow would be well pleased with you," Senator Bishop said with a chuckle, making the reverend beam even brighter.

Mrs. Northe sat at the head of the table like a queen, she fit the regal role so well. She must have felt my gaze upon her for she turned to me, and in that moment I saw how truly tired she was. Not old. But tired. An old soul who was done. Ready to retire. Not from this world, but from the battles this world threw at her. Adding to the list of my many questions, I wondered just what all had happened during her recent escape to Chicago. When she spoke, I wondered if she'd read my mind. Likely she had. She could do that sometimes. At least get the sense of things.

"Friends, I have gathered you here because it should surprise no one to hear that there is still unfinished business. What happened to Lord Denbury and his portrait was one thing. The business at the hospital with the reanimate creature was another. The chemicals given to the Association is another. Master's Society resources are growing, and that's the clock we must turn back. All the assets they've gained we must reclaim. My visit to Chicago was as harrowing and challenging. The experiments that we've been seeing are going on in other cities too. Chicago I know for certain. Possibly others in the East. Industrial towns. The Master's Society has been looking to harness industry. I can only imagine they'd like to do so for their terrible inversion of life, taking the isolated incidents we've seen and mass producing them. Manufacturing horror. There's a deeper agenda at work, that of controlling through fear, but they'll have no stage upon which to play if we gain control of the means of their production."

"How do you know all this? That's quite the sweeping vision," my father asked wearily.

"Yes, Gareth," she replied sadly. It was still odd to hear anyone refer to him with such familiarity. He'd never let anyone so close. "It's the vision my best friend had upon her deathbed. It's why I had to go out to Chicago to be at her side. She needed to tell me what she was seeing. What the possibilities could be if we don't nip this Society in the bud."

Everyone at the table swallowed hard, and I felt light-headed with recollection. The murmur of demons echoing in my mind was all too easy to bring back. My father's hands were clenched, white-knuckled. He didn't want to be wrapped up in this. But the woman he was courting was forcing him to confront what we'd been dealing with for months, and better it come from her than from me. Mrs. Northe continued:

"Spiritualist friends of mine in three major cities have begun to seek out the weed at its heart and rip it from the ground. There is much work to be done. We must pinpoint the epicenter of the Master's Society's New York operation, confiscate any paperwork, and track down the source, laboratory, and masterminds of the latest assault."

Jonathon chimed in, directing all his words to Mrs. Northe, a heavy weight about his generally powerful carriage. "Last week, I received a missive from the London 'Master' with instructions to look in on Doctor Stevens, purveyor of the chemical in Miss Kent's incident, and report back, just as I was instructed to do with Doctor Preston. This is presumably before any news of what happened to Preston reached them, though I'm not sure by what channels it could have; Preston's operation was small and his demonic aide was bested." Jonathon gave Reverend Blessing a small, grateful smile. "However, the address of Stevens and the address of the supposed 'New York Office' were both vacant. Either I was being fooled, or the events surrounding Preston made Stevens disappear. So I've no longer the lead I hoped I had."

I stared at Jonathon. This was news to me, both the missive and his having inspected the premises on his own. I felt betrayed. He knew I wanted to be involved, for him to never undertake playing a demon doppelganger on his own. That a demon had once worn his face was enough to set anyone on edge, but his hiding things only undermined the type of partnership I thought we'd been building. He did not meet my gaze, and I wondered just how much he hadn't been telling me in our past weeks of laying low.

Maybe he felt it was only the little lady who should keep her head down while he was out playing double agent. I balled my hands into fists in the lap of my skirt. Perhaps he wanted revenge against my refusal of his proposal and was reasserting his own ability to take actions apart from me. Would he go meet Brinkman on his own? No. I'd seen the route. I was not about to let him edge me out of this. I hadn't saved his life, risked my life, nearly died twice, and undergone a host of nightmares that would make Poe envious for their morbidity. I realized my soup spoon was loud against the bowl, that I'd merely been turning it, not eating it, and thankfully it was cleared for some sort of poultry in a fine glaze that I'm sure would have smelled and seemed delicious were I in a mood to enjoy it.

"We'll have to face them eventually," Jonathon declared. "With what weaponry, I've no idea. But I feel the pall. I know their demonic forces are poisoning the city. I've seen flickers of red-gold fire across the jagged skyline, treetops, bridge spires. The city will fall to the whispers of demons if we're not careful."

"Yes, it will," Lavinia said, in a frightfully certain murmur.

"Only if you stop being vigilant will the city fall," Mrs. Northe countered. "You, yourselves, have always been the weaponry. Guns or blades may not help you. You know your best arsenal. You must be blindingly bright," she commanded. "Defiantly radiant."

I scowled. "How can I after all we've endured?"

Mrs. Northe's nostrils flared, and she pounded her gloved fist upon the table, rattling all her fine china settings. "Because now, right now is when you need to shine the brightest! Now is when the enemy expects you to be dim, broken, helpless, and afraid!" Her passion was sudden, her words tremulous, eyes hard as she drove a rapier point home to its target.

"If you do not blaze like a dying star, my child, then you might as well be already dead, no longer glittering in the sky of promise God intends for you. You must be spectacularly luminous. Burn far hotter than you're able. Beam for your dear life, child. The world is nothing but shadow and dead ends. Only your own fire can light a way out of the maze."

"Amen," Reverend Blessing murmured.

The rest of our meal was spent mostly in silence, with a bit of small talk about art and a few amusing Washington anecdotes from Senator Bishop. He was savvy enough not to bring real political issues to the table. But all I could think about was what lay ahead and if Jonathon and I could remain the solid team we'd been thus far in trying times. I was a woman of faith who was full of doubt. What could a ragtag band of Spiritualists, a senator, exorcist, a British Lord, a museum curator, and whatever I was—some Lutheran magnet for nightmares and the fancies of demons—do against a wealthy, resourced secret society who distributed murder and mayhem like a calling card to calling hours? I wanted to see a way out of the maze, but for the life of me, and maybe yet the death of me, I couldn't.

As per tradition in fine dinner parties, the men went off to the dark wood and leather of the late Mr. Northe's study to smoke cigars and talk about being masters of their domain or some such masculine chatter, and the ladies went off to the soft, lace-filled parlor to do the same. From Jonathon's reports, that male-driven room had been immaculately maintained and kept nearly overstocked with all kinds of fine liquor and exquisite cigars. I wondered how often Mr. Bishop was over to partake of these treasures as well.

Peter Northe had been gone for at least seven years if I remembered correctly, but it would seem his favorite supplies would be refilled in perpetuity. Perhaps his widow felt some part of him lingered on in the fine things enjoyed by the other interesting men who entertained at her home. I wondered if she heard his spirit speak, what he'd think of the growing closeness between my father and his widow, or just what the presence of Senator Bishop meant, as they too appeared far too familiar for mere friends. The energy between them seemed sibling in nature, but then again Mrs. Northe was a mystery. Just another question to add to my growing tally.

"You've a lot on your mind, Natalie," Mrs. Northe murmured over her shoulder as she led Lavinia ahead of her to the parlor where the maid had set out tea and aperitifs. Lavinia floated ahead as if she were a ghost, her thin frame alighting upon a divan, black layers splaying out, her eyes downcast, her expression lost in some reverie.

I set my jaw, wishing I could better hide things from her, as this was not the time, in a stranger's company, to unload all that gnawed at me. "That I do."

"Whatever you think I may have neglected, I hope you'll do me some credit and believe that I have taken actions on all counts that require concern."

I looked into her steely eyes, bright and powerful, and somehow I was sure she was talking about Maggie. I hoped she'd elaborate at the appropriate time. She then leaned close and murmured, "I'm going to interview the madman Crenfall to see if I can get a hint from him about the root of Society operations in the city. I don't expect much, but any lead is better than none. Care to come with me?"

And in one swift rush, all my doubts and my frustrations were forgotten in the excitement that was being included in secret operations by this most compelling woman. I was under her thrall yet again.

"Yes, I'd like that very much."

"No, you won't like it at all. Asylums are horrid places, but—"

"But I can't bear being useless."

"Indeed, I figure you'd be less trouble if I took you with me. Tomorrow?"

"No, we're..." I looked up in her eyes, and I felt my cheeks color. I was not a good at lying if I was quite sure my lie would be discovered. It was so hard to be artful around a clairvoyant. "Busy."

"Indeed. Not tomorrow? The day after, then. I'll tell your father we're out for lunch. I'll indeed feed you, though I'm not sure we'll have much of an appetite after we're done with the place."

I just nodded, feeling a bit helpless and useless, wondering if, like the times before, the dark magic was just waiting around another corner I hadn't anticipated. But at least my next two days would prove eventful. It was true, I was less trouble if I was busy. After a moment I realized Lavinia was staring at me with an intense scrutiny that surpassed custom.

"You're well intentioned, Miss Natalie. Worried you'll fail, but well intentioned," Lavinia said quietly, before turning to Mrs. Northe and elaborating. "It's odd, ever since the incident, I smell things about persons, subtle scents, but suddenly I feel like I know the truth of their heart. You and the senator are powerful and inscrutable, but similarly well intentioned, though world-weary. I can sense it as if I were to taste the salt air of a long sea voyage." She stopped herself as if she took a moment to truly listen to her own words.

"No, I don't think you're mad, before you ask," Mrs. Northe reassured. That sounded familiar. In the early days of our acquaintance, when I was convinced I was seeing the painting where Jonathon's soul was imprisoned move, she'd said the same thing, bless her.

"Jonathon sees that in auras," I offered. "The ability to judge character you describe. Those of us who have been targeted by the Society end up, it would seem, coming away with more than we bargained for but something that can be useful in the right circumstances, as long as you're brave enough to use it. I look at it as God trying to give us an advantage, a weapon borne out of toil and pain."

I'm not sure Mrs. Northe had ever given me such a proud look as she did just then. I suppose I sounded sort of like her.

Lavinia stared at me, seeming to gain the kind of strength and sense of purpose I felt when I was called to save Jonathon, me and me alone. I found myself liking this girl who seemed to wish to rise to the challenge, not hide from it in fear. But the struggle was there in her pale eyes. I knew that too.

Of course a thoughtful, complex girl like Lavinia Kent would be Mrs. Northe's new project instead of her entitled, narrow-minded niece. Still, I'd have to see if there was something I could do to help Maggie, even if Mrs. Northe wouldn't. The idiot girl had nearly gotten me killed, but I had the sense that I owed her some sympathy and aid. Maggie was a product of her age, her family. When I lost my ability to speak as a child, I'd become an outcast, I had to think of life differently, fend for myself differently. Miss Kent chose an outsider's perspective due to her interests. Maggie was the sort of girl society expected her to be, until she toyed too close to the fires of dark magic and got us burned. But I was stronger than Maggie. I had to earn Lavinia's sense that I was well intentioned. Not only for myself, but for others.

We sipped some sort of sugary liqueur, and Lavinia drank in Mrs. Northe's next instructions as if they were gospel. "Now, my dear girl, you must reach out to the rest of the members of your association and make sure none of them are trying to get ahold of the substance again, and if they are, we need to intercept those channels. Can you do this?"

Lavinia nodded. "I'll make my rounds tomorrow."

Tomorrow. Day by day, fate unfolded. Carefully, wrought with the terrible dread that hell would suddenly open before us. I feared the Master's Society had been busy creating pitfalls for us, traps for us to walk into... My morbid imagination had been given such fodder in the past months that anything was possible, and all I could do was pray. But even prayer felt like flimsy comfort against a widening net that sought to catch us up and feed...

Before long we parted our ways with pleasantries I hardly remembered; they all felt a bit forced, all of us sensitive and aware enough that we sat in the eye of the storm, a maelstrom underground, swirling around us, ready to drag us under like Hades did Persephone.

That night I wondered if I'd dream, all sorts of things having been stirred up. For the past two weeks, my nightmares had been dormant, meaning we did at least have some effect on pushing the dark magic back from whence it came. There were flashes in my dreams, nothing concrete, just vague shadows and the back of Jonathon. Walking away from me... and the hollowness that remained in his absence...

Chapter Four

The next morning I rose early, ate well, and read the paper, glad not to answer to anything. Bessie, a long-time friend of the family who had served as housekeeper since her husband died and our families bonded in grief, was out for the morning. My father and I had enjoyed comfortable silences for far too many years due to the Selective Mutism I had now nearly entirely overcome. But old habits and all... The silence was actually a bit of a comfort, a reminder of when times were simpler. A time before Jonathon.

However, I'd not go back to permanent silence ever again, nor would I ever regret the lord that overturned everything, curses in his wake. Times may have been simpler, but I baffled my father then just as much as I did now. Someday I'd make him proud, just never in the ways he'd imagined. I kissed my father's cheek as I saw him out the door to the Metropolitan, and the bright green eyes I inherited from him glittered. He might never have known what to do with me, and that was likely the same with Mother, but he loved us unconditionally, of that I was certain. Once he was off, I was then free to be consumed with one name, one mission.

Brinkman, this English spy, wouldn't be expecting me. But it was good to meet things unexpectedly. Often a person's true colors shone through in moments of surprise, and Jonathon might see a chink in Brinkman's armor if things didn't go to his plan.

I would walk the many blocks to Mrs. Northe's home, glad for the activity to focus my nerves. Jonathon had been inspecting apartments in Greenwich Village for possible purchase, fancying a home in both Greenwich territories on either side of the "pond," but nothing had been settled. So he remained with our most generous benefactor. I forced aside any jealousy that Lavinia and Jonathon would be under the same roof with each other. Lavinia was utterly preoccupied and over the moon about Jonathon's best friend, Mister Veil. Still, the uncertainty of my relationship with my dear lord brought a heretofore unknown paranoia to my already industrious imagination.

The maid let me in, gesturing me to the parlor where I was relieved to see Jonathon awaiting me. He looked, as usual, dapper and stunning. Having procured finances from his trip to England, he must have gone to the very best in men's shops here in New York for fresh suits, nothing too flashy, everything dark and elegant. This was a charcoal suit with a black waistcoat and deep blue cravat, his blue accents always setting off those heart-stopping eyes. Maggie would've known the brand and store of his attire, surely. She had a nose for such things. I'd have to learn, if I wanted to truly understand Jonathon's world.

So many daunting tasks, from the more mundane function of the ways of the elite to the gravest of hard work ahead: dismantling a deadly secret society. Surely the infamous and aristocratic "Majesty" that had been giving Jonathon orders as if he were still his demon-possessed self would know where Jonathon's suit came from too.

Upon my entrance, Jonathon bowed his head and said not a word as he rose, a walking stick in one hand, top hat in the other, and gestured toward the door. I saw no sign of Mrs. Northe or Miss Kent. Perhaps they were out bonding in the same ways she and I had done months prior. I tried not to fear for my favored place at the center of things, but jealousy has its ways.

"We'll only volunteer vague answers to Brinkman's questions," Jonathon instructed.

"Wait for him to volunteer information first." I nodded.

We took the elaborate route Brinkman had instructed in his note and kept silent the whole way. I'd seen Jonathon play his demon doppelganger eerily well and so was fully prepared for him to take the lead with his countryman. But I palmed the hilt of the small knife I stowed between the stays of my bodice and the corset beneath, accessible via a partly opened seam. This action steeled me. If the spy proved a turncoat, I'd draw and defend Jonathon in a heartbeat...

We were making the last turn of the particular route, the park ahead of us, when a flurry of action at the door to the carriage had us exclaim in alarm. My knife was out in the instant, but so was Brinkman inside in the same, with a cry of, "If you've weapons put them down, I'm on your side!"

The door yawned open as the man's hands were planted upon the roof of the cab and his feet were up and between Jonathon's and mine before a lanky body lithely followed. In another smooth motion, he threw his weight to the side, plopping next to Jonathon. He then bent to draw the flapping door shut once more and turned to both of us with a wide and winning smile, plucking a black wide-brimmed felt hat from his head. He was dressed in a fine black suit and grey striped waistcoat and white cravat, all well-made and tailored but not ostentatious. His features were nearly weasel-like in their somewhat pinched quality, and yet somehow their arrangement was disturbingly attractive. His dark brown hair was slicked back, a few ends turning out in defiance, his eyes were a sky blue, a shade darker than Jonathon's strikingly pale ones, but that just didn't seem fair, as I found Denbury's so hard to look away from.

"Gabriel Brinkman at your service, Lord Denbury," he said in a gently refined accent that I guessed came from a London elite. Though I knew little about England and its regionalisms, I could tell upper class from common well enough. "And who might this feisty young lady be?" he asked, offering a dazzling smile that dimpled lean cheeks. "I saw a telling flash of silver." He bowed his head to me. "An impressively quick draw, miss." He then turned to Jonathon. "Hiring a female bodyguard? Very clever and very good cover, sir."

Jonathon offered a slight smile, but I could tell he wanted to laugh. I said nothing and tried to look menacing. I doubted it worked, but both gentlemen seemed to enjoy it. Jonathon introduced me only as "a colleague" and gave no name. If Brinkman was a good spy, he'd figure it out. Brinkman narrowed his bright eyes at me and did.

"You must be Miss Stewart. I had a look through the files pertaining to your portrait, Lord Denbury, and the goings on surrounding it. Sergeant James Patt seemed all too glad to have your nonsense wrapped up and to have pinned the blame on someone, batty Mister Crenfall, eh?"

"Well, he *was* an accomplice," Jonathon replied. "He was the broker who facilitated the transfer of my portrait and...incapacitated body onto these shores. Justice was served in his arrest, certainly."

"Indeed." Brinkman nodded. "As for the rest of the justice... You've taken that upon yourselves, have you?" While his tone held no judgment, neither of us were sure how we should reply. Brinkman continued. "Patt gave me leave to peruse your diary, Miss Stewart. And am I to presume that it is true?"

I blushed. He'd have read all the kissing bits in that diary. That was *so* unfair.

"It is," I said through clenched teeth.

"I stake my life on it," Jonathon replied. "The life that is wholly in her debt, you'll know from having read her accounts."

Brinkman smiled at me again. That didn't help the blush. "You're a very good writer, Miss Stewart." Even worse. There went the heat of my cheeks a few degrees further. He released me from his stare and turned again to Jonathon. "My contact, Mister Knowles, tells me you met a certain 'Majesty,' and there has been correspondence." Jonathon nodded. "May I see it, please? Do you have it with you?"

Jonathon reached into his breast pocket and withdrew a letter with the familiar, insidious red and gold seal of The Master's Society, the one he'd withheld from me pertaining to the offices and looking in on Stevens. "They have three avenues of experimentation," Jonathon explained. "Splitting the soul from the body, I was the unfortunate test on that. Reanimation had us dealing with poor Doctor Preston. And now, pharmacology, with the chemical given to Veil's Associates." He lifted up the note and proffered it to Brinkman for perusal. "This may have come before what you assume was the undoing of my cover in Doctor Preston's death. How should I proceed with this Doctor Stevens? I went to the offices herein, but there is nothing there."

"Are you entirely sure about that?" Brinkman asked.

"Indeed. I've a way of...seeing things," Jonathon replied carefully, keeping the particulars of his new gifts out of the discussion. "No living soul was present there."

"*Seeing* things?"

"Keen eyes, Mister Brinkman," I offered quietly. "I do hope you have them too."

"Things are never exactly as they seem at first glance with the Society," Brinkman replied cryptically.

"And you? Are you as you seem at first glance?" I queried. "What reason do we have to trust you?"

Jonathon flashed me a warning glance not to be too harsh and was quick to add: "I've my reasons for why I will trust you, Mister Brinkman. But I also have ways of knowing if you've betrayed me to my enemy, so I'd truly not suggest you do so. Are you saying I should try these addresses again?"

"I think you might find *evidence* there. Persons, no. The Master's Society manages to operate with scant personnel that don't keep regular patterns, the bane of any spy."

Brinkman held up the Master's Society letter to the light. He fished in his own breast pocket and produced a small vial with a sponge on the stopper. He uncorked the vial, brushed the damp sponge over the paper and something bloomed forth in response.

My mouth hung open a bit at this magic, and Brinkman smiled again as he explained: "Sympathetic stain. Terribly useful in espionage. Your American Revolutionary rings, that Culper set, were quite fond of it. Your troops gained many advantages passed through unsuspecting pages." He glanced down at what had been revealed, then passed it to Jonathon. It was a date. The following Tuesday. "It is likely Master's Society protocol, then, to encode something important within the letter. Something is obviously scheduled."

"Another experiment?" Jonathon posed. "Should we expect for another 'outbreak' like what happened with Nathaniel's Association?" He turned to his countryman. "We believe we need to find their center of operations to terminate the beast at its source. I hope you'll help us in that quest, Mister Brinkman."

"It changes, they've several offices. I've only pinpointed two, there may be four. They seem to like to commandeer grand spaces."

At this, Jonathon's jaw clenched, and his crystalline eyes darkened. "I don't suppose you've any news of my Greenwich estate."

"The situation will have to be...addressed, Lord Denbury. I don't believe the tenants who overtook your manor are fully in control there; Knowles informed me that he thinks something is a bit off."

"Could that be a center of operations?" I asked.

"In part, perhaps, though their focus seems to zero in on a few cities, London, New York, Chicago. That your estate got swept into this is rather an outlier, my lord," Brinkman replied. Jonathon's leather-gloved hand clenched, and I resisted the urge to put my lace-gloved hand over his. There was no avoiding Jonathon's return to England. This time I wouldn't let him go without me.

"I'd like to know those addresses, and also, do elaborate on how you know someone is 'coming for me' as your note intimated," Jonathon said carefully.

"The former? Intercepted mail. The latter? Let's say instinct. And I was trying to get your attention."

"Idle threats may get attention but not trust," Jonathon countered.

"If I knew exactly who or what or when something was coming for you, my lord, I'd have left you an itinerary. But I do believe they'd rather kill you than wait to see if you bested them, especially without word from Doctor Preston directly. So be on the lookout for anything and everything. Where are you staying? I'm sure I could arrange for protection."

"I am well protected," Jonathon assured. I wondered if Mrs. Northe had increased guards around her home. If so, they weren't visible. The woman was artfully subtle. Brinkman bowed his head. "How can I find you, Mister Brinkman, if I have information to give you or questions to ask?"

"Here is what I know of possible property in Master's Society hands," the spy replied. "And don't worry where to find me, I'll find you." And with that, he was again out of the still-moving carriage, the door slamming behind him.

"Well," Jonathon and I said at the same time.

"He didn't have any aura of the demon about him, but then again, he didn't have any light at all. Generally speaking, when people will be of particular help, they've a soft white light about them. You, of course, were colored in the exact inverse hues the demon sported; thusly, I knew you could stand in direct opposition to its magic. But this fellow, curiously nothing, and for him to be so involved, I'm not sure what it means."

"Could he be a possessed body?" I asked.

"Generally, the possessed have a flicker of fire about them, that odd sulfuric haze. I saw none of that. What do you think, were the eyes off? Did they have that dog-like reflective quality?" Jonathon replied. I shook my head. He shrugged. "Perhaps it means he's neutral."

"You mean he won't help but won't harm?"

"That's all I can think of it."

"Well, that's disappointing." I folded my arms, elbow brushing the knife hilt I'd returned to the unconventional sheath of my corset.

"And troubling," Jonathon added, "if his allegiances are easily swayed." He unfolded the paper.

"You're not going alone," I cautioned. "That you went, with that note, and tried to find—"

"That I did anything without you truly disturbs you, I realize. But you cannot mother me through everything, Natalie," he said, an edge to his tone.

"Mother you? No, I..." I felt sounds die in my throat. *Come on, Natalie, words. Words to fight what isn't fair.*

He sighed. "I'm not ungrateful for anything, Natalie, but I also need to be able to do things for myself and on my own. Not only because I worry for your safety, but also because this is, at heart, my own personal vendetta and the only thing that sets my mind at ease is constantly thinking of the next step to best them. I will try to involve you if it seems plausible. Allow my independence, as you would wish I allow you yours, *Miss Natalie*," he said, driving home the point of my femininity, of the world that sought to confine me and offer me no independence whatsoever. He didn't say it with cruelty, but with a worldliness I could not deny. I had to tread carefully with him. I could lose him at any moment, and while I was not one to beg or plead for anything, I truly wanted him in my life.

His words were not to be argued. But I did take the paper from his hand to examine the addresses before he could yank it back away from me. One was on the Upper East Side, Park and 66, the other downtown, in an area I was fairly sure was industrial, off 14th Street.

"Tomorrow?" Jonathon queried. "Shall we scout?"

"No, tomorrow I'm...busy."

"Busy?"

I considered a moment whether or not I'd tell him, but there was no sense in secrets. It was all for his benefit, to set this madness to rest once and for all. "Mrs. Northe and I have a date with a madman. Crenfall. Mrs. Northe thinks she might glean some sort of clue from him about what to target in the city."

Jonathon made a face and was silent. He helped me down from the carriage as it let me out near the red-brick Romanesque façade of the Metropolitan, a grand building quickly outgrowing itself, where I would go check in on Father so that he could feel as though he were checking in on me. It was now more important than ever that I keep my freedom by making Father think I were subject to his constraints as any good unmarried girl should be. Jonathon bowed his head to me before turning away. The gesture seemed too formal. If the forced intimacy of having met soul to soul receded into the cool detachment that supposedly came with "mature" sentiment, I couldn't bear it. I was passionate, and I wanted to live, and love, passionately. Mutually.

"Do you want to come tomorrow?" I blurted, not wanting him to go, wishing we could replace our last day in the park with a better one, one where everything was said exactly so and unfolded as any girl might dream.

"I doubt a madhouse will do me good, Natalie. I will walk by the addresses Brinkman gave—" He put up his hand as I opened my mouth. "I'll not make any attempts at entry or contact. Merely surveillance. Allow me this while you see what can be gleaned from that wretch who helped imprison me," he muttered, grinding out words through clenched teeth. "We'll be more productive if our team splits up."

I prayed he didn't mean that in terms of our relationship as well, and the fear of this had me blurting again. "I love you."

His beautiful face, as world-weary as it had been in the painting when he feared all was lost, brightened a bit. He took my hand and kissed it softly. My entire body reacted in a sweeping thrill. And then he turned away, gave Mrs. Northe's cross streets to the driver, and climbed in, disappearing behind the lace curtain of the carriage window. Perhaps his wounded pride still sought to punish me a bit, and so he did not return my words of love, but I would relive that kiss upon my hand until he could.

I watched the carriage turn town a side street, waiting for him to look out the window at me. He didn't. I waved at the carriage anyway, biting my lip. I doubted a madhouse would do me good, either, but I'd rather I suffer it than Jonathon. He was truly alone in the world save for me. The young man who had yet to grieve his murdered parents and all that had been taken from him was doing the very best he could in a land that was not his own, and I had to be the best I could be, for his sake. For our sake. Tomorrow might bring us one step closer to answers and closure.

Tomorrow, and tomorrow and tomorrow, creeps in this petty pace from day to day till the last syllable of recorded time... My Shakespearean life would yet unfold day by day, in an inexorable march toward the undiscovered country.

Chapter Five

I watched from the window of my small upstairs room for Mrs. Northe's fine carriage and magnificent mare. When they came around the corner of my block, I darted out to the door. Bessie asked nothing of my business—Mrs. Northe's wealth and high social status offered us that privilege—so I hurried down to the street and hopped in as soon as she opened the door from inside. Before the driver could climb down to assist me, I had already clambered up in a swish of skirts far less fine than those opposite me. I threw myself into the seat a bit like Brinkman had the day prior. It was an impressive skill I wanted to practice.

She opened her mouth as if she were about to reprimand me, likely ready to remind me that wasn't how *Lady Denbury* should behave, yet she only chortled.

"This is the first moment we've had in a while to just catch up, you and I," I began. "I do hope you'll be less cryptic about Chicago and many other things you've been cagy about."

She chuckled again and looked out the window as the carriage sped downtown down an oddly clear Second Avenue. I could tell the chuckle masked grief. I could tell she didn't want me to see the pain in her expression. She kept her voice impressively steady. "My friend was dying, that was no lie. She was a woman of visions. When she bid me come see her onward onto the Undiscovered Country, she told me that she'd seen things I needed to know about. I confess, I wasn't eager to hear them."

There was a pause. The clatter of horse hooves and wheels upon cobblestones was a lulling pattern of sound for several blocks. I patiently waited, but I kept my eyes trained on her so that she knew I was expecting more out of her.

"Every mentor has to step out of the way, Natalie," she added finally. "And allow her protégés to fight their own battles."

I caught my breath, trying to let that declaration and all it may portend sink in. "That's why you went to Chicago, when Jonathon and I, with the help of friends, had to deal with Doctor Preston's reanimated madness on our own? I confess, I didn't like feeling abandoned."

"And I remain torn," she countered. "What my friend saw predicts dark futures ahead. I was hoping she'd reassure me that I would, as I like to do, play the role of guardian angel effortlessly, flawlessly. I can't promise that will be the case, Natalie. So look sharp. Stay safe. And don't look to me as the answer for everything," she said, her tone terribly sad. She kept her gaze trained out the window.

This wasn't something I wanted to hear out of a woman I'd once thought invincible, infallible. But she was human. Just like the rest of us imperfect creatures that fate had bound together against a dark force we still struggled to comprehend. I hope at least fate knew what it was doing even if we didn't.

I opened my mouth to ask about Maggie, for last I'd heard a doctor had been tending her at the Hathorne residence, but I doubted life would simply continue on for the misguided girl—a young woman who was my peer in age, though I was not her peer in wealth—without some sort of judgment, punishment, or internment. I wasn't sure what stopped me this time. But the overwhelming task of what we were up against had me at a loss for words, my occasional difficulty with speech notwithstanding.

A lack of confidence is what had me often fall back into my old patterns of silence. I decided to focus on the task at hand. One task at a time, this day was for information gathering, else I'd lose my mind with worry and wondering. When we disembarked for the small steam ferry and I saw the dreary round island ahead, positioned amid the East River, a place I'd thankfully never had cause to go, there was nothing to do but wrestle with the pit of dread in my stomach. While boarding the small boat, we had to brace our hats—Mrs. Northe's feathered piece far more elaborate than my felt and tulle one—against the river winds, feeling the boat struggle against strong currents as if it didn't want to cross, either...

Good God, what a miserable place. A long, sprawling castle of dark brick out on Wards Island that picked up the howls of patients upon the East River winds. I glanced at Mrs. Northe as I first spied the long, rounded edifice, curving in like a vast crescent. Any hope of getting honest information paled. I wondered if the man we sought would even be recognizable in this gargantuan estate of insanity.

Crenfall, the broker who had seen to the transfer of Lord Denbury's portrait from England to New York—with his soul trapped inside—was an odious man, leering and unseemly. But I couldn't imagine that even the most deserving of creatures would fare very well in this purgatory, just one step away from hell. I couldn't imagine that anyone with a shred of sanity would keep it in a place like this; from the cries and screams I heard the moment the scowling ferryman mounted a rickety calash to drive us up the long winding path to the front doors, it seemed no one had.

"I have to utterly shut down any of my heightened senses, any ability to pick up on another person's thoughts or emotions. It's too painful, scattered, and raw," Mrs. Northe murmured to me as we stepped down from the creaking calash that was all too happy to tear away again, the driver not looking back. I stared up at the towering, formidable building before us as she continued: "I know that Crenfall was an accessory to murder and justice must be served. Still, I feel a pang of pity for those confined here."

An attendant in a dreary gray uniform, a solemn-looking man strained around the eyes, opened the door before Mrs. Northe had even lifted the knocker. He stared past us, out into the wide, vacant lawn, as if ready to run. We stepped inside the daunting doors, and the sounds were far worse *within* than without. I could not blame the man for yearning for that free open space behind us, in such contrast from the overwhelming weight and gloom of the place.

The warden, a stern, broad man dressed in the same somber gray as everyone that could be seen anywhere in the vast open foyer and halls leading off in either direction, looked up in surprise at our arrival. A large ring of keys clinked at his side as he approached. "Can I...help you... ladies?"

"I seek an interview with one of your patients," Mrs. Northe said.

"An *interview*?" The man's eyebrows seemed ready to launch off his skull.

"Yes. Someone who was recently convicted and placed here in confinement, a Mr. Crenfall."

The warden chuckled. "You want information out of him? Because all you'll get is some babbling murmurs about a Master."

I fought back the urge to shudder at that word.

Mrs. Northe was swift to answer. "I'll take what I can get," she replied, her tone not to be trifled with. "It's to do with an investigation."

The man sneered, and I distinctly didn't like him. "Since when did the police let *women* do their work?"

"They don't," Mrs. Northe replied crisply. "And yet we do. Sir. *Do their work*. Every day. It just isn't our job. But we do, in our way. Now please be so kind as to do yours in turn and show me to the prisoner. An attendant guard would be kindly appreciated."

That I wanted to grow up to be just like the woman at my side was hardly lost on me in moments like this. I fought back a haughty look I wanted to give to the man.

"I've got to ask the boss. As this is hardly custom," he said with an exaggerated bow, flashing jagged teeth first at Mrs. Northe, then at me. I quelled another urge to shudder and had to keep it still at bay when I saw the Alienist in charge approach; he was a towering, sour-faced, balding man in an ill-fitting brown suit, the sort of character who looked more like someone the Master's Society would choose as a lackey than the kind I'd like to see tending the mentally ill. The warden was speaking to him quietly as they approached us, and then he walked off, leaving us there in the cold, drafty hall with the head of the place.

"You wish to...interrogate Crenfall?" the man asked with blatant skepticism.

"I realize his lucidity may be limited," Mrs. Northe replied, "but if he's speaking in puzzles, even they, sensible or not, may be of use."

"May I ask what you're working on, and why you've a young..." He turned to me and fumbled for words. "What are you, miss? An... apprentice?"

That the world seemed so baffled by a woman of agency such as

Mrs. Northe was far more irritating to me than a man being baffled by my presence. I typically ought not to be in the situations I'd been finding myself since encountering Jonathon's haunted portrait, but with every new situation, I felt more and more entitled to my purposes and would stand strong, haughty, even, against the withering stare of the disapproving who wanted me to be seen and not heard, home and not out, soft and not strong.

"I wish I could explain our positions and duties, but I'm under orders not to say," Mrs. Northe said with a kindness to her voice that made her less threatening, a good tactic, one that appeared to placate but was unapologetic. "If you've any concerns, I've government contacts to vouch for me, men who will most certainly appreciate your efforts to both allow us to complete an interview whilst ensuring our safety."

I was fairly sure she meant Senator Bishop; he seemed a very useful man to know, and one that was on our paranormal side, a side few seemed brave or open-minded enough to entertain. The doctor shrugged and gestured we follow him into the heart of the gray maze laden with bars and wailing voices.

Dank halls, dirty linens... the men within the cells seemed creatures, not humans. It was a brick building of long, caged hallways. It was a prison, yet worse; they weren't merely being held, they were being worked on. Whatever efforts had gone forward since the Civil War to make sanitariums seem more amenable must not have affected this place for the better.

The doctor seemed to be deploying a host of new advancements, operations, serums, and "therapies" upon his patients that seemed more like abuse from the looks of it as I passed cell after cell of misery. One man was strapped to a chair while attendants dunked him face down into a vast basin of water. I opened my mouth to ask what the point there could possibly be in such treatment when the doctor supplied:

"One has to employ every possible tactic if one is to get anything out of the mad. One never knows what will break them open, what will lead us to another discovery in the great uncharted territory of the human mind. You never know what will lead to progress."

I could see both Mrs. Northe and myself fighting back the urge to argue with the man, but we truly couldn't afford to make any enemies in so miserable a place. Through a metal door was a small rectangular window, and through that smudged frame, I saw Crenfall leaning up against the stone wall of his cell in a baggy gray shift, looking up to the tiny rectangular window that let in a sliver of wan light. The Alienist motioned an attendant to open the door and enter with us, standing to the side but between us and the madman. I noticed then that Crenfall was counting the flies hovering about the window, murmuring numbers.

Crenfall looked up sharply at the sound of the metal door, his beady eyes focusing right upon me, like an animal. A sudden, complicated rush of emotions hit me; if Jonathon hadn't been so strong, if he'd have been more weak-willed, more easily influenced and manipulated, I could be staring at him right now. Thinking of Jonathon, of his inherent worth, how strong he'd been through his own attack, internment, and onslaught of dark magic steeled me, calmed me, and allowed me to focus in on this tragic creature.

"Mister Crenfall, I've some questions for you," Mrs. Northe finally began.

Crenfall kept counting the bugs on the sill of his cell. It occurred to me after a while that it was in a sequence, and it didn't necessarily match the creatures on the sill. I'd never been particularly gifted at mathematics, but I did take note of it, and Mrs. Northe seemed to as well. But I wished to write down the numbers. That I hadn't traveled with a diary frustrated me. Mere months ago I'd have never been without paper, to write things down to communicate as my voice had been absent for so many years.

Mrs. Northe repeated what she'd said, and the clouds of madness seemed to part, and an eerie lucidity shone through like a jarring ray of sunlight.

"You've questions?" he said in wispy voice. "About why I'm here?"

"Yes, please. Tell us why you're here."

"You cannot beat the Majesties, you know. You'll fall under the Master in the end. Everyone will," he said matter-of-factly.

"I'm sure that's true," Mrs. Northe said softly, with a quiet conspiratorial air. "And I've been wanting to know why I've been chosen to see and know some of your secrets." Crenfall narrowed his eyes at her. "I brought

Lord Denbury's portrait into the Metropolitan, Mister Crenfall. I've been trying to learn the ways of this society, but I cannot do that without a guide," she murmured, playing as though she were excited. Crenfall puffed up his chest proudly. "What we should expect and welcome from these Masters?"

"Expect that the gentlemen will want everything. You can welcome his taking of what is rightfully theirs. They are not hasty. Their revolution is quiet and dark. The minion and I were sent from London. Ahead of *operations*."

"The *minion*. Lord Denbury, you mean?" Mrs. Northe clarified.

"No." Crenfall grinned. "But he looked an awful lot like him, didn't he..." The man's ugly, raspy laugh bounced about the dank stone space.

"What sort of *operations*?" I hissed through clenched teeth, balling my fist, wanting to lash out at his casual reference to what had been an experience of unmitigated hell for Jonathon.

"You know, *business*," Crenfall replied, turning a sick smile to me. "New business. *Pretty* business."

I shuddered. The demon had liked to use the word "pretty." A demon who had gotten far too close... I shoved the memories back.

"How many people were sent here?" Mrs. Northe continued.

"Just the *inhabited* young lord and I first. A Majesty will follow. And soon. A shadow has already been cast over doctors. More experiments, you know."

"Business...and experiments, these will be wholly in New York? Or more places?"

"To take preeminence anywhere, one must certainly have deep roots in New York City," Crenfall stated as if that were obvious. "Grand and central, all tracks will lead home."

The word *home* seemed to set him off; he winced and something darkened. "The abyss. We come from the abyss. We return to the abyss. In the end the dark will always take you, so take it first and it will be kind, a soft touch, gentle decay, nothing to fear. The paths are worn deep with heavy tread, those we serve, those who have come before to do the dirty deeds. Such dirt. We are filthy creatures, mankind..."

It was hard to follow, his mental landscape a tangle. He repeated a few choice words, touching upon abysses and filth, eventually leaving his ode to pierce us again with wide, terrible eyes. He continued more lucidly: "Here the new world order shall unfold. The old order. The old shall be new again. The dead, alive. The peaceful, militant. The leaders restored. The striving, crushed. And the content, terrified."

And then suddenly, he rushed at us, shrieking. We scrambled backward, startled by the extreme outburst. The orderly was instantly upon Crenfall, who murmured apologies as he retreated back into his corner once more. "I get these fits, madame," Crenfall whined to Mrs. Northe, sweeping a terrified gaze to me, then to the orderly. "Please, I'm sorry. I'll be better..."

"It's all right sir, thank you." Mrs. Northe placed a calming hand on the orderly's forearm.

Crenfall begged again, cringing. "Please understand. I did not start this with the desire to hurt anyone. I only wanted to serve. For the world to be sorted properly. But once you choose a path and walk it a while...there is no turning back."

Mrs. Northe stood her ground and maintained her gentle but unequivocal tone. "Tell me where your associates meet. Names, if you can."

Crenfall looked at us helplessly, murmuring, wide-eyed, "They're all Majesties. We don't know their true names. Such power in names, you know. Their blood is the finest. And they will situate themselves among the grand and glorious, the central and the vital. Better to seize the heart of the city."

"He's raving, madame. I hope *you've* sense enough to see that," the orderly growled, his fist still threatening. Mrs. Northe offered the orderly a reassuring gesture.

"I'm trying... I'm trying to serve," Crenfall murmured, offering up a soft plea. "Please bestow your grace upon me...for I do grow scared of the dark..." And he was off again, counting the insects round his window bars, only with a few more tears on his cheek, and no other urging from Mrs. Northe garnered any response.

Mrs. Northe turned to me, and I saw a tired, old pain I was seeing more frequently. Or perhaps I was simply more insightful. She spoke softly as we left the cell. "I realize that this branch of doctors, scientists, and analysts are called Alienists because these people are alienated from society, from everything we think of as capable and compatible with our average existence. But their patients are still human. They are not so alien that I cannot still feel them, straining at my mind, their souls reaching out as their hands do. For something. Someone. For a shred of light, sunlight, quiet...anything to grasp."

This was my thought as I walked away, the head Alienist waiting for us, having listened in, his face contorted in disapproval that he thankfully kept to himself.

We made our way back toward the entrance, past chambers of experimental operation, activity that appeared on all accounts to be somewhat medieval and torturous. If I strained to hear it, I wondered if I'd feel the heartbeat of misery. Surely Mrs. Northe did, for it seemed she could not help herself, lashing out at the attending Alienist. "As a rule, are you cruel?"

The man just stared at her as if he didn't understand her question.

As we made our exit, a man in a black suit, with pale skin, dark eyes, and an arm held at an angle entered. Palpable sadness was writ wide within his dark eyes. The crash of water sounded nearby. Likely a man strapped to a chair plunged into a submersion tank, as I'd seen in passing. "Barbaric," he murmured.

"Yes, doctor, so you've said," came the weary reply from the warden at the door. "Do open your own institution then instead, will you?"

I couldn't help but turn to the slight man whose presence was magnetic, whose eyes were so fierce, and smile. He returned it, an action that transformed his face, removing his hat as he bowed his head to me and then Mrs. Northe before walking away, making us all passing strangers once more.

"I was about to decry that there were no persons of true feeling I'd yet seen in a place like this," Mrs. Northe murmured, nodding after the man. "Perhaps there is hope for the hopeless. I always say that there is, as a general rule, but sometimes...those are just hollow words."

Hope for the hopeless. That made me think of Maggie, and as we stepped outside those doors, straining toward that open lawn beyond,

I blurted: "Please tell me Maggie won't be brought to a place like this. What happens when she's well enough?"

Mrs. Northe sighed as we climbed again into the calash that she had instructed come back around for us to take us again to the small steam ferry that would chug gladly back to Manhattan. We sped away from the looming complex, and I did not look back. She turned to me with a withering stare that caused me to shrink back in the bouncing seat.

"Do you really think so little of me that I'd let Maggie, my niece, misguided as she is, be swept away into these terrible systems?" she asked, her voice pained. "These days a woman can get committed for reading a romance novel, let alone "witchcraft," and I swiftly put my sister's vain head out of that notion. It's no wonder Margaret was seeking something more meaningful out of life. Her mother seemed more concerned with the family reputation than whether or not her daughter was well. I'm sending her off to Chicago, to be looked after by one of my dearest friends in all the world, Miss Karen Sheldon. She and my dear Amelia, the one that died, are...were...bosom friends. Maggie will be in the best of care and company with Karen."

"And yet you opened your home to Lavinia Kent, but not your own niece—"

"My sister wanted Maggie sent *away*. This was the compromise. Please don't question me," Mrs. Northe snapped. "I would hope you know enough by now that my friends, to the last one of them, are incredible, I daresay *magical* people. Karen is...inconsolable in losing Amelia, they lived together since they were girls in school, and this mission might just save two souls at once. Karen is very gifted empath and will seek out the root of Maggie's trouble and return her to us well again."

Boarding the steamboat, sprawling Manhattan lay ahead of us, and as always I was stunned by the skyline, the looming towers of the mid-complete Brooklyn Bridge, a behemoth of gothic stone straining to the sky, the churning industry along the river, the bobbing masts of countless ships, and the puffs of constant steam engines. Busy, churning, burning New York. A devil in your midst wants to eat you whole. But does it not underestimate you, grand city?

"So did we gain anything?" I asked, turning the subject away from

Maggie. I was relieved by Mrs. Northe's assurances but still not sure what to think, wondering if Maggie would ever recover, if there was anything left for us as possible friends, even after all the stupid things she'd done.

I thought of what had struck me in Crenfall's words, words that may have meant something. I had grown accustomed to picking apart single words as clues; the magic that had imprisoned Denbury worked off specific words, a direct spell. Words had far more power than people gave them credit for. As a girl who'd spent a good bit of her life mute, I appreciated that fact more than most.

"The *grand* and the *central*," I stated. "Do you think there's something going on near the depot?" I wanted to compare that area to the addresses Brinkman offered Jonathon and see if there was any rhyme or reason to them.

"I do, yes," Mrs. Northe said, nodding, her expression fixed in concentration. "And then there were the numbers. And then the reference to *Majesties*. High-born folk, which would explain the connection with the English, who have more stratifications that we'd like to think we have here, though they merely take different forms, and the discussion of what seemed to be a societal shift. And the ancient power of the name once more. If there are further spells afoot, we must keep that at the core. I ought to have written those numbers down. There is code in madness, and sense in code. Incredible works of scripture and art have been written in odd sequences and fantastical scenarios. But it was familiar to me. I think it may have been related to the golden ratio. But rearranged..."

I blinked at her, hoping she'd explain. She smiled. "I thought your father may have explained that one to you at some point. The golden ratio is a mathematical concept that can be applied to art. It's thought to be divine, a ratio of composition and proportion that is thought to be most pleasing to the eye, a pattern that repeats in nature, something Godly. Ah. Yes, that's why it was odd."

"Crenfall was doing it backward, then," I offered. "Inverted."

"Precisely." She chuckled mordantly. "At least these wretches are consistent in their disregard for the proper order of things. It would seem they'd prefer the world be inside out."

"Just chaos?" I asked. I thought about what we knew so far, the demon's insinuations of a new dawn. "Surely they want more than anarchy. What does mere chaos buy them, other than perhaps entertainment?"

"Oh, there is a greater agenda, but the true scope of it seems to elude me. All the paranormal experimentation has to be leading to something, but I'm just not sure exactly what. I believe they seek weapons of control and terror, the soul-splitting and the reanimation and the chemicals are part of that quest, but to what end they'll be used I'm still not sure."

Having transferred to a trolley car and after a two block walk to her townhouse, Mrs. Northe brought me into her parlor, and I, of course, looked around and listened for any signs of Jonathon's presence, but there were none, to my great disappointment. I'd become used to catching him up on information immediately, and the thought that he was out and about without me was a fresh torture, the kind I'd only felt when he had gone to England to attempt to sort out his affairs.

When I'd first met him, our souls had communed through a painting, and with a flood of guilt, I realized I'd liked it—or at least felt more confident—when he was trapped, as it was a measure of control I'd had over the situation. I didn't like that at all; the realization looked ugly to me when I pondered it within me. I needed to allow him to affect his situation for the better on his own. I'd seen the sort of revitalization of his spirit that his own direct action had wrought. Being his savior had been delicious for me, a power like I'd never known. I craved that sensation again and empathized with the addict of some powerful drug.

Mrs. Northe waited for her maid to leave before she continued with her thoughts, proffering the tea that had been prepared for us. "I've been worried that Crenfall is a liability to us, that if a Master's Society member were to interrogate him it could jeopardize us. But it would appear Crenfall and the demon were lone operatives without a direct overseer. At least not one who could have foreseen the final business with the painting. Considering the timing, Crenfall couldn't have managed to see the portrait in pieces, so I doubt he could be an informant, though we might want to make your father aware that the Metropolitan might be a source of intrigue, if any of them still think Lord Denbury's painted prison still hangs there, and not in pieces."

I stared at my hands, the worn lace gloves I needed to mend a couple of fingertips of, and felt overwhelmed as how could we pick out Society operatives in a city thronged with people. Anyone, anywhere, on any street, could be looking for us. It was maddening. I picked up the teacup and forced myself not to shake; trembling was tedious to me at this point. I dearly did not want to appear as fragile as I felt. I felt Mrs. Northe's eyes upon me before she continued:

"I can't imagine it would have occurred to 'society operatives' that a mute girl would speak the countercurse to set Lord Denbury free, so you may yet be safe while his cover may have to remain carefully in question. We don't know what could have gotten back to London. I made sure that Mr. Smith cleaned up everything around Preston's hospital wing. The staff there was informed of his suicide, and no one seemed very surprised, glad to have the wing reopen without his morbid presence and constant séances."

Well. His *suicide* wasn't entirely a lie; Preston had most certainly brought on his death himself. It was just a bit more complicated, with reanimate corpses and ghosts holding surgical scalpels. The thought of Mrs. Northe's personal guard Mr. Smith stalking about in his eerie, quiet way, tying up loose ends and settling matters with unsettling efficiency, brought a perverse smile to my face. He was the most inscrutable man I'd ever met, but I trusted him.

Mrs. Northe, seeing that there were no more queries or answers for the day, knowing we already had plenty to think about, had a carriage brought round to my home. I entered a quiet house with Father quiet in the study, went quietly to my room in the quiet way that was so often comfortable between us. Then, as I sat gingerly upon my bed, there came the terrible question of what to do with myself next.

My thoughts turned dark, and I knew, before I even closed my eyes, that a nightmare would come.

And I knew it would be one for the record books.

Chapter Six

A hallway again. Of course. The general palette of my nightmares, the backdrop against which terrible things would be painted. In this shadowy realm, I often saw things that would come to fruition. I didn't know that at first, suffering riotous nightmares during Jonathon's ordeal within the painting, but I'd soon found out as murders corresponded with names and terrible images I'd foreseen.

My subconscious had inextricably become riddled with clues, and rather than merely being assaulted with them, I was determined, this time, to utilize them as information that might keep us just one step ahead of the enemy. At least, that's what I told myself when I woke. While dreaming, I was merely terrified, and the idea that this foresight was some kind of gift to fight our enemies was difficult to take comfort in.

The hallway wasn't like that of a house; it was more like an alley, bricks and archways to either side of me, the shadows deep and shifting, the second life of a city once the sun descends. The myriad sounds of a thriving metropolis filtered through to my ear but as if from far away or as though I were hearing them through glass.

And then a horse nearly ran me down. I only heard the galloping at the last minute.

There was a flash of light, a seizure of fear, so many things collided in that moment as I felt a hand shove me against the hard brick wall at my back and a stern voice saying my name. My mother. Saying my name. Pushing me out of the way, just like she did to save my life at age four... Would I always need her to rescue me? Waking, dreaming, always rescuing me.

There were tears in my eyes, for the idea that Helen Stewart was strong enough in life *and* in death to continuously come to my aid, as her spirit had been forceful enough to do even *outside* my dream realm, made me feel as though she were not dead at all, really, just in a different place than my corporeal reality. But still, in her way, she was very much alive. We knew so little, really, of divine mystery and the Undiscovered Country. Those two worlds were closer in distance, perhaps, in dreams. But my mother's whisper crossing the boundaries of life and death to be with me was the stuff of happiness, not nightmare.

But then I heard screaming.

My nightmares liked to remind me what they were, lest I ever be lulled into something pleasant.

As the riderless, unbridled, unsaddled horse ran free, tearing ahead, clattering down cobblestones, and its white form faded into the darkness ahead, I found myself walking inexorably forward, toward a building from whence the noise and commotion were coming.

A lantern swung in the wind of the horse's wake outside a wide-paneled glass window. Within, I saw a figure struggling, wild haired and wide-eyed as if his body were battling with itself, his black-clad form writhing against the wooden bar of what I assumed was a tavern. There were ledges where gentlemen stood with glasses around the perimeter of the bar, and tables of people, all of them looking on in horror.

Two young women, also in elegant mourning-wear, stood at the entrance to the tavern, looking on and screaming. I recognized them from the swaying, enchanted crowd thronging the orchestra pit of Nathaniel Veil's shows; they were members of his Association. I scanned the crowd; all were staring at the struggling gentleman, now a second one beside him in similar throes, a fine-looking man of business, not a youth of the Association. The patrons of the tavern were looking around wildly, as if anyone around them could be suspect. Across the room, leaning against a wall, was a somber-looking fellow, the only one who didn't seem surprised. He was in a long beige coat, the pale color standing out against all the dark din. He stood with a doctor's bag. Stevens.

This was another instance of "The Cure" going horribly wrong.

And then the man turned to look at me. With dark, reflective eyes, shining like an animal's in the night. He smiled a sharp-toothed smile, and his visage flickered as if it were in a flip-book where static images simulate movement if turned in quick succession. In this dizzy shift, I no longer saw a man's face but the gargoyle-like, horrid, twisted features of the demon's pure form, the ungodly picture my mind had attached to the raw, dark energy that had twice physically attacked me. In terms of the demonic possession we had encountered in our ordeals thus far, the senses were not always to be trusted. The man, or creature, reached out a hand, staring at me through the glass, his still and static form so eerie in comparison to all the tumult around him...

A pressure around my throat, all too familiar, had me gasping and choking and bolting up straight into the blinding moonlight as white as the horse that nearly ran me down.

Puzzling over these things as I woke, I jotted down everything I could remember in the beautiful leather-bound diary that had been a gift from Mrs. Northe. I must have slept in past breakfast. Considering I was known to be a fitful sleeper, Father generally didn't wake me and simply let me sleep my fill. We'd not stood on much ceremony over meals through the years; my inability to speak had always made that time somewhat strained, and now, what was there to talk about but the pall cast over us until the evils of the Society were put to rest?

Still, Father and I had gained so much ground in love and trust, and I was determined not to lose it. I was also determined to carve out my niche at the Metropolitan Museum of Art, having been "apprenticed" to the Acquisitions department—which really wasn't an appointment so much as an appeasement of my stubborn spirit, which wanted something to *do*. Still, even though I'd not been given any real responsibility, I would show up as if I had.

But I arrived to find my father kept in a private meeting where it was obvious that a young woman's presence was not welcome. So I then wandered the museum itself, which had always been, since its recent opening, one of my very favorite places, very nearly as sacred to me as the park in which it was ensconced. I was determined not to let the horror that had happened within the building's basement rooms in the dead of night mar the whole of that beautiful institution. I strolled the halls, lost in the beautiful art, drinking in every corner, crevice, and open space of the grandeur of this building founded by all kinds of wealthy New Yorkers dying for this city to rival the great European metropolises. I steered clear of the basement vault rooms where memories lurked like spiders hanging from webs in dark spaces.

Once Father was free, he searched out my restless spirit until he found me in the exquisite company of the sculpture wing. Bidding us take tea in one of the meeting rooms, he excitedly shared the latest plans for funding and expansions at the museum and mentioned a horde of upcoming galas he would need to facilitate and attend. I nodded eagerly at the mention of his various events.

Father busy at the Metropolitan meant fewer eyes upon me and all that I may be called upon to do that he'd hardly approve of. He was sure to add that Mrs. Northe would see to my chaperoning, which he said with some trepidation. He probably realized at this point that the woman he was painstakingly courting—though he and I both faced the daunting class and wealth differential between our respective prospects—was as much an enabler as anything.

Still, as long as we went through all the motions of propriety, in this there was some consolation for a man who had always struggled to know what to do with the headstrong girl so much like his late wife. A man who found himself again in the thrall of someone as imperious as Mrs. Northe. My father the mouse, my mother the hawk, Evelyn Northe the eagle... Perhaps the species could get along, like in the visions of God's kingdom...

"Evelyn has invited us for dinner this evening," Father added. "She might be out when we arrive, but she's instructed us to make ourselves comfortable in our various spheres."

My father did enjoy a fine cigar, and there were no shortage of those in the late Peter Northe's study, which was kept lively by the comings and goings through her home. I'd have no problem entertaining myself in her massive library, wondering if I could pick the locks on some of her glass cabinets of the rarer and potentially scandalous kinds of books a good girl was not supposed to read, like advanced physics and mechanical engineering and maybe the odd book on the occult. I would, of course, hope Jonathon would be there. He had yet to report on his scouting of the addresses. I had a great deal to share with him in turn. I would have to do my very best to make sure there was no awkwardness, to assure him that I wanted us to move forward as a team, a couple, betrothed...

I smiled and took Father's proffered arm, hoping warmth could offset the dark circles beneath my eyes from a sleep full of harrowing dreams. My quiet demeanor and pleasant expression seemed to placate him. I would do what I could to maintain that facade for the man who only wanted my happiness. Truly, I knew that was his foremost concern, hoping for a less paranormally augmented life for his daughter than had been granted by fate. He didn't ask about any news, evidence, or anything about Jonathon at all. I was sure he'd pressure the proposal still, but perhaps he was giving us a bit of breathing room, and for that I was grateful.

No one seemed to be home at the Northe residence but a new maid I didn't recognize—perhaps with all the entourages of various guests in her home, she'd hired more staff. The Irish woman, Sally, (who was surprised that I asked to address her by name) said she'd likely be home soon so I could wait for her in the parlor, as there were always "people that Mistress would be expecting," and I was one of them.

And so I did. At first I just sat, taking in all the fine things of the room, the brocades, the flocked wallpaper, and richly paneled wood, the fine curtains with tassel and trim, the marble fireplace with a mantel topped with stained-glass lamps and two dancing bronze sculptures, the fine curio full of delicate china and figurines, a lacquered harpsichord in the corner I wondered if she knew how to play, and of course, a lavish writing suite.

There was a letter laying out upon on her desk. I stood. I knew I shouldn't spy or pry. But knowing you shouldn't and actually stopping yourself from reading what's lying out in the open... But the first sentence caught my eye:

My dear niece Maggie,
It's up to you whether the devils will have you or not...

And then I was absorbed in all that Mrs. Northe hadn't wanted to tell me, but what she'd clearly left out for me to see...

Chapter Seven

My curiosity about the letter overtook my propriety. Mrs. Northe knew me. Quite well. If that was lying out in plain sight, I was meant to see it. At least, that's how I justified sitting down to read it.

My dear niece Maggie,

It's up to you whether the devils will have you or not... Karen tells me that you seem detached from the reality that you are in, in that you are not taking responsibility for your actions but are blaming them on others. Me, for one. Natalie, another, Mr. Bentrop and that book still more...

Here is where I have failed you. I didn't know about that book until it was too late. But some part of you had to know it wasn't a good book, Maggie, didn't you? You've insisted on trying to get information out of me. Why wouldn't you have brought that book to me? Mr. Bentrop turned you against me? Over the course of a couple of dinner parties? He is not a nice man, Maggie, nor are his associates. They are trying to pave roadways for the type of terrible energy that nearly killed you, the kind you willingly brought into your own home, resurrected in an altar in your closet.

I beg you to see that I dissuaded you from the wrong types of paths; I encouraged you to sit with our simple, quiet séances. But they were not flashy enough for you. It was not exciting enough, it seemed, to merely set a soul to rest. Power was more entrancing for you, and parlor tricks to charm a crowd. There are plenty of charlatan spiritualists out there who can train you in the ways of the trick table to create knocks as if a spirit were corresponding. That isn't my brand, it isn't my way, and I'll not encourage mere theatrics. I've told you this countless times. But I want you to see these convictions of mine in print, on paper, here in this vulnerable hour, I want you to understand the difference between the type of evil you courted and the type of peace and light in which I strive to live. And, yes, of course, there is a harrowing gray area between.

I know that you are jealous of what Natalie and I shared. I am fond of Natalie, and I always will be. She was called by God to do something very specific. She had to be the one to rescue Lord Denbury's soul. You must accept that as fact and move on from it.

And now you, dear Maggie, are called to turn your life around.

In doing so, I daresay you might be far more powerful than you could ever have imagined. For you stared down the Devil, after inviting him in and now you have the chance to repent and say no. It is brave to recognize you made a mistake and to devote your life to a different path. There are two paths. Two walks in this life, and in the life of a soul beyond its body. This is the point at which you must choose.

You must take Karen's words deeply to heart. She and Amelia were the two brightest spots of my youth, and when all of us were beset with dark energies, we pulled each other through into the light. I have to believe Amelia is there as a guardian angel, willing you into that same better day; she was always powerful in spirit.

Please don't ever think you haven't been important to me. Your soul was crying out for attention, and I was fixated upon Natalie's particular dilemma. For that I apologize. But I did trust that you were strong enough to not be overcome by darker whims. Prove that to me now in showing me you know the difference between the darkness you courted and the light that your family and friends offer you. Don't worry about the retribution of your family, you leave that to me, I'll make them come around.

I hope you might be moved to write back. Natalie has asked after you; she wants you to be healthy and happy as much as I do. If she can forgive you, seeing as she almost died due to your lack of understanding, you are further along your path toward a greater power. Embrace it.

Your aunt,

Evelyn

I set down the letter and sat slowly upon the nearest settee, my heart very full. I prayed very hard for Maggie. For Mrs. Northe. For myself. I sat in silence until Mrs. Northe swept in, all grace, graciousness and grandeur.

Dinner was quiet and lovely. Lavinia had dinner sent to her room as she was tasked with correspondences to all of her Association, trying to make sure no further lambs were lost in the dark wood of chemical temptations offered by wolves. But my dream haunted me and I wondered if I should warn her. But what could she do? She was already trying to assess the damage done, and she was perhaps psychologically still at a critical juncture. Jonathon was again out. With no explanation as to where. The thought that he may be avoiding me made my stomach twist in a terror as gripping as my nightmares.

Home once the sun set, I returned immediately to my room. Diary in hand, I sat at my window, looking out at what I could of the city, the avenue beyond. It was all right that I was restless. So was New York. The city had always, in its own way, understood me. Then I looked down and examined the words I had written.

White Horse.

Tavern.

Chaos.

Stevens.

Bits of conversation came back to me as I stared at the first two lines of my notes. The new White Horse Tavern. I'd heard my father's friends at the Metropolitan talking about its recent opening. That would be the site of the next attack. And if I knew my dreams, the result would be within days of the dream. I had no time to lose; I had to investigate. Tonight.

Chapter Eight

I'd done this before: dressing in men's clothing in order to investigate a scene.

Last time I'd ended up in a part opium den, part brothel in the Five Points, on the trail of a murderer, trying to protect innocent victims. It was certainly one of the braver things I'd done.

This time, simply donning men's clothes so as not to be questioned or accosted while I examined a mere tavern near Greenwich Village after dark seemed like far less dangerous quarry. Still, upending my gender and pretending to be something I was not has its anxieties.

I stared at myself in the mirror, dressed in one of Father's plain brown cast-off suits that I'd had secretly tailored down to fit me during my first foray into subterfuge, back in the days when saving Lord Denbury's soul was a methodical process.

Looking at the youthful creature in the mirror, my auburn locks tucked and pinned up beneath a newsboy's cap, I felt far less certain about the exact right course of action. Though my instincts were strong, I now had experienced more trials and errors by which to second-guess myself.

The fact that I'd survived against all odds with the help of God, mentorship, love, and some benevolent spirits didn't make me feel much better about tempting fate once again. At what point would God deem me foolish and stop watching out for me when I was obviously putting myself in situations where I might need divine intervention?

The danger of crying wolf seemed a distinct possibility here, and yet I didn't know any other way to confront the clues granted to me in my dreams but this. If I did nothing, I was a coward without a gift. This was a way of taking my knowledge into action without dragging anyone else along with it, in case my dream world was entirely wrong. I didn't want to make anyone else liable for my mind's unpredictable eye. Along with any sort of power, a great responsibility comes hand in hand. That was surely a certainty for the ages.

I stared at myself in the mirror in the same way I'd done when I'd first donned men's wardrobe for the sake of espionage; surprised at the young boy before me, I knew that I was me, and yet here I was certainly not as society would have me. It was a nice blending wardrobe, nothing too fine, nothing too shabby, brilliantly and forgettable in the middle-class range.

I snuck out of the house by ten, blessed by early and heavy sleepers on Father's and Bessie's count. I was far more the night owl. Watching men's gaits to try to embody their strides, I went out to Lexington Avenue to hail a cab. My allowance for penny candies, ribbons, and newspapers had been increasingly co-opted for spy-craft. I corralled a downtown-bound hansom cab, and the small compartment clopped and bounced down cobblestone blocks until the streets went at odd angles, and old New York streets took over, donning family names and early histories, banishing the numbered grid to the uptown streets it had served since the beginning of the century.

The White Horse was as you'd expect of any tavern: loud, raucous, filled with liquor and men. I sidled up to the wooden bar and ordered a drink in a low voice, whatever I'd heard the man a few steps ahead of me order. I knew nothing of liquor or beer; I'd sip the glass and not drink it as I scouted for my target, not wanting any substance to make me any less sharp. It didn't take terribly long to find the man in question.

I nearly physically recoiled at the sight of him. Somehow my dreams had foretold enough about the man that even though the description hadn't been clear, my gut knew exactly who it was. The predatory nature about him, his stance, his eyes, the way he seemed to sniff more than breathe, all of it had the air of animal more than human that spoke of a possessed body. His behavior wasn't overtly so, otherwise no one would entertain his presence, but it was subtle enough for me to feel and see that something was a bit off. But obviously the man was targeting those with little to lose, easy prey, who tended to overlook such things as eyes that shined a bit too oddly and movement that was a little too much like a puppet.

He was holding court, it seemed, looming over a table of bleary-eyed young fellows who were considering the man's words, one with skepticism, another with hope, one with desperation, and one who seemed a bit too intoxicated to focus. I wondered if somehow I could distract them, break the spell this man seemed to be casting over them like a pall. But then directing the man's focus onto me seemed like a bad idea, considering the dream. I knew I was staring at all of them a bit too intently, rudely, but hopefully from the shadows I kept to, no one would notice.

And then I felt arms slide around me from behind, and just as I jumped, about to cry out, I heard a familiar, delectable British accent purr my name. The whisper in my ear stilled me immediately.

"Shh... Natalie. I know it's you," came Jonathon's murmur and the action of his arms and the murmur of my name made me weak in the knees. "The trouble with disguises," he continued with a bemused chuckle in my ear, "is that, when it comes to *me*...I can always see your light. You can't hide the vibrant color of your soul. Not from me."

I drank in his words. We'd had such awkwardness, such distance, I was afraid the kind of dreamlike words and intense passion our relationship had been built upon had been banished to the world of his painted prison, I feared our poetry was lost in the "real" world. It would seem he still had fine words for me. Perhaps it took a bit of unexpected espionage for them to return. Thankfully we had magic to bring us home. He could see the colors of my aura, the clue that had allowed his soul the agency to communicate with me even in his prison. And it would seem I was illuminated by magic still...

"I love it when you find me, Jonathon," I whispered back to him. "And I always want you to..."

He kissed my temple, breath hot against my ear as he murmured: "You ridiculous thing, you, what on earth are you doing here?" My body thrilled from head to toe. I relaxed in his hold and leaned against him.

It was good that we were wholly in the shadows, considering how I was dressed. The bohemian freedom championed by such circles as Nathaniel Veil's Association had no precedent here, and so two *men* embracing in this sort of intimate manner was simply not allowed in society at large.

Maybe someday it would be. For my part I didn't see anything wrong; love was love, a soul was a soul, I'd learned firsthand that the spirit defines the person, not the body it was in. But society, I knew well enough from the disability that still cast its occasional silent shadow over my life, didn't like things to be anything but "normal," expected, traditional, unquestioned. But considering paranormal had become my normality, all things had to adjust accordingly. I could only consider my own spiritual, psychological, and physical well-being and say my own prayers, knowing I'd gotten this far by a faith that was larger than the time and the constraints in which I lived. I couldn't count on society to know how to adapt alongside me.

"How did *you* know to come here, Jonathon?" I murmured, turning my face to graze my nose against his fine cheekbone, warmed also by the fact that he wanted to touch and be close to me no matter the clothes I was in, a reassurance that reached across myriad boundaries.

"I asked you first," he countered.

"A dream. Foretold," I answered. "You?"

"I followed him." Jonathon indicated the man in question, who was ordering a round of drinks for his captive audience. "From one of Brinkman's addresses. He was coming around from the back of the building. I saw a sparkle of the red and gold of the demons' light bounce about him, the color flashing out of the corner of my eye. No other addresses seemed to wield anything of particular interest or note. I'd watched each for many hours. I didn't really think, I just came this way."

"Same, once I put the pieces of the dream together enough to evince the clues as leading to this location, I donned this disguise and made my move."

"Is this what you wore the last time you went someplace a lady shouldn't go on her own?"

I nodded. Jonathon held back a laugh. Whether I was or wasn't convincing, he didn't say, and I didn't get the chance to ask before the man we were watching pulled a few glass vials out from his long, pale coat pocket and put them on the table, where the youthful audience stared at them with a mixture of hunger and apprehension. Jonathon seized my tall glass of stout and a second glass of ale that had been abandoned upon a nearby ledge. Gesturing for me to stay put, he then suddenly he stepped out from the shadows. I noticed he'd dressed down considerably, to mere shirtsleeves, suspenders, and trousers like a regular factory worker. A grubby cap with the brim pulled low concealed his fine black locks and a bit of soot was smudged over a chiseled cheekbone.

It's true that his more lordly appearance might have given him away, and in this case he didn't seem to wish to play the demon to this Stevens fellow, just in case he was being sought as such. We both had come in covert costume, it would seem.

Jonathon stumbled artfully forward, careful not to tip the glasses, until he jostled toward the table. He ran right into Stevens, first spilling the dark stout onto the man's beige coat, then spilling the second glass over the glass vials, overturning them, sending a tiny puff of red powder near Jonathon's face. He batted the particles away with a faux drunken movement. I wasn't sure how potent or volatile the substance was, and I hoped there was no effect from his proximity to it.

Disrupting the whole scene rather brilliantly, causing far greater hubbub and commotion around him, Jonathon fumbled over an apology—in an impressive New York–styled accent—before stumbling on to say he'd go get someone to help clean it all up. Stevens barked after him not to bother, the man's dark and troubled eyes flashing, his drawn face scowling as the youths at the table blinked and reacted.

Jonathon circled round the tavern, I lost sight of him in a cluster of bodies for a moment, and suddenly he returned to me in the shadows. Upon his return, he was sans cap and wearing a dark black jacket, blending into the shadows with me.

"Where did you..." I gestured to the coat.

"Hung upon a coat tree in the back of the bar," he replied. "Brinkman wrote me a note with a few tips. Useful things, really." Before I could ask further about fresh communication from the spy, Jonathon continued. "Watch for any changes or anything to do with those vials or the content. I'm going to speak to the management about someone coming and trying to make sales of products that were not sold by the tavern itself, something that might keep Stevens watched, and hopefully reported to the authorities." He stalked off, and I watched the unfolding reactions at the table.

The four youths seemed to have broken from a trance. They stared at Stevens and at the dripping mess before them alternately, their brows furrowing. Three of them stood to clean themselves off and walked away as if they weren't exactly sure of themselves; one just turned from Stevens but remained sitting, using a kerchief to wipe down the surfaces directly around him, his shoulders hunched, either tired, drunk, miserable, or all three. Stevens clenched his jaw and turned to pace in the dim light of the tavern lanterns, thinking no one was watching.

Just as the group dispersed and the moment was foiled, I noticed two young black-clad women in short black cloaks and hats with net veils peering in through the tavern window from the street beyond, arm in arm. They waved at one of the young men within, and his visage brightened at the sight of them.

My heart pulled, as all of them reminded me of the characters in my dream. In my dream, there had been screaming as young men were turning into monsters, transformed by insidious means, dehumanized to wretched experiments meant to keep the victims in fear. Here, there were only smiles. I wanted to cry out in triumph. We changed the fate of the night...

Inside, Stevens turned, his sallow face hard and haunted. I wondered what drove that man. Was it as misguided as it had been with Doctor Preston, reanimating out of love? What made Stevens want to alter a person so? Or was he merely a possessed body, the actual original researcher having long ago been dispatched?

He stole a glass from a ledge where a few smart-looking fellows were hotly debating politics and downed the beverage. His fist clenched and his arm raised, seeming ready to throw the glass before he then thought better of it as one of the staff approached him. I overheard the manager gruffly ask about whether he'd been trying to sell products in their establishment. Stevens was immediately contrite and ordered more alcohol. I wished in that moment this "doctor" of questionable repute would have picked a fight so that a local police officer would have been called to take him in. I thought about throwing something to seek escalation, but escaping a bar brawl wasn't in my particular expertise.

Confident the doctor wasn't going anywhere as he sat back at the table now wholly abandoned, defeated, a glass of liquor in each hand, I took my eyes off the man and searched for Jonathon. Feeling so vindicated by Stevens's failure to incite another incident, I turned to Jonathon upon his return to the shadows surrounding us and nearly threw my arms around him. Instead, I merely stood very closely, hoping to regain the scorching intimacy we'd had from the moments our souls had first met within the magic of a canvas...

"Let's not be strangers, Natalie," he said, reassuring my foremost concern as if he'd read my mind.

"Let's not," I replied eagerly. "I've been so worried, can feel you withdrawing—"

"I've a lot on my mind," he interrupted, his voice hard. "Dark things, Natalie. I don't want to burden you—"

"I want—need—to know everything. I want to bear the weight of that burden *with* you, just like when your spirit kept darkening that painting."

He sighed heavily. "Home is calling me, Natalie. I'm going to have to return to the estate at some point. I can't avoid it any longer."

"I'm coming with you," I declared.

He just gave me a pained look.

"I don't want us to be apart," I insisted. "I want us to be together and for everything to be perfect, never pressured, never looking over our shoulders, but just perfect."

He stared at me, and I could see the flicker of doubt in his eyes. "So you will accept me? If I were to ask...again?"

My heart jumped at this, but it still had to be for the right reason. "If you ask for no other reason than for your own desire. Not because anyone forced you to. I've never wanted to say yes to anything more," I whispered, achingly. He nodded, biting back a smile, seeming in part placated, in part still nervous. "Besides," I added, "don't you think the forces at work would like to see us split apart? We can't give them that opportunity."

"True," he agreed. "Tonight, I do think a crisis may have been averted."

We had intervened before further victims had been ensnared for Stevens's experimental purposes, sowing seeds of chaos. I felt a proud surge flood my body. We were clever, resourceful, and gifted. We were more than the enemy would expect of us.

As we left, for we could not stay out into the night indefinitely, we had to step from the shadows and into the brighter gas-lit entryway. I cast one look back over my shoulder. The man, Stevens, was staring at me. Right at me. Through me. His eyes flashed oddly, unnaturally.

And suddenly I didn't feel so clever anymore.

Chapter Nine

Jonathon and I shared a hired carriage back to our respective residences. I doubted he'd have to sneak back into Mrs. Northe's in the way I'd have to sneak back home; men did not have to answer to their whereabouts. Lord Denbury was lord of his own domain, and that would never be questioned. A young woman was not afforded such freedom of destiny.

But the particulars of freedom were lost to me the moment that Jonathon closed the cab door behind me, shutting us into the dark compartment. Somehow being truly alone together in full cover of night gave us permissions we hadn't allowed ourselves of late. The intense situation we had just shared brought us back to each other, to the partnership and perils we had become so familiar with. With those perils also had come passion. He and I must have been of a mind, for the moment I reached for his hand, he took the opportunity...

"Will you permit me a moment of not being entirely gentlemanly, Miss Stewart?" he asked in a hot murmur in my ear. "We've been trying to be so proper and behaved—"

"You're permitted," I nearly gasped. He tore the cap from my head and entwined his fingers in my hair. Pulling me into his arms, he kissed me deeply, again and again, hands roving, until the carriage slowed its pace. East down the block stood my home, and I could not remain locked in his embrace indefinitely.

With a reluctant groan, he released me to catch my breath. I was just as woeful to be let go. But the driver wouldn't just sit there without question or further payment, and we did not dare to be suspect in our actions. Silent as I descended the carriage—I was afraid my voice would tell tales of me—I donned my cap once more, hoping no one was watching the front door of the divided townhouse, and that I could quietly ascend to our top floor rooms as undetected as I'd descended.

I was in luck in returning to my bed unnoticed, though the eyes of Stevens still haunted me, as if I could see him hovering at my window like some creature in my beloved Gothic yarns. The sorts of tales that had once so titillated me left a far different taste in my mouth now that I was living what would only be believed as fiction.

That night came a nightmare, as if the night's victory was just a tease, as if I couldn't possibly be afforded a sensual dream of Jonathon's kisses alone, heaven forbid. Just as I was beginning to feel we were gaining ground as lovers and partners once more and winning against enemies in our waking hours, the dread fear and reality of his looming departure was writ large over my unconscious hours and the dread I could not entertain while awake had full reign while asleep.

This time the dream was shared with Jonathon, as we used to when our souls met in the painting and our consciousness was linked in dreams, a life-saving particular his curse could never have predicted. I was so glad to see him in my mind's eye, thrilled that he had returned to my resting self, but it seemed he didn't see me down the hallway from his striking silhouette. He was preoccupied on something before him, far, far away down the endless corridor that was such a continuing construct of these dreams. Always a corridor, with different particulars. This time it was the long hall of a house. A fine house. Perhaps his...

Something was calling him, voices, murmurs. From the empirical evidence of our horrors thus far, I knew that a swarm of murmurs in my mind meant that the dark magic of demons was amassing, building, coalescing, drawing him out and away from me...

This was the darkness gripping hold of him as he'd intimated to me at the tavern, and I called out:

"Jonathon, don't follow shadows..."

He looked over his shoulder, back at me. His bright eyes were at first pained, but then flashed oddly, like the demon's once did. He turned back, away from me once more, and kept walking. Ahead of him was a familiar old room, his study, in Greenwich, England. The study he had been painted into, a painted prison we had both become all too familiar with. I couldn't think he was walking back into it willingly... Forces would fight for him, yet, would he ever fully be free and could he ever regain his home? Could that place ever feel safe? What place could feel truly safe again when demons invaded with little care for doors or decorum, rejecting the sovereignty of soul? But thankfully, even though the devils wove their way into my dreams, so did the angels.

Jonathon cried out far ahead of me, there was a burst of light, the door to his study splintered. He cried angrily and ran off into the darkness, pursuing something as all the gas lamps around me suddenly lowered their flame.

They're coming for you... A warning whisper in my mind.

If the devils had anything to do with it, they would part us. Separate us and pick us off one by one because as a team, we were invincible. Or, at least, had been thus far, thanks in no small part to some divine intervention. In our separation would lie our downfall, I was sure of it. Why in the world had I turned down his proposal? It was just what the devils wanted. Maybe they were at work within us more than we knew.

The nightmare meant that in the morning I rose at the time my father rose. He always did take to the morning better than I. Before I could face anything or anyone, I jotted down the details of the dream in my diary; purging the images was cathartic, and yet I still had to log details of the dream as potential clues.

I'd been careful to take the time to be fond with Father, and with Bessie, our housekeeper who moved in after her Irish husband died building the foundations of the Brooklyn Bridge. A friend of my mother's from protestant civil liberties circles, Bessie had angered both her own family and her husband's by the sheer fact she was black and he was not. She hadn't had options, resources, or legal recompense when he died, and being a friend of the family, she filled a necessary void here, my widower father not knowing much what to do to keep the house when I'd been away at school learning Standard Sign.

"I assume you'll be going over to Mrs. Northe's today?" he asked, when I knew the question really meant if I would be seeing Jonathon.

"As one would only expect, and as she should," Bessie said matter-of-factly, shifting a piece of bread from her plate onto mine when she saw I'd taken to my food rather quickly. I caught her winking at me. I returned a wink when Father wasn't looking.

Bessie must have been encouraging Father not to be so worried about Lord Denbury's proposal, as he simply didn't press the issue further after her comment. She knew all too well the damage various familial pressures could do to true love across boundaries.

Father shifted the conversation to acquisitions, and I mentioned what I thought the collection lacked, and then we were all off to our respective duties and errands.

I spent a little longer on my appearance, pinning up my hair with seed pearl pins Mrs. Northe had gifted me, sure to wear the nicer of my two lace-trimmed cream blouses, noting the slight tear in the sleeve had been repaired. Bless you, Bessie. I wore my best overskirt with its slight bustling at the back, a deep plum, my favorite color, with a little matching plum vest trimmed in mauve that made the piece seem like a whole ensemble. After the delicious kisses he gifted me the night prior, I wanted to be at my feminine best, though my best dresses were ball gowns I'd been given as gifts. A mere trip to Mrs. Northe's parlor did not necessitate a ball gown, fine as the parlor was.

The maid let me in, gesturing me into the parlor, and ran down the list of who was in, who had been in, and who was out. It was quite the rotating guest list. Mrs. Northe and Lord Denbury were both evidently out, but Lavinia was looking a bit lost in the parlor. The maid was quick to fetch us both tea. The black-clad girl, hair partly up and partly streaming down her back in a fetching deep red stream, looked like a Pre-Raphaelite Brotherhood painting in mourning.

"Natalie, I'm very glad to see you. I wanted to tell you something I heard. One of my associates dropped this note for me." She referenced a small card in her lap. "He was out at the new White Horse Tavern, downtown, and he thinks he got a sense of the man who was behind the substance. And he said he thought someone looked familiar, someone who...interrupted the man in question, just as he was pressuring a group of lads. I don't suppose...Lord Denbury is on the trail of anyone, is he?" she asked hopefully, as if my Jonathon could be the hero she seemed to need.

I shrugged. I wasn't sure that we were letting on any word of our activities to anyone. It wasn't that I didn't trust Lavinia, there was something about her that compelled me, but I would let Jonathon be the one to share what he'd been up to. I assumed perhaps he was taking Mrs. Northe to the location in question, from whence he'd followed Stevens. Before Lavinia could press me further, there was some commotion at the front door.

Suddenly, I heard a familiar British accent crying out: "Darling, I've come for you!"

Lavinia looked up, wide-eyed, partly in ecstasy, partly in shock, as if she couldn't believe her ears. And then her cheeks turned as red as her hair. We both knew exactly who that voice belonged to.

Nathaniel Veil had returned from England. And it would seem he was on a mission.

I could hear the maid protesting with him that he needed to be announced, but he charged right into the parlor in an imperious swoop of black fabric and flying locks of hair, not bothering to take off his cloak, tossing aside his top hat onto a nearby chair, and practically diving across the parlor and onto his knees before the divan where Lavinia perched so gracefully.

Enter Nathaniel Veil.

Tall and wild, the Gothic actor—all in the finest black, tailored vestments—did not leave his persona behind on the stage once he took his bow. Instead, he lived his theatricality in every moment, to the fullest, the energy and powerful presence entirely overtaking a room. I had to stop myself from laughing, not because I found him foolish, but merely because I was so entertained by his full commitment to being unquestionably dramatic. It was contagiously delightful.

And Lavinia's expression was rather priceless. I could see the joy on her face, but as he took her hands in his and kissed them with flourish, a fierce pain took over, and her whole demeanor darkened.

"Ah, you finally pay attention to me now that I've gone and done something terrible?" she murmured. "You fly to the side of your injured toy?" He looked up at her in horror. "And you might want to be just a touch less rude, Mister Veil," she added, "and say hello to Miss Stewart, who does happen to be in the room with us at present."

"Hello, Mister Veil," I said gently from across the room. "It is so good of you to come. I am sure your Association will derive great comfort from your presence."

Veil sprang up and instantly was across the room and back down on his knees again, taking up my hands in his this time. He did not kiss them, thankfully, for poor Lavinia's sake, but he did hold them to his breast and spoke with absolute earnestness, his accent every bit as delectable to me as Jonathon's was. "Miss Stewart, I am so frightfully glad to see you, too, have you been taking good care of my dove here and my best, bosom friend? Where is that glorious cad *Den*, anyway?"

"I... You mean Lord Denbury?" I said, trying to hold back a chuckle, having forgotten Veil's pet name for Jonathon, a name I was not allowed to utter under any circumstance. *Ever.*

"Yes. Where the devil is the man?" Veil jumped back to his feet again. A towering presence, he paced a few steps before throwing himself onto a pouf. I opened my mouth to answer, but he was onto another subject, addressing Miss Kent. "I've sent a call to round up my Association. We can't have anyone trying to take advantage of them again, so we'll rally the troops here. How are they, *Vin*?"

It seemed everyone important to Nathaniel had a pet name. I cringed at "Vin." He dared not call me "Nat"; he could save that nickname for himself, surely.

"They are all passable. Trying to mitigate any damage done," Lavinia answered, her tone even. "As Miss Stewart said, your presence will do them good. However, I suggest setting a firm tone. We can't have this seem like errant behavior will make you come running." She stared into her teacup. "And before you ask or assume, I was not trying to do that to you. I was genuinely interested in...options."

Veil crossed the room to her again in a mere step. Even though there wasn't room for him, he sat down beside Lavinia, edging her over, her own skirts spilling over his trousers, the two of them a streaming splay of black fabric. If his next words were an act, then he was a very good actor indeed, for he seemed utterly sincere. There was nothing he did by halves, but his truly contrite and earnest tone could not be denied.

"Promise me you'll talk to me before you turn to anything else," Veil said gently. "All of you. I want all of you to feel supported. Is that clear, Vin? I didn't start my Association out of ego. I started it to save lives. Do you remember how many near suicides we had our first year as acquaintances, all brought together by some old dark loneliness that was sown down deep in our bones?"

"I do remember," she whispered, barely audible.

"The point is we have each other, rather than substances, rather than drastic measures. In the Association, all are cared for," he murmured. Lavinia wouldn't look at him, merely nodded. He took a black-gloved finger and placed it under her chin, forcing her to look up at him. "And some are cared for more than others."

"Nathaniel, please don't," she murmured. Even though he had turned her face to him, her eyes still refused to meet his. Blushing furiously, she was surely uncomfortable that I was in the room still. This kind of intimacy was rather shocking to be shared with an acquaintance in the room, but Veil didn't seem to care; he flaunted custom regularly, the whole of his life and his actions public and unapologetic. I was amenable to honest conversation between lovers, but Lavinia didn't know me well enough to know I would not judge her for it.

"Where are you and your Association meeting, Mister Veil?" I asked, lest he try to press the intimacy issue further and publicly kiss her, a shock indeed.

"Why here, of course," Veil replied as if that were obvious. "Mrs. Northe did say I was welcome in her home when she wired me."

"Ah. Yes." I smiled. "But does...Mrs. Northe know about potential... company?"

Veil blinked a moment. "You don't think she'll mind, do you?"

I took a moment to choose words carefully, stifling a surprised chuckle at his oblivious regard for anyone but himself and his own. "I'd think she'd appreciate a bit of an advanced notice, as would the staff, Mister Veil," I finally replied.

Lavinia just stared at me with a wide, horrified stare, trying to mouth an apology. It only made me want to laugh again, until I imagined what it would be like if I were the staff. Maybe I'd go help them. I had benefited from Mrs. Northe's acquaintance, learning how the upper echelon lived, but when one was as distinctly middle-class as I was, life could go either way and so would my empathy.

"Yes... I suppose you've a point there, Miss Stewart..." Veil murmured. "Did I mention you're looking lovely? Purple. Suits you. One of the rare colors I'm fond of."

He bounded up again and darted into the hall; it was impressive how quickly he moved, preternatural almost. It fit with his persona eerily well. I heard him call into the hall: =

"Lovely young miss who I entirely, rudely, bowled past at the door, would you do me the kind favor of preparing for guests?"

My jaw hung open at the sheer cheek of the man.

"How... many..." I heard the poor, beleaguered young maid reply.

"Oh, I'd say about forty," he offered cheerfully. "Give or take a few."

"For...ty...give or take..." came the frightened response. There was a scuffle down the stairs to the kitchens below, and I heard a clatter of a few pans and fire irons.

"Thank you, beautiful!" Veil cried after her and bounded back again to Lavinia's side. She had been able to do nothing but stare after him, helpless to stop the tumbling, sweeping force of nature that was the man she so clearly couldn't help but adore. "So. Darling," he said, edging back onto the seat, practically in her lap. "I think just a good meeting, all of us, among friends, would do a lot for morale, don't you think?"

Lavinia nodded.

Veil then looked over at me, remembering his earlier question that had gone unanswered. "I say. Where *is* that charmer of yours, Miss Stewart?"

"I appreciate that you think I'm the keeper of Lord Denbury's whereabouts, Mister Veil," I said with a chuckle. "But I haven't a clue."

"Well, would you find a way to fetch him?" Veil said as if exasperated. "Otherwise, he'll miss a bloody good show! Impromptu parlor shows are my *favorite*."

"Neither Mrs. Northe nor Lord Denbury seem to be in at present, Mister Veil," I said in response to Nathaniel's insistent belief that I should know the whereabouts and goings-on of my suitor at all times. "So we'll just have to wait."

"Unless they ran away together," Nathaniel said dramatically. Lavinia snorted.

I didn't bother replying. Considering Mrs. Northe was the wisest woman I knew, I didn't think she was the type to run off with someone who could be her son, no matter how attractive he was. But then again, jealousy was a funny creature and flared up at the most inopportune moments. She had always been keenly interested in his welfare and well-being...

Before the green-eyed monster could entirely run away with my sensibilities, the maid I recognized as having been with Mrs. Northe for years, a thin woman who must have been hiding from all the commotion, bobbed her head at me before handing me an envelope. I could feel Nathaniel's keen, dark eyes upon me like a hawk.

"This place is full of secrets and missives!" he exclaimed. "I felt, from the moment I entered this fine house, caught up amid plots and espionage!"

Lavinia leaned forward from the settee, a fond smile on her face as she said in a stage whisper: "Everything, even the smallest thing, feeds his imagination."

"Oh, but it is espionage, Mister Veil," I replied with a wink and opened the note.

"Ha!" he exclaimed, seeming rather delighted. But my humor was short lived.

My heart faltered a bit. The letter was from Maggie. Nathaniel and Lavinia were lost to a bit of banter as I was lost to the words of the misguided young lady who was as much enemy as friend, yet a girl whose destiny I felt was awkwardly entwined with mine.

Dear Natalie,

I write this to you from Chicago, which is an odious place compared to New York City. It's crowded, loud, smelly. Not that New York doesn't have its foul districts, but this swine-butchering city seems so uncultured comparatively. But Karen is trying to endear Chicago to me, and day by day she wins a bit of it over to me.

I'm sure this letter sounds very frivolous thus far. That's probably what you think of me. Frivolous, shallow, with no idea what I've done.

But I do know. Please don't think the worst of me. I realize I nearly died. And I nearly dragged you with me into the madness.

I realize I nearly killed you.

I do not know what else to say but that I am sorry. And I am so very glad that you, Jonathon, and Rachel, and whatever forces were on your side, managed to save us. I owe you my life, misguided as it is. But seeing as I'm still alive, I might as well make the best of it. Though the fashion here in Chicago is at least a year behind New York. Not that I've had much time for shopping.

Karen is teaching me myriad mysteries I don't even begin to know how to describe to you. Perhaps you will see them in person. I long to return to New York, but I am advised that the dark magic needs space and separation. Something you probably already knew.

But things are afoot here in Chicago, Natalie. There are other "doctors" doing other "experiments." Auntie was out here, having left us to our own devices, and her and Karen and the late Amelia did a bit of snooping, and it seems there's a subterranean racket of missing bodies and body parts, of possessions and soul-ripping. Karen said other recent instances might also be related to the collective trying to grab hold in the strangest ways.

But really, is what they're doing entirely evil? Is there not a point to experimentation? Asking questions? Seeing what the limits of the body, mind, and spirit may be?

I wonder these things, and then I wake with carvings on my arms and Karen has to bless me and wash my arms down with holy water. Karen says that Amelia is watching over me, she's sure of it.

I cannot help but wonder if Karen and Amelia were more than friends and were actually in one of those "Boston Marriages." Could you imagine? How scandalous. You should ask Auntie about it, though I doubt she'd tell me the truth. She never did like me being nosy in other peoples' business. I can't blame her. It has gotten me into trouble.

Karen said that Auntie told her that you suffered the same markings as I have. Runes? Some ancient language repurposed for something terrible? Perhaps you can share with me your thoughts and how the terror of it made you feel, for right now I am feeling rather put upon and wholly alone. I've never done well with solitude. Perhaps that's something I could learn from you too.

Not that you're alone, now, with Lord Denbury... I burn with shame. I don't know what else to say upon that count. That's another apology and contrite plea for forgiveness for another day. Though I doubt it would surprise you to hear I'm still rather jealous. What woman wouldn't be with such a catch as he?

Rachel has been by to check on me, not that we can communicate other than by notes we write one another. I can't imagine what it would be like not to be able to speak, and yet she is full of joy and hope, the sweetest soul. I can learn a lot from her about being grateful. That's another thing Auntie always said about me. Ungrateful. But not Rachel, who bears her burdens lightly and with grace.

Rachel says, well, wrote, when she came over for tea, that she's very busy putting all the souls to rest that were pulled to the reanimate body that a researcher here was working on. She says she feels a sense of purpose in fighting all this dark nonsense and that sense of purpose is something I'm trying to cling to.

What about voices? Do you hear voices, Natalie? Whatever you can tell me of your experiences with the forces that Karen refers to as "the Society's darkness," will likely be of great help.

Or, you might tear this letter up, wanting nothing to do with me ever again, and I could not blame you for that, even though I would be sad. I might not have ever been a good friend, but maybe, in the end, I can be.

With hope,

Margaret Hathorn

I sat with these words, a ponderous weight upon my heart, not sure whether to be amused or appalled by Maggie's flippant, socialite tone shifting so effortlessly between gossip, deadly matters, and plaintive soul-searching. I went back and reread her previous paragraphs.

She was so close to what I would consider a redemptive tone, and yet she still justified the experimentation. Until she entirely denounced them, it was likely that the dark magic would still cling to her, call to her, and worse. It might still work through her.

I had denounced the demons entirely, and yet the runes had still managed to invade, carving their ways onto my arm as the dark magic sought me out. What was it doing to her, when she so clearly was still tainted?

I had been staring so intently at Maggie's words, as if I could somehow will further meaning, insight, and direction from the paper itself. Frankly, I wasn't sure how much time had passed. But at the sound of rustling fabrics and soft murmurs, I looked up.

The number of persons in the room and milling in the halls and stairs beyond had increased dramatically, though the sound had not. Mister Veil's Association could be an eerily quiet bunch.

"Oh..." I murmured, my cheeks burning from the realization of sudden, further company. "I see it is time for a show..."

Chapter Ten

There was a cluster of dark-clad persons shifting silently in the hall, moving slightly on their feet as if they were feathers on a breeze or ghosts not touching the floor. Others had quietly entered the parlor.

Two waifish, lovely women sat draped on either side of Lavinia, having entered silently while I'd been reading the letter. Their legs were tucked up on either side of the settee but fabrics trailed down to the floor. Lovely heads rested with a preternatural stillness on Lavinia's shoulders. One was raven-haired and the other was dark brown–haired. Their expressive eyes were kohl-rimmed and their lips were painted a dark red. And then I realized what was slightly scandalous about one of the women. She was in trousers. A fine riding suit coat and *trousers*. And I didn't think she was, like I had recently been, participating in espionage, and so this was simply her choice of evening wear rather than a choice of safety and subterfuge.

"Natalie, please meet my best friends, my kindred spirits," Lavinia said softly, gesturing to the compelling persons at her side. "Raven and Ether."

"Hello, Miss Stewart," Raven replied, in a voice that was a lower register than I'd expect of a rather consumptive-looking woman, and then it occurred to me that Raven and Ether weren't women at all. But young men. I took this in a moment.

They were the ones in my dream. These two were the women outside the White Horse Tavern. I looked at them, one to the other, trying not to stare, trying not to be rude, simply trying to take them in as they would wish to be considered.

I had lived most of my life with a disability. I knew the *precise* look I did not want to give them, a look of confusion or pity, a look that made them feel as if they were just as much the outsider as I'd always felt, a look that they were somehow *wrong*... No, I was better than that... This whole company was better than that.

As a child, all I'd wanted was simply to be accepted for who I was, without others' demands of what that might be. If I had never begun talking again, I would still want to live a full, whole life. Not a half life. Not a cast-off life. Being my own person ran contrary to the idea and expectation that I was to give myself over entirely to the stronger sex and a more dominant will... Clearly these two didn't want to give themselves over to that idea, either and instead were presenting quite an uncommon alterative. It was bold. It was something I had never encountered. But lately, the world saw fit to throw me new challenges.

Nathaniel Veil's Association was a safe haven for those who wished to buck society's expectations in an increasingly dramatic number of ways. Raven and Ether could surely see me puzzling through this, over them, and their choices in presenting to the world. They merely returned my gaze with a gentle patience that was admirable, considering that when people had given my inability to speak a similar baffled and pained, pitying expression, I was far quicker to scowl. Their gracious attitude made me want to be more generous in how I looked at others, most especially when surprised.

"Raven, Ether, a pleasure," I finally managed to reply, and smiled a genuine smile. Ether's sallow face suddenly transformed as he returned the smile, all without breaking the wistful pose against his friend's shoulders. Raven's darkly stained lips curled up in an engaging smirk.

"We saved one another's lives," Lavinia murmured. "We'd had a pact, all of us, that if we couldn't see the light, then we'd all die together in the dark."

"But he stopped us," Ether whispered lovingly, nodding toward Nathaniel, who was greeting Associates at the door with handshakes and kisses on cheeks to each and every one, filing them into rows and places.

"He was known as the Dark Angel around London," Lavinia explained. "He'd find out who in our social circles were at their wits end and try to rally them back, by his sheer force of will. Or, if they went ahead and attempted to take their life, if they were unsuccessful but injured, he brought them to Lord Denbury, who would dress the various wounds of the afflicted, and any other family members would be none the wiser, or none the poorer, for the service. I came from wealth, but not many of our Association do, and your gracious lord's clinic saved many a life that London could have cast aside without a second glance."

My heart swelled with pride at this, and I ached for my valiant Jonathon, who had done so much for this world in his young life thus far. I wished so dearly he was by my side, especially as our reconnection after our bit of espionage had been so...passionate. In this place, with these people, we could simply be ourselves and not worry about censure or propriety. We could simply be loving creatures who had become our own Dark Angels to one another.

It was inspiring, the emotions these quiet and sometimes awkward persons around me exhibited merely in their expressions, their choice of dress, tone of voice, movement, words, the interesting weight of their souls, some lighter, some heavier, depending on their inner burdens. We said so much to one another without even saying a word. From years without speaking, I could read bodies, expressions, attitudes and energies, gestures and physical quirks like I were reading books. The stories that these bodies and faces told were amazing novels in and of themselves. And every beautifully dressed person that entered, each with their own distinct style yet all adhering to the mourning dress as a unifying characteristic, was a new story.

But before I knew it, the room was utterly filled with eager-faced persons of dramatically different class, race, creed, and age. The binding factor was the fashion, and the figure before us, and his themes. And Veil, the master, was ready to put on a show.

"My darling ones," he boomed, accentuating a London upper-class accent when his own was slightly less defined. "We are gathered here today to reaffirm that we are the masters of our own destiny. You shall not give over that mastery to any other thing, person, rule, substance, or vice. You may only give it over to spirit, to love, to something vital, not something draining or cruel. You may only give over to that which makes you better. Never something that makes you less. My dark stars, take your place in the sky. Shall we begin?"

Applause, cries of happiness, gasps, and murmurs, the joy of anticipation launched him into his natural place: center stage of life.

He took stage in the front entrance foyer, visible by all those who had gathered in the parlor, and visible by those waiting on the stair, an impromptu gallery and balcony, concentric circles of dark colors and black crinolines, velvet bands and heaps of ribbons and bows, veils and cloaks.

The keening strain of a violin came from atop Mrs. Northe's grand staircase. From the chair where I sat I could see the musician at the top of the proscenium frame that the parlor pocket doors made. One of his associates, a tall, sturdy woman with skin nearly as dark as the clothing she wore, was playing, her dark limbs, swathed in black lace, moving the bow as if gently raising and closing wings. Her eyes were closed, but now and then when a note hit a resonance that vibrated in our bones, she would flash a slight smile, a bit of white teeth a glint against dark skin, lips, and fabric. That little twinge of joy was the ebbing and flowing crux of Veil's show, and we the audience were caught up in all the sparks of life amid talk of shadow and death.

Veil began to sing, soft and sweet, a melancholy Shakespearean sonnet on themes of pining love. With the violin wafting down to us as if it were from on high, it was like it breathed with Nathaniel's beautiful and resonant voice, vocal and strings equaled one living thing. Several of the audience members clutched at their hearts. Some reached out for Veil with trembling fingers as they knelt in pools of lace and tulle. Some leaned toward him from the banister as if tethered to him by invisible strings.

I must have been more sensitive, far more raw, than when I'd last seen Nathaniel's show, for it touched down deeply within in ways I hadn't allowed it to before. The Gothic themes of his shows, composite pieces of existing text, poetry, and popular fiction dealing with the natural, the unnatural, the supernatural, the veil between life and death, and all the great mysteries, it simply hit too close to home. I think it did for all present, everyone raw and on edge.

But it was just what we needed.

He coursed through his show. I'd never seen the same show twice; he plucked different texts from Walpole, Shelley, and Le Fanu, from the great romantic poets, and of course, a running threaded theme of Edgar Allan Poe, my personal favorite and that of this crowd. If I'd found this Association earlier in my life, perhaps I'd never have had such terrible nightmares, as all my darknesses could have found a healthier home in this circle.

But then again, we are granted the friends we need exactly when we need them. Mrs. Northe had instilled that particular confidence in me. I needed my loneliness; it was how I knew I could survive against other odds. It was how I knew I couldn't just wait for someone or something else to save me. But knowing that I could get by with little else but my own wits and company and *then* finding community, that was a long overdue comfort.

I could feel the group dynamic breathe and shift like a woman adjusting to the stays of her corset and arranging her skirts, sitting poised and on the edge of delight and discovery, all of us gazing at our captor, Nathaniel Veil, who paced the space at the center of the packed circle like a great and graceful wild animal, clutching us all by the throat with his captivating presence—at one point he did clutch a few people directly by the throat in one of his stints as *Vampir*—and making every one of us swoon; whether for him or for the gentleman or lady in our hearts, he brought out all the passions within us and exorcised them exquisitely.

And then suddenly the quiet, seductive, safe bliss of the show was shattered by the door flinging open and a flailing form tumbling into the foyer, blowing past Nathaniel, and nearly trampling a few of the youngest Associates who were clustered upon the floor.

A tall, round-cheeked man, marked as older than many of Nathaniel's Association by his graying hair, but similarly dressed in mourning finery, seemed in the throes of agony, droplets of red—blood, surely—staining his face and throat, shining stains upon his black waistcoat, the sight of him evoking gasps and screams from Associate members. He raged and snarled and made a move to overturn the fine table, vase, and mirror near the door, but Nathaniel, who was a head taller than the struggling man, charged up to him and clamped a hand on his shaking shoulder.

"George," Nathaniel said sternly. "This is not you. You've been affected by a toxin." The man, George, gurgled a cry.

"The city can't be safe," George snarled. "For the city is the toxin. Chaos the only cure."

George tried to struggle with Nathaniel, but the imperious actor was stronger than he looked, or he was channeling his presence into brute strength; perhaps seeing that he was the protectorate of this fascinating coven was its own enhancement.

George cried out in pain again before peering a head around Nathaniel's broad shoulder and eerily piercing me with a darkly reflective gaze.

He dropped to his knees, dust flying up, a red dust. Perhaps it wasn't blood all over him but powder that had mixed with his perspiration. I thought of Poe and the Red Death coming into the party...

And then the man spoke. But as he looked up at me with oddly reflective eyes, something green and violet shining in them, reflected in them, the light of my own aura and power, I knew he was no longer a mere man. But something terrible had taken him over.

George flung himself across the open space between us and crumpled before me in a heap of red powder. Before he lost consciousness, he spoke.

It was a voice I knew all too well. The voice of a demon. He pierced me with a phrase the demon had once used to address me:

"*Hello, pretty...*"

And then his eyes closed and his head struck the floorboards. He was either unconscious or dead.

Chapter Eleven

The body remained too near to me as it fell flat, but even though I wanted to scramble away, shock and terror rooted me.

There was then, as one might imagine, panic in Mrs. Northe's fine home. A few screams pierced the suddenly fraught room, awash in murmurs and stirrings, our collective trance so rudely jarred into a living nightmare.

Lavinia rushed up to Nathaniel and murmured in his ear. He placed a protective hand upon the small of her back, nodding confidently as she shared something insistent. She drew the tulle veil that spread back from behind her feathered, beaded fascinator around her face and cupped the gathered fabric against her mouth with a lace-gloved hand.

"No one breathe freely," Nathaniel cried, putting his red silk cravat to his mouth, and others followed in his example. Lavinia made a move to withdraw, but he held her close and through the veil, I saw her fair cheeks redden.

"It's the powder to be careful of," Lavinia clarified for everyone's benefit, her usually soft and timid voice now carrying with the weight of necessity and authority. "Take care."

Everyone did as instructed; cravats and silk scarves, shawls and gloves, all created a shield. I did what I could with my sleeve, wishing I had some of the draping, flowing fabrics so many of the Association boasted.

"Stay here," Veil instructed to his crowd. He moved toward the front door in order to survey all of his crowd at once rather than having his back to anyone. "We must see if George was followed, if there were any others targeted. Were any of you approached? Have any of you been pressured by any 'doctors' or anything bearing the seal printed on that original leaflet?"

His coterie shook their heads. "Then Lavinia has taken good care of you indeed since the first incident. We must remain vigilant."

"Is he dead? Georgie?" asked a mousy girl draped in black velvet, pointing a satin-gloved finger at the floor. I peered closer. There was a slight hitch of breath from the man's back, barely perceptible but there nonetheless.

"Not dead yet," I stated, hoping to help keep calm, as a death among us might trigger any number of unfortunate reactions. I wiped at my nose with the edge of my sleeve.

Veil gestured to a slender man in dark, embroidered silk whose black hair was slicked back and braided—Chinese, I assumed, though in the cultural fugue that is New York City, one should never assume. The intensely focused man nodded and slipped out the front door, his compact frame tensed. Perhaps he was Veil's bodyguard, this quiet man who I hadn't noticed until that very moment he was drawn out, as he'd blended with the more ostentatious crowd, a good safety measure.

Just then I heard a familiar voice of someone who was clearly surprised by a stranger at her front door.

"Excuse me, and you are? This happens to be my home. Did I summon for a party I forgot having thrown?" Mrs. Northe, key in hand, stood framed in her grand doorway of beveled glass, decorative ironwork, and carved wood.

Just as lovely as her home, she wore a deep green satin dress that was neither casual nor formal, the very definition of elegance in all she presented to the world. Her slightly off the shoulder dress was made more modest by a gray shawl that glimmered with silver beads. Her lace-gloved hands, the only part of her that showcased any tension, were fisted tightly about her keys, fan, and reticule. Were the situation not dire, the look on her face would have been pricelessly amusing as she took in her home overrun by a coven of striking, black-clad creatures positively dripping off her stairs and furniture, filling her halls and parlor, wide-eyed and trembling.

"Well, well," she murmured as she swept in her front foyer, shaking off apprehension so that her presence might command the room in nearly as impressive a manner as Veil. "I've an unexpected murder of crows to host, do I?"

Murder was an unfortunate word for a cluster of ravens, considering the circumstances. I doubt Poe would have written this scene; he'd surely find it distasteful and a bit much.

"The lady of the manor, I presume!" Veil cried, bowing, his ascot still cupped to his mouth, though that had no effect on his being heard. His voice could boom no matter what obstructed it. Mrs. Northe gaped slightly. He maintained his bow as he continued.

"Nathaniel Veil at your service, madame."

He swept his hand about him, presenting his compatriots. "If you'll forgive us, Her Majesty's Association of Melancholy Bastards here needed to host a meeting for our collective safety..." Veil stood upright again, towering over the woman whose home he had overtaken as she looked up at him blankly. "But as you can see from the supine body of Mister George Fernstock there, our little soiree has been interrupted and compromised. And a damn shame, that, as I was putting on a right good show.

"'Tell me, my esteemed lady, do you advise we call the police on this matter or just hope for the best?" He gestured around him. "Oh, and do be aware of a red powder. It seems to be the culprit of madness. That's a very lovely embroidered shawl you have there, madame, I'd suggest breathing through it."

Mrs. Northe blinked, unable to look away from Veil as if he were a fascinating species of creature she'd never encountered up close. She'd seen him on stage, of course, but close and in person, his quality as force of nature was truly something to be reckoned with. After a moment she brought the shawl draped elegantly over her shoulders to her face. She searched the crowd, met my eyes, and her shoulders eased slightly. I gave her a look that hopefully read how glad I was to see her.

There was a questioning look in her eyes that made me uneasy. I never liked noting her in any attitude but firmly in control, cool and collected and exuding a confident plan. But I needed to remember she was human, not my guardian angel, not my fairy godmother of mythic quests. We were all just trying to stay one step ahead of madmen, to varying degrees of success. And something wasn't quite right—man lying unconscious at my feet aside.

"I do think at this point, Mister Veil," she replied finally to his query, "that the police will need to be involved. My associate in the clerk's office and I have gathered enough information about some of the Master's Society property to prompt proper scrutiny, and I'd rather leave that up to authorities. I am not a vigilante type, and I'd not suggest that course of action for any of your associates, either."

The black-clad crowd shook their heads. Like most people I'd ever met, they simply wanted to be left in peace and given leave to be their own masters and mistresses.

Mrs. Northe approached me. She bent, and unceremoniously, she proceeded to draw me away from the body on the floor. Through her intervention I felt able to move, though I was oddly light-headed. The room spun a bit as I stood.

"Have you seen Jonathon?" she asked quietly. "He and I were supposed to investigate a site that may be the very crux of the Society's New York operations, but he didn't show. That isn't his style…" She trailed off, frowning as she stared at me. I didn't like her words, and I didn't like the look on her face even more so.

She wiped something off my lip. There was a bitter taste in my mouth. She brushed her fingertips over my face, and then over my collar. Her lace gloves came away red. I felt a dull sensation blossoming in my stomach becoming sharper as panic opened into full bloom.

"What?" My voice sounded far away to my own ear. "What did you say?"

"Jonathon," Mrs. Northe continued. "Not that you're his keeper, but I thought perhaps he was with you… It didn't seem like him to not turn up… I don't mean to worry you…"

"Jonathon," I murmured. "*Jonathon.*" The sound of his name was an exotic spice upon my tongue. He was the whole of my heart, and he was absent. That was…unacceptable. I cocked my head to the side in an abrupt movement that felt foreign. My breath was heavy and strained against the stays of my corset that were suddenly violently tight against my rib cage.

Damn Jonathon Whitby. Damn his beauty. Damn his hold over me. Were there not greater things to be held in the clutches of?

I heard laughter, low and far away, deep and rumbling, like thunder.

It was not mine, and it did not seem like the laughter of anyone in the room, which had dimmed significantly. Whispers coursed past my ear like wind.

Oh, that couldn't be a good sign. Whispers in my mind, unless they were warnings from my mother, were to be avoided. My mother was dead. This was not her whispers. It was a crowd. That meant something else entirely.

I closed my eyes. My body shuddered with strange sensations that were both seductive and vaguely disturbing in their sudden sweeping intensity, as if every inch of my skin were suddenly on fire and sensitive to suggestion. And pain. There was a deep, widening, vicious chasm of pain...

And then the curtain was drawn on rage. A pure, unchecked, heretofore unheard of rage took center stage.

"Where is Jonathon?" someone shrieked.

It took me a long moment to realize that someone shrieking was me. I think I tore at something. Or someone.

That's the last thing I remember before darkness overtook me in a swift and obliterating shot.

Chapter Twelve

Awake or dreaming? I couldn't tell what state I was in, other than that it wasn't a good one. All I could sense concretely was that there was pain, throbbing pain as if I were on fire. My mind swam.

I was laid out horizontally, in what I assumed was a bed, from what I could tell by the feel of my back, but I was not lying in comfort; everything was pins and needles. Every sense and sensation felt raw and chafing. I was warm and perspiring, and yet my teeth chattered, and a constant, slow, undulating tremor went up and down my body as if I were my own tide, rolling in and out.

Trying to open my eyes was a gargantuan task I was not suited for. My eyelids would not respond, so I remained in a shallow darkness and tried to discern meaning.

There was the constant sound of screams. Whether the screams came from my mouth, my mind, from others, from nightmares...I was not at liberty to say, for I was not at liberty at all. My faculties were entirely compromised. I was not free. Something had taken over me. Some part of my mind was still my own, as I wondered if this was what it was like when a body was overtaken by a demon.

If I was entirely far gone, or entirely overtaken, perhaps I wouldn't have had a sense of self at all. It was said that people who were truly mad did not ask if they were mad. So perhaps, in this terrible state, there was hope for me.

The first thing I remembered as a product of true awareness, rather than swimming in a timeless sea of discomfort and confusion, was that

I was laid out somewhere familiar, and there were voices. Outside of myself. But there remained many voices within myself too. I had to take a moment to sort out one versus the other.

After some time trying to pick apart the noises and distances, I began to recognize the exterior voices. Mrs. Northe. My father. The low, deep resonant voice repeating prayers. Reverend Blessing. He was praying over me. Was I being exorcised? What had happened? Had the demon, in speaking to me through that poor wretch who collapsed on Mrs. Northe's floor, transferred something unto me? Into me?

Was the pain I felt actually all those runes again carved onto my flesh? Was there any hope for me, or was this the beginning of the end? What had I done? Why did my wrists feel so sore?

A particular searing scream from my own mouth shook me fully alert, and I looked up into the dark-skinned face of Reverend Blessing, who was anointing my head with oil and murmuring scripture.

I renounce thee...

I tried to help him in my mind, to echo, to reiterate, to join in the scripture by my own renunciation of the evil that had clung to me, but only unintelligible noises were coming from my mouth. My cheeks burned in shame; it was like the ugly sounds I made when first regaining my atrophied voice...

That's when I noticed I was bound.

What had I done that required that I be restrained? A turn of my head revealed that my wrists were done up in long white strips. Ripped fabric from sheets or pillowcases were wound round my wrist and tied to the metal headboard in one of Mrs. Northe's pleasant guest rooms that at this moment felt very stifling and utterly unwelcoming.

My stomach churned in a sickening roil and clearly that nauseating sense of horror read on my face, for my father rushed to me with an awkward reassurance that was hardly reassuring...

"It's all right, Natalie. You didn't hurt anyone. Too badly." He chuckled nervously, miserably. "Just a...scratch or two, it was fine—"

I made some kind of sound of protest or shame, my blush further ignited by humiliation and frustration.

"Nathaniel and I held you back as you turned, before anyone was hurt,"

Mrs. Northe added. "You received the brunt of the toxin borne in on that poor fellow... And that stuff...changes people. It makes sane persons into animals."

I wanted again to retch at this, but something stopped me, something small and lovely. Even in my fevered state, I noticed Mrs. Northe take my father's trembling hand in hers, not in a measured gesture of comfort but a motion on instinct, a gentle act that was so natural and intuitive to her that wanted to join in that collective comfort, for us to be a family. Whatever fear and confusion raced inside my scattered mind, those same raw emotions were writ large directly on my father's face... I wanted to be well again for their sakes, for Jonathon's sake; all that was important to me bolstered me. I regained some sense of myself in my regard for my loved ones, as if I touched the foundations of some sacred site and the divine reached down to steady me in return.

I seemed not in a fit state to respond to them, so I merely bit back a sigh, a cry, a heaving and exasperated curse. I felt my body conspire against me and the whispers near my ears threaten to drag me back under into the murky depths once more. Before I lost consciousness again, I overheard Mrs. Northe say something about Jonathon.

His name was the one thing that could keep my eyes open.

"Where?" I managed. Mrs. Northe and my father exchanged a look. The nauseating feeling I was fighting returned in force, but now layered with a fresh terror.

"What...*what* about Jonathon!"

"He's gone. We don't know where. It's been two days."

My eyes rolled back in my head, my whole sense of self and sensation pitching and roiling as if I were tempest-tossed in the worst of seasick throes. Before I lost myself again, I prayed with all my heart, then, that I could dream, and in that dream, find the man I loved and see where he'd gone and what he'd need of me if I could shake off these dreadful curses of ours...

Chapter Thirteen

When I thought I had the very worst luck a girl could possibly encounter, then the heavens proved me wrong in giving me a helping hand, extending down into my tired, addled brain and granting comfort and a useful turn. God or the angels or merely my clever subconscious, granted me my wish. Unsure what to thank, I said a prayer of gratefulness to all.

A dream. At last. A shared dream. Like Jonathon and I used to have when his soul was bound to a painting and I was his one tether to the tactile world. Some part of that original bond of soul to soul held on and connected. Love and truth will out.

Never mind the dream ended in nightmare. My dreams always did. My dreams forecasted unerring doom on sliding scale. It would be up to Jonathon and me, our waking selves, to make the tragedy into a happy ending. My nightmares were riddled with roundabout clues, gifted from some higher power than I could give myself any credit for, and their ignominious end, those terrible moments right before I wake, were the worst case scenario that we had no choice but to risk our lives to avoid.

But what I was presented with in the depths of my fitful rest was no solution, only information. But a tether to a missing lover was far better than no exchange at all.

I was getting very tired of the endless dark corridor in my mind where the dreams and nightmares take place, the narrow playground of terror, the dark, dank space where all things come to pass, where all clues are unfurled amid various horrors, my vulnerable mind unable to suitably brace itself against the inevitable onslaught. I wondered if at some point in my future I would see that hallway in my actual life and I would know that something important if not abjectly horrible and life-ending would take place there.

I did not know what of my dreams was clue and what was fancy. 'I had never known that balance or how to structure it. I dreamed and then I woke. How else can one live life, but to make sure their waking life is full of love and actions of grace? I could be held accountable for a mind in shadow that reveals what it would.

But there he was, Jonathon. Paces ahead of me down the dimly lit corridor that had no discernible light source and yet was luminous as if by an eerie phosphorous.

The British lord stood stiffly elegant in his fine black frock coat, navy waistcoat, and an azure ascot, his striking figure a greyscale palette with a splash of blue highlighting the spectacular color of his eyes. He was all the more striking for being against the run-down corridor, like in an old grand house but with wallpaper and paint peeling, wood panels cracked and splintered, foundations slightly askew so that the world was like a carnival mirror.

Jonathon's innate grandeur set against this sickened space made him all the more beautiful in contrast, and I could feel, with a swift punch to my gut, his absence from me. I could feel his distance as though a needle were pricking into my skin and drawing away something precious, threading out my heart in a thin bloody line of passion.

Immediately, upon seeing him there in my mind's eye, in this corridor where our minds entwined, I somehow knew that he was no longer in New York City. I shuddered as I tried to take steps forward in this rotting corridor toward his handsome form. But my feet were uncooperative and the length of the corridor just kept lengthening, drawing us ever farther apart.

He stared at me longingly, then turned that beautiful head and began to walk away. As he did, a low and rumbling chant began to lift into the air as if a storm was rolling in and fast. I called to Jonathon, and he stopped. He cast a sad look over his shoulder.

"I've gone back to England once more, darling Natalie," he said. With great effort I raised my lace-swathed arm to achingly reach out to him. He continued, with a weary, grim tone. "I have gone where you cannot follow. There was no time. I was dragged along, bid not to write to you for fear of tracking. But you've got to look to the numbers. The toxin will go wide. There was a sequence. Find it before it finds the city."

And then the corridor around us started to collapse. Jonathon in his paces ahead began running. But not to me, away from me.

"Let me go and save yourself," he cried. If he said anything further, his voice was overrun in a horrid din, and I lost sight of him in the shadows.

There rose into the air, filling my ears like a violent swarm of insects, a chant of terrible numbers. A fog of red smoke rolled in like water filling the moldering corridor. And then the walls came crashing down.

I fell beneath the force of the rubble, and my last sensation was of the life being pressed out of me as my lungs filled with acrid, stinging smoke...

I awoke with the gasping cry of, "I have to go to him."

No one was with me in the room, one of Mrs. Northe's fine guest rooms where I was still bound to a bed. I couldn't be sure when I'd be well, released, or safe around anyone, let alone the man I loved and was desperate to join, no matter the danger. Was I not in danger here in New York? Was I not in danger no matter where I went, when the demons seemed always able to pinpoint me, their insidious instincts by now having trained on my scent?

I closed my eyes, moaning in pain, burning physical aches. I thought about what Jonathon had shared. His words. There was something in them to stir results. I had instructions to give. I couldn't find any numbers or any sequences while tied to a bed. I figured I'd better start being useful by screaming for help.

Chapter Fourteen

The sound of my screams certainly sent the house staff scrambling. The door to my guest room–prison was opened, and two starched-hatted maids in black dresses and white aprons peered blanched faces at me before darting down the stairs in a cumbersome tandem, gingerly calling for the lady of the house.

I heard Mrs. Northe muttering under her breath as a swift tread up the stairs came closer and closer.

"I have to go to him, Jonathon," I cried. "He's in England." I could feel my panic rising, calling out to her even before she entered the room. "He said to let him go and save myself, I don't know what to do, what he'll do, I have to—"

"You're not going anywhere, Natalie," she murmured, her tone more weary than I'd heard it for some time as she turned the corner into the room. She was dressed down; in a plain workaday linen skirt, white blouse with sleeves rolled up, and an open linen vest; she must have been at work on something. She moved to a water basin by my bedside. She dipped a cloth in water and ran it over my forehead that I only now noticed was warm for the contrast of cool water.

The next piercing physical sensation was how much my wrists hurt. I must have been wresting against my restraints in whatever level of precarious state I'd been in. The sight of the bonds made me freshly fierce.

"I will find him, I will find Jonathon," I cried. A wave of anger that felt foreign and reckless, huge and unwieldy, crested inside me like a cat extending claws. While the impetus of emotion was mine, it's scope was something that I could only imagine that the Master's Society would want to exploit in their endless drive to further misery... I tried to trade the anger for pleading, thinking I might get further on that sentiment, staring up into Mrs. Northe's wide, piercing hazel eyes that missed no detail and seemed to know me too well. "I know where he is, he told me, I have to go—"

"You know I can't enable a mere sentence from a dream," Mrs. Northe said gently. "But tell me more about the dream." She dipped the cloth again and soothed my brow, fussing over me but making no move to undo my restraints. "I do appreciate that you often reveal clues—"

"Don't treat me like a prisoner."

"Tell that to the man you threw a punch at before Nathaniel managed to wrestle you to the floor downstairs," she replied. I could feel the color drain from my face. "Not that it was your fault," she added, "but we must take the greatest care. I think you're in the clear now, my dear, and I'd like to unlash you, but let's be careful here, let's see how you deal with what you're telling me, let's just talk a bit, you and me, so I can ascertain your mood and your physical reactions."

"Did...did the demon overtake me?" I asked sheepishly, trying to think back to what I dimly recalled as maybe having been an exorcism... "The demon, the one we destroyed, it...it spoke to me through that poor man George... At least, I thought it did..."

"I believe you were merely in the grip of the toxin. Parts of you remained distinctly...you. Stubborn. Passionate. Opinionated. Hating to be restrained." She chuckled. "Reverend Blessing was here with me as I would suffer no possible risk to your soul. Your father was relatively terrified, but seeing that you had a small army around you, save Jonathon, he knew you were being taken care of. It didn't follow that you were actually possessed. Truth be told, I think you're too spirited for anything to have room in there," she said smiling, tapping me on the sternum.

I felt a partial smile break through my anxiety. I tried to get a read on my body, my heart rate, my skin, the parts that ached, what seemed natural or unnatural. I tried to breathe and relax as she spoke. I needed to appear well. I needed to *be* well. Mrs. Northe continued, maintaining a calm, soothing tone as if her words were extensions of the cool compress.

"And I'm not sure we should be thinking of the demon as just one, but rather, a negative force. I've been in my study, writing letters to my gifted friends to see if they've wind of a shift in their séances or communications with the dead. I've been trying to make contact with spirits myself, to seek a window in, to see if a whole army of hell is upon us or just isolated bodies of negativity seeking hosts—"

"Mother," I blurted. "Did you speak with my mother?"

Mrs. Northe shook her head. "She remains elusive. Not out of love, I'm sure, but..."

I looked away, another wave of emotion threatening to drag me under. I needed to remain sane. I needed to get out of this damned bed, and no further fits would get me out of it any faster. Mrs. Northe took her cue and changed the subject.

"If something was possessing George, it left with George, who remains comatose in a nearby hospital, with a police officer on guard. It would seem the toxin does like to feed upon emotion. Hence Veil's Association being quite the group to target. Lovely people, truly, though I had to eventually insist they all leave my home after all the events."

"Did they overstay their welcome?"

"Ah, no, they just like finery as a whole, it would seem, and I'm not sure any of them are much used to fine homes, so they were a bit entranced here. I admit, I did, once you were seen to, have quite a wonderful conversation with Mister Zhee about Peking. Amazing city, Peking. I'll have to take you sometime." Mrs. Northe said this so casually as if China were not on the other side of the world but just a train ride away. I supposed, for the wealthy, distances were not as long or as implausible. She was examining my limbs and skin as she continued speaking.

"He misses it very much. His wife, of course, he misses more so. What a shame this country won't let the women of his country in. Who can begrudge a man for taking work when it's offered and wanting to be with his family while he does it? Is this not a city were the world comes to make their way?"

This was news to me that only men of China were allowed here and not the women. How painful. Mrs. Northe seemed satisfied with the look of me; at least I couldn't discern any concern on her face, and while she did not unwind my bindings entirely, she did loosen them as she continued:

"It seems one of the Association members managed to extract Zhee from a crime syndicate that kept him as if he were a slave. Frightening what people will exploit from the needy. That Association"—she shook her head in amazement—"is filled with amazing stories of resilience and reinvention. No one there is exactly as they seem, and every last one of them has a fighting spirit in them that utterly defies their romanticisms. Zhee is now a valuable asset to Veil, a guard and friend, teaching Veil about the East and about the various disciplines he practices. Veil is like a sponge. I've never seen anyone drink up and absorb more details; he is an endless student of the world. Ridiculous and irascible, but what a good heart inside that restless, attention-seeking body. Maybe one day he'll even commit it to that poor, pining Lavinia." She chuckled, leaning close to murmur the last, as Lavinia was likely in the house, still "recovering" until she made her own way.

I hoped, for Lavinia, that Veil would do just that, help them build a life together now that she'd lost her parents' blessing, good will, and fortune. Fortune.

"Now, can you speak about the dream without an adverse reaction?" Mrs. Northe prompted.

I took a deep breath. I thought of that terrible corridor and tried not to relive the horrible sensation of its collapse, of being trapped, of watching Jonathon disappear from me...

"Jonathon is gone," I managed to say after a moment. "Back in England or at least en route. He was telling me I couldn't follow, and something about numbers, about the sequence, about that being important."

"Would he not have told us he was traveling again? He said nothing to me, were you informed—"

"I think the spy must have dragged him away before he could write," I replied. As Mrs. Northe's eyebrows raised, I bit my lip. I remembered we hadn't ever told her about Brinkman. I swallowed hard. "Oh. Yes. There was a spy in town."

"Really? Is that so? And when were you going to mention that to me, pray tell? Were you ever going to—"

"For his safety, we thought we'd not—"

Mrs. Northe batted her hand to stop me. "Well, Rupert—*Senator Bishop*"—she hastily corrected herself from the easy familiarity—"will want to know that. I knew you were hiding something, something important, but I thought maybe it was just that Jonathon had stolen your virtue or something—"

"No!" I protested, my face growing hot with a furious blush. "He's a *gentleman*—"

"A spy," she continued, as if she hadn't even heard me. I blushed even brighter but lest she think "the lady doth protest too much," I let the matter go, and she continued. "How very interesting. *Espionage*. And you think this spy made off with Jonathon?"

"Why else would he not leave a note? Or send a telegraph via Morse, for transcript from the steamer? Information in our dreams could not be trusted without circumspection. I'd like to think he'd not hide his exit from me unless it was hasty, and that he was in danger. Society operatives must have trailed him and found him, so he ran. I hope I can trust Brinkman to keep him safe in the meantime. Until I can get there."

"You're not getting there, Natalie, I can't possibly—"

"You can't expect me to just lie here—"

Her hazel eyes now flashed at me like lightning. She was shaking. "I could never live with myself, I...I just can't, Natalie. There are things I know, things that Amelia told me before she passed, things I've intuited—"

"About what? You can't play that game with me again; you withheld things from me before, about what the spirits said, about what my *mother's* spirit said—"

"The simple fact is if you go to England, your father will never trust me again for putting you in direct danger. And he'd never again trust you. And he shouldn't—"

"Why? Why do you even care about my father? More so than me?" I blurted finally. She turned to me and smiled, and in that smile and the soft, nurturing look in her eyes, I felt the full breadth and scope of my youth in comparison to the life she'd lived, and I felt very small.

"Natalie Stewart. Let's not play games with who has more of my affection."

"What do you even see in my father?" I grumbled, suddenly very resentful I woke up screaming and he was not there, as if this whole maddening part of my life just didn't include him at all. "When I went under, did he just stand in the corner being terrified, when you were doing things, or did he step up and acknowledge what's going on? Where is he now?"

"He is at *work*, so you can keep the roof over your head—"

"But truly, I ask you, what do you see in him, he's not of your league—"

"Natalie Stewart, you listen to me *right* now! Don't you dare for one more moment let that toxin inside of you make you more ungrateful than you already are." I'd never heard her take such a scolding tone, and I was taken aback. She took a deep breath. "Your father is a quiet, kind, intelligent man who treats me not as an inferior species. You'd be surprised how rare that is. While aware of my wealth and status, he does not put me upon a pedestal, for that is just as alienating. He meets me eye to eye and mind to mind. He shares his thoughts and is interested, *genuinely*, in mine. He has a quiet confidence that does not seek to dominate me but allows me my strengths as I would allow anyone theirs. This is a *very* difficult quality to find in men of this age, my dear."

Her tone shifted from this spirited defense of my father to something more gently world-weary. "You've been spoiled by Jonathon, a man of a forward mind, dear. You don't really know the sorts of *gentlemen* that are out there, seeking to strangle a woman and keep her forever at heel, forever seen as solely domestic, forever out of realms of thought, employment, rights, and issues considered too intense for our 'delicate' sensibilities." She bit upon her words as if they were sour. "Delicacy be damned. Delicate is for lace, and I look damned fine in lace, but my spirit should not be confused with what I wear."

I sat with all these words a moment, utterly taken aback by this chastisement, surprised by the depth of response, and suddenly I felt a pride in my heart for the man who had always tried to do right by the women of his life. I imagined, from what I'd heard about my mother, she'd have said something similar. Seeking out powerful women only meant he was confident enough in himself not to have anything to prove. Nothing but love. And the pursuit of art. Ah, what a poet's soul I'd come from. The emotions that had been so thick and violent within me now made me want to do nothing but weep. I had to hold myself together.

And I had to do right by my father. I couldn't just disappear to England, even if I did manage to escape from under Mrs. Northe's watch and board the next steamer. I owed him more than that. But he'd never let me go. And yet I had to go. Would it come down to choosing which of the men in my life was more important? The man who raised me or the man I hoped I'd someday marry? That wasn't fair, was it, to have to choose?

I looked up at her pleadingly, and that was no ploy, it was simply how I felt. "I have to do something. I can't just lie here... Surely there's something to do, to stop the evil creeping in..." I trailed off, remembering what else Jonathon had said. "The numbers. The numbered sequence. I think he might have meant that sequence that Crenfall was repeating. It's important. Very. I truly think lives hang upon us knowing what it refers to."

The look on her face proved she was taking this as deathly seriously as I was, altered state or no.

Chapter Fifteen

"Yes," Mrs. Northe agreed to my prompt. "Yes, we do need to think about those numbers. About any and all connections we can draw. Let's apply our thoughts to the paperwork I've managed to get hold of in the past few days."

"Paperwork?"

She smiled craftily, rising from my bedside and going toward the door. "It's good to know people in clerks' offices. For the devil is often in the details, my dear." She disappeared into another upstairs room and returned a few moments later with a few brown folders with papers inside.

"It would seem," she began, taking a seat beside me once more, "the Master's Society has been making major investments in New York City, by all kinds of means. Some overhanded, most under." She held up a stack of deeds, receipts, and a ledger. The top papers were stamped with the distinct gold and red dragon-flanked crest. "These transfers of assets, and general encroachment, have been happening within the past few years. A great deal of the property is centered around Grand Central Depot. If you recall, that poor madman Crenfall was on about the 'grand and the central.' When Lord Denbury and I were out examining various suspected Master's Society properties before he disappeared, we concluded there must be a hub of something that will either be built or will occur around that area."

"I hope it's enough to take to authorities to examine? What can people like us do about mere property? Will anyone believe the underhanded aims of the Society enough to, what, what would we even suggest, raid these premises?"

"I'm not sure if the truth of the Society will be believed, if my dealings with the New York City Police Department are any indication. They don't take kindly to the idea of the paranormal. Well, they're not particularly hostile, they just don't believe—"

"At their own risk," I grumbled, and Mrs. Northe scowled.

"Well, yes, but you tell that to the sergeant who still has your diary in custody."

I felt my face go hot again. I'd truly like to get that back... There were so many personal details that just should *not* be public record...

"I've been discussing all this with Lavinia, to see if she has any insights," Mrs. Northe mused, gazing out the small window that presented a tiny sliver of a courtyard between her property and the townhouse beside. "Somewhere, between all of us, we'll figure out the chink in the demonic armor. She needs to feel empowered by what has happened around her, and not a victim. What happened here in my house, with all of the Association present, to that poor fellow George, and then to you, it dealt Miss Kent a bit of a regressive blow. 'She's not been seen out of her room much. I think she still feels this is somehow all her fault."

I sighed angrily, trying to move. "It isn't, none of this is anyone's fault but the fault of evil—"

"She'll appreciate hearing those reassurances from you, and I encourage you to tell her that."

"I don't suppose you'd like to let me up?" I said, shaking at my bindings.

"Ah." Mrs. Northe flushed, embarrassed. "Yes. I'm sorry. You do seem to be behaving yourself, so I suppose it's time..."

I looked up at her, trying to honestly remember the extent of the madness I'd glimpsed, those indistinct hours that were taken from me. It was all so hazy. But I'd never forget feeling so horribly compromised. Having a distant sense of faculty and having control taken away from you was, as Lavinia had said, the most horrible cruelty. "Was I really that awful?"

"I'm sure you could have been worse, the effects could have been worse. You could be like that poor George and still be comatose." Mrs. Northe sat upon the edge of the bed, leaning over to undo the bindings upon my wrists.

As I turned them and winced, rolling them in an aching stretch once released, Mrs. Northe picked up a minty salve from the bedside table. With a generous dab of the cream, she gently rubbed and treated the raw skin, mothering me as she continued. "The toxin is not to be trusted nor believed. Turns lambs into lions. Thank goodness it managed to stay contained within my house and we cleaned up the residue without much damage, else I'd not have had a house left."

Mrs. Northe helped me up to a seated position against the headboard, and I groaned, all my muscles aching and on fire from the lying down without being able to turn and all the struggling I must have done. The way she tended to me, I lost all the resentment about being bound up; she'd done it for my safety and for that of everyone around me. She had such a maternal way about her, and part of me wanted to ask about children, what she really thought about not having any, even though she sort of had surrogates in me, in Miss Kent, in Maggie...

Maggie... I hadn't told Mrs. Northe about the letter. There wasn't anything in it that was particularly private or damning; it was mostly just Maggie being her usual self, but it was worth mentioning the fact that I read her as still hovering on the edge of vulnerability and needing all the prayers and support she could get. She was precarious, and while I felt I should write back, I wasn't entirely sure what I should say. I was precarious too. Hardly confident. False reassurances from my sickbed would be of no use, the ailing counseling the ailing...

"What is it now?" Mrs. Northe asked, looking at my expression, which must have been telling. That, or her extraordinary depths of perception would have allowed her to feel the shift within me as much as see it.

"In all the madness," I began with a sigh, "I forgot to tell you a letter arrived from Maggie. While you're looking at paperwork, you might as well read it. I would like to know if you think, as I do, that she still has a ways to go until we would call her recovered... The letter is on your writing desk in the parlor if you'd like to take a look."

Mrs. Northe nodded. "I will." She exited to collect it and any other extraneous evidence.

The desire I had to help Maggie, wayward as she'd been, was nothing compared to the wave of panic that again crested inside me when I thought about Jonathon, out there on his own.

Mrs. Northe would not let me go anywhere, without a fight. My father... Well, of course in his mind anything remotely questionable, much less outright dangerous, wasn't an option. But I would go one way or another. Better to ask forgiveness later than permission now, especially when I knew the answer would be a resounding *no*... The hesitant forgiveness given from others would be nothing compared to the lack of any I'd ever give myself if I lost Jonathon. If the worst came to pass and I didn't try to find him... I was not worthy of the divine intervention I had earned thus far.

Not to say I was infallible, invincible, immortal. I was, most certainly, mortal. And here I was, ready to tempt every fate I'd yet encountered. How reckless. How necessary.

I simply had to go... It was inevitable, truly, and I'd learned that there was a certain magnetism to inevitable things. Once I knew something had to be done, it simply had to be so.

Whenever I could be assured that the sequence Jonathon warned me about would lead to one mystery solved, he himself would be my next case. I just had to figure out how a young woman traveled across the Atlantic unaccompanied... I'd have to put on the suit again, pretend. And I'd also have to steal some money... I wondered how much a steamer ticket to England would cost me...

Lavinia Kent interrupted my musing machinations with a desperate cry, wild-haired and wide-eyed at the door.

"Nathaniel's gone! Utterly gone! It isn't one of his tricks, he has *vanished*."

I stared at the lovely red-haired young woman, framed in the doorway, clad in a black velvet robe that was somewhere between a dressing gown and a priest's habit. She appeared like a fraught archetype that one of the Pre-Raphaelite Brotherhood's painters might have dreamed up, perhaps a rendition of her own ominous name utilized in one of Shakespeare's most gruesome tragedies. But since I'd had plenty of experience with cursed paintings, I'd take Lavinia's three dimensions over canvas any day, though the reality of her panic and worry cut straight to the bone, her passionate heart exposed for all to see.

"And do you have any idea where your dear Mister Veil may have gone to?" Mrs. Northe replied, rising to her feet and going to the door, keeping utterly calm in the face of Lavinia's panic. "It seems we've a rash of handsome Englishmen disappearing out from under our noses."

"No," Lavinia fumed. She began pacing in the hall, like a nervous raven, black fabric swirling as she stalked. "I do not. But I have my suspicions. I believe he has returned to England. He said he wanted to help Jonathon. He was looking all over for him yesterday. So I assume he's at least part way across the pond."

My heart seized with many emotions, firstly hope and pride that Jonathon had such good and loyal friends to rally around and help him. But I simultaneously seized up in pain, for I was not there, not a part of the chase, not immediately following after. After all, I had as much of a claim to him as a friend had... I was his love... I wanted to be his wife... Why the hell was I still in New York when my heart traveled across the Atlantic? My whole body ached to run out the door and down to the piers right that very moment...

Mrs. Northe was eyeing me, and I had to keep my calm, for she was gauging me, and I had to keep in her good graces. There would be no going anywhere if she suspected me...

I spoke very gently in my most reasonable tone. "Do you happen to know if Jonathon told Nathaniel he was leaving for England? Because he didn't give me any clue—"

"No," Lavinia replied, stopping her pacing to come into the room and speak with me. "He said he was hoping he'd have seen Jonathon but was struck by a memory of the persons who targeted the Denbury clan to begin with, a night he still feels guilty about. And I'm sorry to be so rude and think only of myself and my heart... But are *you*...feeling better, Miss Stewart?"

"Do call me Natalie, I insist, and yes, I am, thank you. Thank you for helping keep order in the house, I understand it was...difficult. I am sorry for—"

"You apologize for nothing. It was I who brought this whole terror upon us—"

"The Society targeted you, you couldn't have known—"

Lavinia's bright eyes flashed darkly. "I should not have let anything in," she moaned. Shame made her cheeks burn nearly the color of her hair. "I should not have given a substance faith that I didn't have in myself. I should not have allowed my Association, my treasured comrades, think, for even one moment, that there was a shortcut to their health when we've all taken such great and measured strides together." She clasped her graceful hands together. Her every move was theatrical, whether she knew it or not, and yet all of it entirely sincere. "Proven medicine for ailments is one thing. Risks like what I undertook? No. I hope one day I'll forgive myself, but today is not that day. Now, if you'll excuse me, I'm going to write some letters of inquiry on Nathaniel's behalf." She bowed her dark red head and disappeared.

Mrs. Northe was about to open her mouth and comment on the situation when the doorbell rang and the door was opened unto my father, who was shown upstairs, and soon after, the maids rushed about to make sure all of us had tea in nearly the blink of an eye. None would look at me. Surely they were frightened. And yet they remained in this house. Mrs. Northe created that kind of unbreakable loyalty.

"I... I'm so relieved you're recovered," was all my father could manage, coming into the room. I struggled to stand for the first time in what had evidently been a few days, wincing from the aches, but it felt so good to be upright.

When my father looked at me, he still blanched, as if he were staring at a ghost. Mrs. Northe had been through enough séances and exorcisms, it would seem, to not have been phased by the toxin's effects upon me; she treated me no differently, and for that I was grateful.

But for my father, though the inexplicable things that had followed Jonathon and then, by default, me, become commonplace, they could never be fully understood, never fully accepted. And yet, despite this, he cared enough for me and for Mrs. Northe, for this family of fate, to try his best to stare it all fully in the face even though I knew how utterly terrified he was. I wondered if he heard my mother's whisper, ever, in his mind, and if it steeled his gentle heart that was so full of love it sufficed for strength. I'd like to think he did.

We stared at each other for a long moment, as if summing one another up. My heart twisted in anguish for what I knew I had to do, break his heart all over again and disappear once more. He might never forgive me. I had to take that risk. And looking at the kind, distinguished face of a man who simply wanted to love me, for me to be happy without threat... It nearly made me ill, sick, and enraged all over again. What right did any evil force have to try to sunder something so lovely as the persons I had in my life?

I thought I was going to finally go home with Father. I hadn't had the heart to ask precisely how long I'd actually been Mrs. Northe's crazed invalid...but he stopped me as I started gathering whatever of my things sitting around the vanity had been brought from home during the interlude.

"Natalie, not that I don't want you home, but perhaps one more day under this roof? To truly make sure you're...yourself again? I just..." And he looked at Mrs. Northe with a mixture of fear and wonder. "I feel you're safer around Evelyn than you would be around me. She can...protect you better than I could. She knows... I was helpless. I suppose your Jonathon knows too... I just...wouldn't... I don't know what to do..."

He was the same man who desperately wanted the best for me despite his own personal cost. When faced with my disability, when I stopped speaking after Mother died, he sent me away from home to the finest school that the country offered so that someone more skilled could help me. I only just now understood, looking into those eyes that seized my heart with the force of their love, that cleaving me from him for my own good was the hardest thing he ever had to do. He'd lost his wife, and here his daughter kept needing expert care that he could not provide. And yet he did not let his pride withhold what I needed. What trust in grace. What wondrous love.

I moved to my poor, overwhelmed father, and embraced him. Hard. "Go home and rest, Father, you look like you haven't slept in days."

"I haven't," he admitted.

"I'll be fine. I've gotten this far, haven't I?" I said, offering him a smile that he returned.

"By the grace of God," he murmured, kissing me on the head and slipping quietly back down the stairs. Mrs. Northe escorted him to the door, and I heard him thank her gently in the downstairs foyer. "I'm sorry for all the trouble, Evelyn," he added.

"You're quite welcome, Gareth," I heard her reply. "And no trouble was had. But if there had been, your family would be worth it."

There was a long moment before I heard the front door close. I actively did not think about what that long silence might have meant.

Mrs. Northe did not come back upstairs. Perhaps she was pondering the same things I was, how beautiful and rare it was that a loving gentleman left the women he cared most for in the world to their own devices. Not because he was not interested, or thought himself above the goings-on. But because he trusted us. Despite all we'd both done in direct opposition to what would have engendered trust. Surely, the late Helen Stewart was somewhere helping our family cope... Or, maybe, my father didn't need any help at all, he was just very gifted at letting people do what they did best and caring for them as they did so.

I was left alone. I found I didn't like that fact, as I felt as though I might jump out of my skin, impatient and restless. So, as with anything I didn't like, I sought a remedy for my state. I poked my head into the hall. Down the lavishly papered and plush-carpeted hall, Lavinia's door was open. I padded down to its frame and left one rap upon the dark wood.

At the sound, she looked up from a small Turkish suite where she sat writing by the lavender light of a gas lamp with a purple glass shade. It make her look oddly spectral, slightly ghastly. I was sure she'd like the effect, provided it was in her control. It was clear the Association appreciated theatrical morbidity but wasn't fond of violence or actual threat. They sought to make light of death, not actively court it. That's where the Society had misjudged them.

Lavinia gestured me in and rose to close the door behind us.

"So," she murmured. "We're in a similar *boat*, are we not?" As she emphasized the word boat, I wondered if Lavinia was, in fact, thinking exactly what I was thinking.

"I'll never be let out of here at this point, I fear," I replied. "Mrs. Northe knows me too well. But I have to escape. I have to get on a steamer, and I have to get to London. To Greenwich, to his estate, wherever he is... The trouble is," I said, wringing my hands, feeling helplessness rise inside me like the raging tides so recently had, "I don't know the first thing about England, or international travel."

"Well. Good thing I'm British, then, isn't it?" she replied. "*I'll* take you to England, Natalie. I have to follow the man I love. As do you. And I feel much better about it not undertaking it alone. Everything happens for a reason, so they say, and one cannot fight the types of battles we've been chosen to fight on our own." I stared at her. Her lovely face, one I'd seen so often scared and nervous, was stalwart and resolute. I wondered if I'd looked the same way when I'd made the dangerous decisions I had in protecting Jonathon in any number of ways. Do not stand between a resolute lady and her love, that's for certain.

I nodded, squeezing her hand. "Yes. All of this, yes, Lavinia, thank you. And I hope to leave as soon as possible—"

"Tonight. I've packed a bag, I've secured money. I knew my parents were tiring of me long before they cast me off, so I've gathered and saved a considerable amount, and I've been clever about it, lest I lose it all to one unscrupulous thief on the boat."

I stared at her, impressed. "Your parents were wrong to cast you out merely for company you keep. I think the Association is wonderful, creative, and true to themselves, and there's nothing inherently broken about any of you. It's the world that needs assimilation when the individual needs only one's self. I am glad that if I've been subjected to the hells I've been subjected to, that it's been alongside fairly spectacular company."

She beamed. "There's an early-morning steamer, but we'll be seen by house staff in the morning, so we'll leave tonight, at midnight, prevail upon a friend of mine who lives not terribly far from the Cunard offices, wait out the midnight hours, and tomorrow morning, we begin. It takes too many days to cross the Atlantic to waste a single one more. Go to your guest room and gather what little useful you can. We'll have to procure other items in transit." She moved to the large mahogany wardrobe across the room, opened it, and handed me a hat box. It wasn't luggage, but it would have to do.

I nodded at her and moved quietly into the hall. I remembered what had felt best when anything frightening had been placed in my path, and that was to move around it. To act. Paralysis would kill me. The only thing to fend off any recurrence of the madness that had overtaken me was to again stare the demons down, one by one. The Master's Society and all its misguided experiments preyed on a mixture of fear and chaos leading to conditions for domination. I had to hope the demons and their agency hadn't factored in the spirited rebellion of those they crossed. But it did make us marked targets.

I hoped that night I could dream, to pluck details from Jonathon's innermost mind, wherein I would also see, surely, clues to my own doom. I had to believe those warnings could be avoided. If some increasingly slippery part of this ungodly puzzle would come for me regardless, I might as well meet it in battle...

Chapter Sixteen

Lavinia and I had agreed upon a time. We had packed what we could.

In each of our respective rooms, the bedclothes molded under the covers of each bed looked convincingly like a sleeping body.

We thought we were very clever.

We met in the hall at the appointed time, using the soft chime of the grandfather clock at the end of our corridor to mask the sound of the opening doors, the jostle of bags and the hatbox that served to carry far more than a hat, and our careful tread. Sneaking down the staircase as the bell continued to softly toll, we were painfully aware of every creak and slight murmur of the house, wincing at any and every sound.

We reached the downstairs landing. I could feel the tension thick in the air as we turned to each other. This was it. The point of no return. We were going forth unto an unknown world, an uncertain destiny, a future from which there might not be any coming back... And yet neither of us felt we had any other option. That was what the demons had done, propelled us forward on a terrible course that we could not begin to fathom the end of.

And then there was a movement from the shadows, blocking our path.

"Oh, no, you don't!" Mrs. Northe scowled, turning the gas-lamp key of a front door sconce and throwing us into illumination.

So much for clever.

She placed one arm on either side of the doorframe to block us; the lavish bell sleeves of her thick satin dressing gown trimmed in fine lace spread and unfurled like formidable wings.

Lavinia shrank back, her shoulders falling, and she stammered in an effort to defend us, though her tone was one of distinct guilt. "Mrs. Northe, forgive me, you misunderstand—"

"No, she doesn't misunderstand," I murmured gently, ruefully. "She knows *exactly* what's going on. Clairvoyance, and all..." I set down the hatbox before I went to her. I took one of her hands in mine, moved by the fierce quality upon her face, the face of a mother protecting her brood from leaving the safety of a den to run directly toward predators. "What? What is it that you see that has you so concerned when you know that avoiding the inevitable does us no good?"

"Death," she choked.

I swallowed hard. "Death if I go, or death if I stay?"

"I...don't know," she said, looking at me helplessly. A helpless Mrs. Northe was one of the more terrifying things I'd encountered. Lavinia just looked from one of us to the other worriedly.

"I can't take the risk of staying behind," I said finally.

"How can I bear the risk of letting you go? I can't let you. When I went Chicago to help my Amelia pass onto the next plane, she warned me that death lay ahead. I can't allow you to doom yourself—"

"But the doom will find me if I am marked for it, you know that. It will find a way, but so will I. You know me—"

She closed her eyes as if the threat that next came out of her mouth was as intolerable to her as it was to me. "I could have you sent to an asylum—"

"You wouldn't dare," I said.

"I'd dare anything to protect you—"

"You have." I fought to keep my words gentle. "You always have protected me. You always will. Just...let us choose our paths."

"Your father will—"

"Never know, because you'll make up something brilliantly creative—"

"Natalie, I sense *death*," she cried. "You're not prepared—"

"Do you see *my* death? Or simply death?"

"Not precisely, no, I can't forsee a specific fate, but danger and death is a certainty, I cannot risk you—"

I sighed heavily. Lavinia was ashen pale at my side and yet still resolute. "I've faced death awake, I've faced it dreaming. I don't like the idea, but I've a strong notion it will come for me regardless. I'd just rather it not be expecting me."

There was a very long time where Evelyn Northe and I simply stared at each other.

"You realize you're the bravest girl I've ever known," she said finally. I felt tears threaten to sting my eyes, but I fought them back.

"I learned bravery from the mother who pushed me out of the way of a carriage and was run down instead. I learned bravery from a stepmother who doesn't flinch at dark magic."

Mrs. Northe blinked a moment. Then she realized that "stepmother" meant her, and it was then her turn to blink back tears.

But the moment of deep sentiment was short lived. Mrs. Northe's expressive hazel eyes rolled back entirely, and her tall, slight form began to shake uncontrollably. A voice came from her that was not entirely her own, it was singsong and eerie. "They've gone to the house, and it is ashes...ashes..."

"What...what's going on..." Lavinia said, looking at Mrs. Northe and then to me, terrified.

"I think... She's channeling something," I said slowly. "I hope it's a spirit..."

"Let's go," Lavinia said and stormed to the door, blowing past our suddenly incapacitated hostess. "Natalie, come on. This is our chance—"

"But we can't leave her—"

Lavinia rushed back into the base of the landing to emphatically ring the maid's bell, picked up my hatbox from where I'd dropped it and shoved it at me, grabbed my hand, hoisting her satchel over her shoulder, and we flew out the door.

`Out the front door, I heard Mrs. Northe cry out: "Beware...all ye who journey there..."

It was hardly the parting words I wanted to hear. I wanted benedictions, not warnings. But then came a telling, shrieking addition.

"Heed the sequence," Mrs. Northe cried, from whatever forces were utilizing her. "The order. The *book*."

And that, I knew, was a clue. This was too chilling of a note to leave my mentor and spiritual warrior upon, but as Lavinia was physically dragging me away, I'd take whatever help I could get.

I paused outside just a moment, to see if there was anything else to be gleaned, but the maids had descended about her then; I heard fussing, and I could see the grouped shadow inside the beveled glass of the door. I was confident she'd be taken care of. Hopefully her staff would call Blessing, or maybe that senator, one of her powerful friends—if she didn't come to after some time entranced.

At least the spirits were trying to help us.

At least I *hoped* it was the spirits speaking through her and not something else...

Chapter Seventeen

What happened to get me onto this steamer was an elaborate process that I undertook without pausing for reflection or consideration. Lavinia and I agreed to banish sentiment and second-guessing, like discarding excess ballast from a ship, in order to make ourselves light, efficient, dynamic, and quick. Uninterrupted by fears or beset by counterproductive worry.

She had planned this out on her own, and I was not a hindrance to that plan. Rather, I think my presence emboldened her. Having spent a life without speaking, I was quite used to doing things on my own, and where Lavinia faltered, I stepped up with confidence. Where I was out of my league in the business and details of international travel, Lavinia filled the breach.

We passed the few hours until the next boat out with one of Lavinia's Association friends down near Pearl Street, a convenient walk from Cunard offices for the tickets. From there, it was a brief jaunt to the pier and then out on the first express steamer possible. I kept looking around for Mrs. Northe, or my father, fully expecting either of them to try to intercept us there—it wasn't like steamers to England kept their schedules private.

Part of me wanted them to stop me. But the rest of me knew this, just like everything else the dark magic had wrapped us up in, was inevitable. Mrs. Northe was likely still recovering from what had been a somewhat violent-looking channeling, and my father was still asleep. I promised myself I would write and wire him whenever possible. I owed him that much and so much more than my circumstances allowed me to give.

I moved, acted, and reacted as if I were a horse with blinders, staring straight ahead at my next immediate objective, unable to heed my mind's various cries, denying the sense memory of what it was like to have that dark magic breathing down my neck and prickling upon my skin. Though those discomfiting sensations threatened to overtake me one by one, I beat them back with sheer will. I drove myself like a draft horse pulling weight, moving onward toward a specific task.

It was the second or the third day in—the days began to blur immediately—that I allowed myself to truly pause for breath, staring out over the vast and unfathomable Atlantic Ocean under a brilliantly moonlit sky that I hadn't seen quite so unhindered in some time, due to Manhattan's constant gaslight. I permitted a moment to take stock of myself and my state. My anxiety kept pace at a dull thrum to match the steam engines decks below my boots. I had hoped against hope the steamer would make a bit better headway and arrive to port a bit ahead of schedule.

This large, impressive boat made me nervous. While the view above me and around me remained spectacular in theory, the truth of it was terrifying. I had never been this far out on the ocean, and I didn't realize how much it would unsettle me until it was far too late to turn back. The steamboat was indeed a wonder, but its behemoth engines were also like strange monsters of this modern world that seemed at any moment able to turn into dragons that could eat us all alive. My father was right. My imagination was far too fertile.

Every now and then I felt tears itching at the very back of my eyes like small pixies, emotional imps demanding I pay attention to all the things I refused to face. All the potential realities. All the potential finalities. But I bit everything back. Perhaps the rolling crest of seasick nausea was its own blessing, for it was quite a distraction.

In the pocket of my modest linen pinafore, I palmed my notebook in a trembling hand. That simple action allowed for my tensed shoulders to fall just a fraction. Each of my notebooks through the years always proved such a comfort as they were the infallible way I communicated with the world. On a page, I could converse and present arguments with my inner self that needed to externalize its thoughts. The written word had proved in my life to be far more reliable than speech ever was. I'd had far more years writing and communicating in Standard Sign than I'd had actually speaking. The written word held a power that the ephemeral spoken word did not, and I valued the written word like I would a vow.

I flipped through to the latter pages of the notebook, where I'd managed to write down Mrs. Northe's final warnings. I knew better than to ignore or disregard anything out of that woman's mouth, especially if she were in contact with the spirit realm.

A book. A sequence. Whatever had overtaken Mrs. Northe zeroed in on those items. I wondered if any of what had come before, the countercurses we'd learned, the ways of a split soul, beating the Society at their own games and particular experiments would serve us anymore, or if we were instead dealing with another layer of puzzles. The aforementioned clues would crop up, surely, and I hoped I would know them when I saw them and have an instinct as to how to solve their mysteries.

But first, the only sight I was desperate to see was Jonathon Whitby's beautiful face. I wondered if he missed me. If he'd propose again. I'd not hesitate. I'd say yes. Every moment away from him, every circumstance keeping us apart, proved that I simply didn't want to live a life without him. Here I was placing myself in danger just like I'd always done for him, because I simply couldn't take a reactive stance. I had to *do* something, and it was for his sake, because he was *such* a good soul. And I'd seen it, held it, cherished that soul. I'd never met another quite like his. Never would. Never needed to.

Everything around Jonathon had been targeted, as the powers of evil always gravitated toward the brightest lights. And we now sought to control the epicenter of that outbreak.

I wondered if there was yet a reason to be revealed as to why Jonathon and his family had been chosen as an initial point of entry for the Master's Society, besides Jonathon's inherent goodness. What of his family? The Denbury lineage? Was it as noble and good as its heir?

The fleeting thought crossed my mind that Jonathon might be dead. I swiftly blocked that from even being a possible reality. Not only did I pray for God's help but I demanded of God's will that Jonathon lived. I needed to dream of him again, to keep me going, to remind me why. I needed him to be there when I landed. I needed something solid.

And then, at the corner of my ear, came a whisper, a tiny kiss of sound upon the wind, a flicker of white at the edges of my vision. Mother. Mother's whisper, that had haunted me so beautifully since I lost her so early in my life.

She was there to remind me why too. From her perspective, she didn't want any more demons walking the earth than I did. She was protecting not only her daughter, but the whole fabric and web of life around me. While I might need something solid, so too did I need a shade.

There was so much of the spirit world to cherish and appreciate. It was not all a world to fear. It was a world that had helped me against the demons as much as the living had. Somehow my close contact with the spirit of my mother made death's sting less terrifying. The demons counted on fear, fear of them, fear of chaos, fear of death. My mother vastly mitigated my risk, and the demons had vastly underestimated us.

In that moment I truly understood the lesson my soul being split from my body had taught me. There were two worlds at work every moment of our lives: the tactile and the spiritual. Each and every one of us lived a double life. Body and spirit. Solid and shade. And there was, of course, a constant battle over them. We needed to make friends in both worlds, because there were enemies in each.

And just because Mrs. Northe saw death, it didn't mean it was mine. She specifically couldn't pinpoint the future. And that was for the best. I needed to believe in the power of free will as much as I needed to believe in God. Being a puppet of a divine puppeteer never suited me; it would be with God's help and my own will that we would conquer the problems laid before us. I didn't overestimate myself. But I was damned sure of my calling.

I'd not risk anything before finding Jonathon. We were a good team, and we couldn't dare be separated further. That's when the demons had leverage. But the demons hadn't accounted for my guardian angels that had passed on. I was reminded I was not alone. I had friends in both worlds.

The wind took a stronger turn, and I felt the need to retire, and I ducked down the narrow stairwell and down two levels toward our room. Lavinia had procured us distinctly middle-class comportments. She denounced first-class passengers as a nosy lot that would ask too many questions, but that steerage would simply be too miserable. Middle class was all I'd ever known so I simply tried to move as invisibly through this trip as I'd moved all my life as a mute female. I'd been cast out of "proper society" so long ago, frankly it afforded me far more freedoms than the scrutiny Lavinia had to seek actively to avoid.

It unsettled me that at dusk the dimly lit corridor leading unto our bunks resembled the constant corridors of my nightmares. As I opened the narrow door to our tiny room, Lavinia was laying on her stomach on the top bunk in a pool of sumptuous black fabrics, writing. She nodded to me as I entered and kept writing.

The realization about the familiar corridor must have affected me on a conscious and unconscious level for sure enough, that night a nightmare came in all its resplendent horror.

Why couldn't I simply have a pleasant dream about nothing at all? That might be the greatest gift my mind could give, an entirely mundane dreamscape. What a lovely interlude. Maybe, some night, I would be granted that simple pleasure. Tonight was not that night...

It didn't surprise me that I was in a corridor again. That a simple corridor could take on as many troubling dimensions as it did in my nightmares was perhaps a credit to my powers of invention and manifestation. But a sinking realization hit me during that dream. The corridors were leading up to something not metaphorical but real and what might be found there would mean life or death at some future date. The corridors would lead up, eventually, to one. Or, at least, to several corridors. But halls all in one place.

The Denbury Estate.

Jonathon had once described his home to me while we communed soul to soul when he was trapped in the painted image of his Greenwich estate's study. The architecture before my dreaming eye followed his descriptions. I stood at the end of a very long, shadowed corridor with gaslight sconces down several sets of doors, all of which were open, some dim threshold manifesting in gray gaps of light amid the dark structure of the house itself. Dark wooden paneling and deep purple wallpaper, arches and carving all in gothic styling, an aesthetic akin to something the Brontës would write about. My life had followed a relative Gothic novel style thus far, why stop there? These were just the culmination, the inevitable final chapters, were they not?

Looking from side to side, I noticed there were numbers painted haphazardly on each door. In a specific sequence, winding down from higher numbers to lower. The pattern; the one Crenfall had been repeating in the asylum. That was odd; houses didn't generally number their rooms. So perhaps I was to consider that a metaphoric clue, not literal.

I'd honed the skill of logical deductions while dreaming illogical things. By now I'd had a bit of practice. Perhaps my mind knew that my life would depend upon it and my every faculty was expanded as a result; perhaps when my soul had split from my body, the part of my mind associated with these realms had taken on greater strength, capability, and a certain dominion over what was presented.

But before I could ruminate further on the nature or logic of the numbers, the hair rising on the back of my neck reminded me that I was in a nightmare and that something dreadful was about to be seen, done, heard, felt, or any combination of the lot. It was the most terrible of inevitable things, to have become so familiar with that dropping, sickening dread swinging like the pendulum in Poe's ungodly pit.

I took stock of the corridor once more. It was empty, and yet, I felt I was not alone. The hallway stretched for a length that seemed absurdly long even for a grand estate, as if all proportions were off. At the end opposite me, an uncomfortably far distance indeed, I was faced by an oval portrait of a person whose details were too faint to make out. Anemic sconces on either side cast a subtle haze over the portrait's façade. I tried to walk toward it, as it might be yet another clue, and it was the item pulling focus, the only thing truly lit with any brightness in this dim setting.

But, per that terrible convention of dreams, my least favorite of all the unfortunate tricks of the troubled mind, I could not move. Not forward, not backward. Not that I could go anywhere. A wall was to my back, the corridor's end. Cool, carved wood paneling crested at the nape of my neck in arched patterns set within the fine mahogany. Leaving me to face the empty corridor with open doors and an unknown portrait. If I found my footing, at least I could go into the other rooms. But what might be *in* the other rooms was a question I doubted I wanted answered. The corridor answered for me.

With a slam all the doors at once shut of their own accord, and I started, backing against the end of the corridor behind me.

And then, one by one, in a frightening, invisible procession forward, the gas-lit sconces went out. First the lights illuminating the oval portrait went out. Doused. Instantly. Utter blackness lay in direct opposition of my place at the other end. And then from the end of the corridor forward, one by one, each set on either side of the narrow walls were snuffed out as if by a great wind. But there was no wind. And no one there to turn the key. Just an encroaching and all-encompassing darkness, creeping toward me. One set of sconces at a time. Like footsteps, but there were no footfalls. I tried to step back, to turn and run, but still damnably rooted. I tried to call out for someone, anyone, Jonathon's name upon my lips, but no...

And then the darkness was upon me. My eyes were wide, the blackness thorough. There was a terrible, *terrible* pause in which I was helpless and sensory deprived.

Then an icy, unseen hand closed around my throat.

"This time *you're* coming for *me*, are you?" came that horrid, familiar whisper of the demon in the pitch dark. Warm breath contrasted its icy strangle as it threw its own words back in my face.

Oh, God. It would be waiting. A congealed but yet incorporeal evil could never truly be killed, could it? It would just keep lying in wait... In New York, or England...it would always know me. Could it ever be bested?

I renounce thee... My mind screamed, words that had helped to keep the beast at bay more than once.

The inhumanly cold vise tightened, and I choked a gasp into the encompassing darkness.

I awoke with a start, nearly hitting my head on Lavinia's bunk above. Breathing heavy, I choked but managed not to have screamed, which was for the best. I doubted making a scene or a fuss involving others on the boat would have helped my seasick nerves.

I took a moment to wonder what I could have learned from that dream, other than the obvious demonic pall. Clearly, if I was to travel to the Denbury estate, I should do so with a torch in hand. And a weapon. And avoid corridors. Noted. Also, try never to be alone. To be alone in a nightmare was a most despairing condition. Even worse, to be alone with potential dark magic swarming the air.

I thought of someone else alone in her own mind, and I pulled out my trusty notebook, neatly tore out a few pages, and began writing a letter to a girl recovering from demons' thrall far, far away. A girl who wasn't nearly as accustomed to loneliness as I had been. Despite all her faults, the Master's Society had taken too much to additionally take away the one peer, the one possible friend she might still have, and the only one that could actually understand her plight. That was me, and I needed to rise to that designation. For I bet the demon haunted her too.

"Margaret Hathorn," I murmured to the page before me. "I owe you a letter."

Chapter Eighteen

Dear Maggie,

I would have liked to have written you sooner. But I fell ill. I was, in fact, targeted again, sought out by the demon's tendrils, and laid low by the Master's Society's most recent experimental horrors.

Regrettably, the journey I am on currently will mean it will take even longer for this letter to arrive at your doorstep in Chicago. I embark upon a journey in hopes of resolution, as you have done. I hope you will keep me in your prayers, along with anyone in this dire situation who tries desperately to turn evils around into justices.

From your perspective, considering the expansive and bold contents of your letter, there are things I would like to encourage of you and things I would like to discourage. Not because I think I know any better than you. I chafe at people acting like they "know better" than me. What I write, I write simply because I am trying to take my own advice.

But first, allow me to thank you.

Not for what you did in almost getting us both killed.

But in being willing to reach out, to write a letter, to try and salvage something of what might someday be a truly beautiful friendship. For that, I commend you. It is a brave thing to reach out to another person. I spent most of my life being quite solitary due to my lack of speech, so I understand what breaking isolation means when you've been forced by circumstances to withdraw from average society. Society, for you, meant so much more to you than it ever did to me, so I'm sure your separation from it is all the more troublesome.

But, there are always consequences for actions, and this ostracizing is the unfortunate consequence of your letting the demon in. I believe you are weathering it well, but I would not be a friend to you if I did not share my perspective on these most unique and peculiar and dangerous circumstances.

I encourage you to appreciate Chicago for what it is. My trip out west made me only appreciate New York all the more, so I hope you can truly take in the contrasts as perspective. Absence making the heart grow fonder for home will allow you to reclaim your own self more fully upon your return. You are displaced there for a reason. In my case, I did not weather the effects of dark magic well because I was too quickly wrapped up in it once more, snapped back to New York before the evil had worn off. You need this time, distance, and space for cleansing yourself of the spiritual grime and stain of the demon's making.

I encourage you to listen to the counsel given you there. It is a precious gift. Karen is your guide, as is the lingering presence of lost Amelia. Treasure them as I treasure my deceased mother who yet guides me. Internalize their words and sensibilities down to your core. People like them will save your life. Mrs. Northe gave you the gift and protection of her friends; please see this as her taking care of you. Do not believe for a minute that she doesn't care. She always has, though she hasn't always expressed and acted upon it as thoroughly as she should, in my humble opinion. I do believe she grieves for what more she should have done with and for you. Allow her the opportunity to rectify it here, by sending you somewhere safe, with her dearest companions.

I beg you this: do not entertain the Master's Society's aims in the least.

Do not try to see the perspective of the darkest nature and lend it credence.

Yes, you must understand the enemy in order to fight it. But thinking it has any right to do what it has done or that its agenda is somehow worth considering only gives it more space to breathe. Like a fire that needs air to expand, do not blow upon the embers of the Society. It is already ablaze in several major cities, and the firefighters may be outnumbered. (Well, at the least the police in all cities are entirely unequipped for these *conditions.) We'll see how it all plays out. There are many conflagrations that require stamping out.*

But, I am dead sure that the answers the Master's Society seeks are to unnatural questions that should not have ever been asked. One cannot invert and pervert the ways of God's kingdom so. I do not believe that the processes of science are meant to undermine God, but the Master's Society members are not scientists. They are backward upstarts, seeking to pervert progress unto chaos.

Most of all, do not feed anger and misery. Do not let it grow within you. That's another way for devils to enter. Don't give them the threshold. Don't show them the door.

The phrase of scripture "I renounce thee" will serve you well. If you were not a person of faith before, I encourage you to become one now, in whatever liturgies or practices that empower you, provided they are about love and not hate, graciousness and not omnipotent power, free will rather than enslavement. Otherwise, it is no faith at all but a prison, one in which your mind and soul will rot.

I look forward to all the ways in which we can become better friends and confidants. And, when we're back in New York, let's us go shopping, shall we?

Your friend,

Natalie

I stared at the nearly sermon-like response I'd crafted, thinking it might sound a little too grandiose or a little too much of a lecture, but the young woman needed help. And true friends gave sermons if they felt that something needed to be said, for the sake of the friend in need. I'd appreciate this if the situations were reversed. The strange calm I had when I was delegating and instructing others was one I wished I had when I turned inward. But that's the trouble with advice, it's easy to give and hard to take.

I wasn't about to reveal my location or any of the latest clues in that letter, as I didn't feel either were appropriate or useful. And if for some reason this letter were to find its way astray, or heaven forbid, the

Society was still after Maggie and had a way of getting to her, I didn't want anything incriminating or too revealing to cause me (or Jonathon) trouble.

Something I had written unlocked something for me. The natural versus the unnatural. The sequence. Mrs. Northe said the Master's Society had a penchant for inverting that which had a divine pattern. I would need to consider the orders of the things I would see. In that, I would know where to look for the *disorder*, the sinister path veering off from that which was right and true. And therein I might find the chink in the armor of dark magic. Deducing its dissembling pattern and righting it again, subverting the subversion back toward something loving. The simple good in the world they sought to upend.

I knew that this battle, this odd adventure, might upend me. Upend my life. Result in the death that Mrs. Northe feared. I wasn't, despite this impetuous flight, ignoring the base possibilities. But I simply couldn't give them traction to derail my forward momentum. I couldn't stop to think enough to talk myself out of what had to be done:

Find Jonathon. Fight. Enlist the best help along the way we possibly could.

Much like how I knew I had to aid Jonathon from the moment his painting changed before my eyes and gave me clues to help him, I *had* to do this. Make this journey. See this through. Meet the Society face-to-face. I think I'd always known, somewhere deep within me, it would lead to this, from the first moment I heard the demon wax rhapsodic about the Society's aims there late that night in the Metropolitan.

The world was made by single people doing brave things. Or it was unmade by single people refusing to do what fate decreed.

Chapter Nineteen

Another uneventful few days passed where Lavinia and I spoke of life, dreams, and spent nearly a day hashing out our favorite novels. Austen and the Brontë factored in as our lady heroes, though a wealth of Gothic novels crowned Lavinia's favorite muses above all else. Whereas I gravitated more specifically, solely, to Edgar Allan Poe. Because there was a truth to his words, stories, poetry that resonated with me more than the sweeping romantic gestures of others. Lavinia, like Nathaniel, enjoyed the theatrics. But I understood Poe's pining, his loss, and also, his horror. That hit, unfortunately, so close to home.

And of course we spoke of our loves and of hopeful futures. We attempted to be consummate ladies on a delightful, carefree journey, taking tea in the finer tea rooms specifically to distract ourselves with pretty place settings. It seemed an unspoken agreement to entirely ignore the dread that sat in my stomach, and I'm sure hers too.

England now was closer than it was farther, and I allowed myself a bit of excitement about docking. I'd be seeing Jonathon, surely. Somehow, I'd find him; I knew names and locations, and perhaps, once we were there, he could take a moment to show me his world, his city, a place I'd always yearned to visit.

A part of me was sure he'd be slightly angry for my making the journey. The rest of me was sure he was absolutely expecting it.

But still, I had to let him know, and as he'd given no itinerary, no specific instructions, I was left to my own devices in terms of communicating with him. So, I used our unique and unparalleled connection: our meeting of the minds and entwining of the souls.

Thusly, I forced myself to dream of Jonathon, and thankfully, enough of me knew my life was on the line to agree to a subconscious demand.

Shockingly enough, no corridor in this dream! I almost didn't even know I was dreaming. I was presented with an entirely literal dreamscape, at least at first, a desperate telegraph from a desperate woman.

I was standing on the deck of a ship, this ship, the one I would remain on until we arrived to port two days or so from now. There was a great gale around me. I was wet, struggling to stand, hearing the crash of waves upon the steel hull, the splash of water across the deck, feeling the sting of whipped moisture across my cheek, but I held to a rail and shouted into the storm, for there before me, a few paces away, stood Jonathon. He was turned away from me, but as always, distinct.

I knew it was him—black frock coat, black shoulder-length hair whipped back in the wind, his frame, his stance, his height, and the way my heart pulled toward him like a magnet.

"Jonathon, I'm coming for you," I called.

He whipped around as if he were tossed by the gale, his bright ice-blue eyes luminous in the moonlight, ethereal and otherworldly. His expression was pained.

"That's what the demon said to you. Do you say that to me...because you have been compromised, my beautiful girl?" he asked, calling across the gale, anguished.

"No... Those were the demon's words, but that's hardly what I mean," I protested, reaching out to him, trying to move forward to him, but the pitch of the ship nearly made me lose my balance. Jonathon reeled a bit and regained his footing, still space between us. "I hope you know I'd never let anything within me hurt you..."

I hated that space between us. I needed to be in his arms, to prove what my words only hinted at. I needed his body fully against mine. I needed to kiss him. To go even further. To accept his proposal and act like the betrothed, with certain permissions... I felt a wave of heat radiate down my body. We were not meant to be so separated. Not in spirit, not in body.

"I am coming to England," I clarified. "I must help you. Because I need you. I want you."

He let those words settle in, in the myriad ways I meant them. A lady could say this to the man who was her hero and partner. I could not be ashamed of what neither my body nor my mind knew was right and true.

"Why, Natalie, of course I want to see you. Of course I feel the same. But we don't know what we'll face, this was foolish—"

"You know me better than to think I won't come for you—"

He laughed wearily. "That I do. But take care. People may be on to us. I am not sure when or where we can meet, safely, there is so much sniffing about. We're trying to be the bloodhounds, but there is an arsenal of similar dogs trying to out us. We've tried to play our cards brilliantly, but we maintain constant vigilance."

"How shall I find you?"

"I will find your steamer. Do you know what day you arrive?"

"Dusk. Two days hence. Lavinia is with me."

"Oh, is she?"

"She planned this, separately. She'll not allow Nathaniel to slip away any more than I will you."

Jonathon smiled. "He'll be glad to hear it—"

"So he is with you?"

"I seem to attract the best company. Don't find me, I will find you. And when I do, just... You'll have to trust me. Do you trust me?"

"I do," I cried, wishing that were another proposal if not a wedding vow.

He grinned. "We are so lucky our dreams are like letters and telegraphs. Only better, because I get to see you... And oh, *look* at you, you're all wet..." His noble voice descended in pitch, to a purr that somehow still carried across the storm.

And suddenly he was the one to close the distance between us. He seized me roughly and drew me into a furious kiss, the saltwater of his lips crashing over mine like the waves upon the ship. My soaked dress revealed the full contours of me to his bold and questing fingertips. Perhaps the fury of the storm was an excuse to be rough with me. Never has a girl so welcomed a squall.

He pinned me against a large cabinet bearing life vests, and this steadied us for our deepening kisses, soft cries, bold and searching caresses. And in this storm, we sunk together into our desperate need, as much of a force of nature as the pitch and roil of the boat. I noted all the ways in which I knew he desired me, and I blushed into the gale, and I wanted more.

I welcomed this abandon that would risk all, as I had always welcomed our physical trespasses. I could not think of anything carnal between us as anything but sacred, for magic had bid us be lovers, and being lovers was its own magic.

"Come to me, then, Natalie Stewart," he growled, his words thrusting against my ear as he did against my body. "And let's finish *all* that we started…"

I woke up perspiring, my nerves making the moisture of the gale real, and my body was alive. Shaking. Humming with titillation. Furious that I was now awake and no longer his willing captive.

It dawned on me that this was the first dream in my memory that wasn't a nightmare.

This didn't change the fact that I faced a *living* nightmare ahead of me.

But for now, my love, my lover, my pride and joy, he transformed a troubled mind into a paradise. Even in the storm.

Chapter Twenty

I was taking in what details I could of the English coast as we dropped anchor at Port Brimscombe where we would then make arrangements for a train on to London, and prepared to disembark.

I was rendered breathless by the Port, appreciating the sweeping landscape before me. As dusk set, lamplighters were busy at their trade; creating a winking path of golden streetlamps blazing forth to illuminate the lines and depth of the brisk seawall. Streets ahead led under arches and down busy lanes.

Two other similarly impressive ships as ours had moored ahead of us and the bustle surrounding the docks resembled a swarm of insects over the boats. Ours was apparently the last big ship scheduled in for the evening.

I drank in the sea at twilight, pausing for a moment as the sounds of the harbor washed over me, the chaos and hurry, the business and the comings and goings, meetings and partings. There was great beauty before me; I found myself enthralled by the sound of so many different classes and ranges of accents. I couldn't worry about how Jonathon would find me, for there were men and women, families, friends, all finding one another, somehow, through the chaos. Bonds will out. Longing and fondness will bring the missing reunited. Surely, it would be a matter of moments... We'd come this far by faith.

What was one more seeking out...

Ports were full of endless possibility, and I sensed the raw emotion of meetings and partings, of dreams setting sail and hopes deferred, of quests and longings, of departing citizens already dearly missed. The charge and power of a harbor was one of the most invigorating hubs of any society, and I thrilled and thrived in it here, as I did in New York. A sea of passengers buffeted around me as I descended the broad gangplank and onto first the wooden dock, then ahead, the cobblestones of the bank street.

When I looked around for Lavinia, realizing I'd been separated from her in the thick of the disembarking masses, she was nowhere to be seen. This was the first swift kick of terror to my gut.

The second came when I was seized and thrown over a shoulder.

And *that* was a far more terrible terror indeed.

My cry of surprise was lost in the din as I was taken into an alley. I tried to kick, but my legs were held fast, and though I pounded my fists against a broad back, soon another set of hands put a gag around my mouth, seized my wrists, and bound them with a thick piece of fabric, and I was thrown inside a carriage where Lavinia sat wide-eyed, bound and similarly gagged.

We stared at each other, the panic upon our faces was evident, and I prayed so hard that somehow my message to Jonathon in our previous shared dream would mean that since he was expecting me, he'd notice if I'd gone missing. Somehow, he'd come find me. Somehow he'd know how to save me, just as I had done for him. It was what we were meant to do. A princess who saved a prince who saved his princess...

I wondered if Lavinia was thinking the same thing, wondering if somehow Jonathon and Nathaniel were working together, thinking together, plotting, and problem solving together, would rescue us together...

I looked around at our unexpected prison. It was the finest carriage I had ever been inside. It was spacious, an imposing black lacquer space with silver fittings and detailing, with dark green velvet curtains and the same green velvet covering the benches that faced each other.

Lavinia had been deposited across from me, her lovely black gown fitting for this imperious space were she free to enjoy it. But her bright eyes darted about as mine did. I shifted, hefting myself forward, and as the carriage lurched, I came down on my knees on the dark wooden floorboards.

With a groan of pain, I shifted my torso so that my bound hands behind me could fiddle with the carriage handles, seeing if I could open a door. Lavinia watched me with hopeful eyes. The carriage was locked, that was quite clear from my wresting, shifting efforts with the door and the latch that should have opened it. It must have been secured upon the exterior by another lock or pin.

Lavinia nodded, seeing my efforts, and she then tried to stand. Her red tresses jostled against the dark, carved wooden ceiling as she tried to draw back one of the curtains to see out the glass windows we could only glimpse the edges of. But it would seem the corners of the curtains had been secured in a way we couldn't gain purchase upon, tacked down by ornate silver pins. She tried to wrest the heavy fabric one way, then the other, which only succeeded in her throwing herself inadvertently from one side of the carriage to the other, colliding against the green velvet benches. Her face contorted in a wince of pain.

We sat back down together on the same side, each of us hearing a rip as a hem of our skirts tore. We had no hands to ensure the safe shift of the layers of fabric from one position to another. There was a long moment of us just breathing heavily, swaying and bouncing as the carriage trundled on.

This was the carriage of someone of means. That surely didn't bode well for us. People with means had many resources at their disposal to do with women what they pleased. I could feel the familiar panic of being in a life or death situation—a feeling I did not like but seemed so ridiculously accustomed to by this point—rise within me, the heat of my body, the thump of my heart, the drying of my mouth, the plummet of my gut, the prickling of my hairs, the desire to scream...but none of that physical reeling would keep me or Lavinia alive. Somehow, my mind remained sound.

I tried to get a sense of where we were, any telling clues of sound or scent, but the jostle of the carriage and the occasional neigh of the horse team that was hefting us along at a great clip was din enough; no details surpassed the clatter. At some point we did cross from cobblestones to earth, so we were heading out of the city proper.

At least an hour passed. Maybe two. Time was hard to tell in captivity and helplessness. The fact of how little we'd slept the night prior was catching up to the both of us, and at one point we realized we'd folded over each other in an exhausted collapse, lulled by the constant rhythm and steady pace of the carriage flying over well-packed paths.

When one of us started awake, the other did, all we could do was look into each other's eyes and feel empathy. This went on for some time until the carriage came to an abrupt halt with the sound of a male shout, the piercing whinny of the team of horses, a clatter of the harnesses, and a lurch of the cab.

There was the sound of footsteps climbing down from above, the carriage rocking slightly in the effort, a thud of feet on both sides. And the sound of two deadbolts being thrown back, simultaneous. A hand upon each carriage door. The lever turned...

Lavinia and I stared at each other in abject terror. At least one aspect of our fate was about to become clear. Our heads whipped back to each respective door. I wanted to face my abductor and stare him down with whatever strength I could muster.

The doors on either side of the carriage were flung open, and in leaned our captors: two handsome, black-haired gentlemen, looking *rather* pleased with themselves...

Good God, if it wasn't Jonathon Whitby, Lord Denbury himself, that leaned into the carriage about a foot away from me, resting on his elbow somewhat jauntily. Nathaniel Veil appeared on Lavinia's side with an expectant expression, looking like the wild, theatrical twin to Jonathon's more tamed elegance. But in that moment, I wasn't thinking of their black-haired beauty; I was only filled with fury as they both broke into grins at our blushing faces.

My cry of, "What in God's name?" thanks to my gag, came out as one jumbled, inelegant, "*Aah ih aw ehh!*" I threw my body forward, onto my knees, and tried to say, "You untie me this instant!" but that didn't come out any better than the first attempt.

I shook my head like a horse trying to throw off its bridle and wrestled my shoulders. Lavinia was, by contrast, sitting quite still and staring.

"I said I'd come fetch you," he replied, shifting forward to undo my bindings. I didn't like being tied down when I'd been subjected to the toxin, so I certainly didn't like it now.

The minute the fabric was unwound from around my mouth, I launched into a tirade, though the language was so much quicker in my head than I was able to spit out. My tongue, due to my disability, still remained at a pace behind my mind, and it only made me blush hotter.

"Jonathon Whitby! You...should be ashamed of yourself. This is not how you treat ladies. Much less ones you're courting," I murmured vehemently. "We had no idea what was going on. That was...simply cruel!"

I looked over at Lavinia for support, expecting a mutually incensed young woman.

Instead, I found Lavinia looking rather dreamily at Nathaniel as he undid her bindings. We wore the same blush, blooming brightly, but hers seemed far less borne of anger. As she leaned toward him with hitching breaths, I rolled my eyes. I supposed, in her Gothic novel heart, that this was somehow very romantic.

Jonathon noted with discomfort that I was not so swayed. He opened his mouth to reply, but I cut him off.

"Why such a show of abducting us, what good did that do save scare us to death?" I asked, keeping my tone hard. "And I hope you'll give us the small courtesy of telling us where we've been swept off to."

"It's good to see you, too, you know," he said, frowning.

"Don't you *dare* pout at me! You nearly drove us mad!" I snapped. I felt my whole body grow hot with the delayed panic, as if the blush were a rapid contagion, my survival instinct now overturned with relief and yet replaced by a thorough and violent anger. "After all we've been through, to do something like that? It's not a game! It's not a game when I honestly thought I might die," I said, tears springing to my eyes. "When I'm scared I might soon die, with your help or no, these dangerous circumstances—"

Jonathon climbed in the carriage and took me by the arms and spoke earnestly. "I'm so sorry. This was what was advised to us." I wanted to break away, but his embrace felt divine and his warm breath on my ear so delicious. I cursed giving over easily, though my heartbeat still pounded like the thump of rolling trains. "I thought you'd know it was me."

"You could've said something," I murmured. I glanced over, glaring at Nathaniel. "You could have whispered something, either of you—"

"No," Jonathon replied firmly. "We were both advised against that as your body, fight, and struggle would have changed in the moment, and even a hitch could have cost us the ruse. Please understand that we feared eyes upon us, we had to keep up appearances."

"Advised by who—"

"Gabriel Brinkman," Nathaniel piped in. I noticed that as he stood at the side of the carriage, Lavinia had gravitated to him, sitting midcarriage between the benches in a pool of black satin and ensconced in her paramour's arms. I furrowed my brow.

"Ah, Mister Brinkman." I turned back to Jonathon, pulling back to stare him down fully. "He who ferreted you off without allowing you any chance to tell me you were going?"

Suddenly Lavinia seemed to recover her dignity and self-awareness. "Or me!" she piped in.

Both gentlemen sighed in tandem.

"Time was of the essence. And to tell you the truth, Brinkman so passionately convinced me to just come directly to London that it was precisely the thing to do. I telegraphed a note to Mrs. Northe with addresses I'd found in my searching on the streets of New York, several Master's Society properties that had that fiery red and gold aura about them, the demon's mark."

"You wrote Mrs. Northe, but not me—"

"It was encoded, and nothing could be traced. I didn't know how to send you something as efficiently that wouldn't give too much away. Please, Natalie, your need to be included shouldn't overreach the caution for my safety and that of your own."

"No, it shouldn't," I agreed. "But I do hope you'll explain why this show of force was necessary." I fought to take the edge off my voice, trying not to let the tears of panic I'd held back now flow forth in relief and displaced anger. My stubbornness was not so easily worn down.

"Brinkman said that there was a Society tail that he thought was closing in on me in New York, and had reports that things were escalating in England, that the Society was keeping an eye out on any of their scientists, experimenters, and operatives. We chanced that if I returned to England and convinced the Master that I was still my evil half, then they might be more forthcoming in general while giving me leave to move and interact with more freedom."

My jaw fell open. "You chanced meeting with that man again? He could've had you killed!"

"Brinkman was at the ready with police should I have signaled distress. But I convinced the bastard." A furious flash of pride crossed over his lovely, albeit haunted, face. I wondered if playing the demon again had the same distressing affect that his soul had shown when his body and mind were failing in the painting. "Dragged Nathaniel into it with me, he was brilliant."

"How did you earn his trust?" Lavinia asked, looking up at Nathaniel, her voice breathy, impressed.

"By saying I wanted to see the breadth of his power as I could see my Association was under attack, and that they indeed had presented themselves as a test group of willing subjects. I told him if I could bring the Association into the fold of something more powerful, then I was willing to become a devotee in turn," Veil said convincingly.

"I played the same part as before," Jonathon continued. "I've seen the mannerisms and the pointed, eerie ways of the possessed enough to know how to mimic them. He asked questions of my conquests, and I invented elaborate stories." His shudder inspired my own. "And I made some promises..." And here his expression suddenly grew sheepish.

"Promises? I'm not sure I like the sound of that, Jonathon," I said, my voice lowering. "What kind of promises?"

"Bait," Nathaniel replied with a nonchalance that disturbed me. Our respective gentlemen looked at each of us.

"*Us*?" I was immediately indignant again.

"Only if you're willing," Jonathon rushed to reply. "I had a feeling when I met with the '"Master"' that you'd be coming. Natalie. You have that way about you, a certain predictability..." He offered a fond smile that threatened to undo my indignity. "And I know you want to eliminate these bastards as much as I do."

"*Or* I could convince others within my Association here in England," Nathaniel added. "In no way did we predicate this plan on the assurance of your involvement, most esteemed ladies. I am sure I could find other willing women—"

"I'll do it," Lavinia blurted. I set my jaw and nearly growled.

"But..." Jonathon leaned forward again to cup my face in his palm. "It would be far better to have the bravest woman I know there at my side. To have someone beside me who knows the enemy better than anyone else? That's the safest option. For in the baiting, there is the trapping, the snaring of the fox." Here his bright eyes lit with determination.

"Go on," I urged. The fact that we were discussing intense and dangerous plans while in an open carriage was questionable, but they must have taken us somewhere far from civilization indeed, as all I could hear outside were the sounds of nature and wildlife at night.

Jonathon continued excitedly. "Brinkman will have guards posted in the secret passages of my home, and just when the true depth of the depravity is revealed, as I hope to get him onto one of his rhapsodies about his plans, the authorities will swoop in and apprehend the villain."

"And the context of this baiting?" I queried pointedly.

Lavinia looked at me with a certain overwhelmed gratefulness, as if it was all she could do just to keep up and she was glad someone was asking the right questions. This kind of mindset and these sorts of situations were not the kind of thing any "good, upstanding" young woman would ever have been trained for. I simply had grown somewhat accustomed to the sort of twisted tale I seemed to have lived into, a strange extension of the countless adventure novels I consumed and loved since I could read.

"Why, you bring all the *best* bait to a lavish dinner party, of course," Veil replied with a winning smile. "A meeting of the depraved minds."

"I am hoping it will bring out others within the Master's Society for their arrest," Jonathon added.

"But..." I began, furrowing my brow. "Couldn't that mean we might end up being outnumbered? For what if Brinkman can't be trusted? What if he is just serving us all up directly into the hands of the enemy? Who vouches for this stranger who just conveniently, unexpectedly, showed up in our lives?" I thought about the day he swung uninvited into our carriage near Central Park, and this abduction plan seemed like his handiwork indeed. I wondered if he was lurking somewhere nearby, listening to everything. "Arriving knowing more about you than I'd like a stranger to know?"

"He isn't about to serve us up," Jonathon said gravely. "He's playing the double agent just as I am. Though unlike me, he's not doing his part as a possessed creature. But he is entwined in the same dangerous game, I assure you. Playing for life or death. For someone he loves."

"Trust us on that count," Nathaniel murmured. Though I didn't know the situation, from the look on both their faces, something horrible was at stake, and I felt a pang of pity for Brinkman. To have garnered such an unquestioning response, it must be something terrible indeed.

I nodded, though something nagged at me that I couldn't shake, the certainty that this couldn't possibly go smoothly, no matter how well thought out or imagined.

"You still haven't answered where we are."

"Ah, yes, that!" Jonathon smiled. "Now that we're away from watching eyes and listening ears, I shall present our next task. Surveillance." He offered his arm. Glancing over at Nathaniel, he did the same; a matching set of black sleeves, a similar engaging smile, a glimmer in Nathaniel's dark eyes was mirrored as well as in Jonathon's ice-blue ones. It was clear these two were best friends, kindred spirits, and impossible to resist. Even after kidnapping. "Shall we?"

Chapter Twenty-One

The gentlemen helped Lavinia and me out of the carriage, and we stepped down onto soft green moss. From what I could see by the lit lanterns hung on each corner of the fine carriage, we were surrounded by trees, the team of horses having stopped in a little clearing. A bright moon hung high in the sky.

The horses were steaming with their exertion, seeming very glad to be nibbling at grass once Nathaniel removed their bits and patted their sweaty hides. He spoke to the two horses with such fondness, calling them by name, so I now knew this was his carriage, his team. Veil had done well for himself, it would seem, for those were just as fine a set of horses as the carriage itself was of the highest caliber. Perhaps he had a few wealthy patrons. I knew nothing of his lineage, but this wasn't the time to ask, as a peculiar arrangement lay before us.

A few paces ahead of us sat a circular, dark brick wall draped in climbing ivy that just surpassed Jonathon's tall height.

He took two of the lanterns from the carriage's four exterior hooks, then handed one to Nathaniel and strode forward, the beams of light bouncing and illuminating only lush greenery around us. The rest beyond was thorough darkness. Jonathon fished in his pocket before procuring a large iron key that he inserted into just as large of a lock. The solid metal gate opened with a rusty groan, and Jonathon gestured all of us forward.

He led us within the curved wall. Inside were the long-lost remnants of an untended garden that may once have been exquisite.

Up the path sat a small, single-story cottage of dark brick that was nearly entirely overgrown with ivy and climbing roses. The roses, either white or pale pink, I couldn't quite tell in the light, were the only things looking thoroughly healthy in the area, their tumbling glory utterly unheeding the dilapidation of the building they climbed upon.

We walked carefully up an overgrown flagstone path. Weeds and briars slapped and snagged at my skirts. Jonathon led us up to a splintering wooden door.

This reminded me of a fairy tale. We had somehow crossed into an enchanted forest, and in this hut we would encounter either profit, an oracle, a witch, or some other Grimm doom. Though I had to admit, the scenery had more romance than magic or dread to it, wistfully abandoned.

I wasn't sure what this place was or once had been, let alone how we could attempt surveillance from so remote a location. Though I had no direct experience with English lords, I'd seen enough of the wealthy to know what an estate was and was not. This was not an estate. But it was curious indeed.

The same large iron key opened the door, paneled in shaded glass as if wanting to keep something within obscured. If there were windows, I couldn't see them in the darkness for the coverings of ivy and rose briars.

"Where are we?" I asked, looking around at the interior of the small, dusty cottage.

Jonathon took a thin taper sitting on the plate of a sconce by the door and began lighting the candles and lanterns within the place, and pool by pool of light revealed an intriguing space.

While petite, it was lavishly appointed, having obviously kept someone in great state. But considering the forest and wall around it, someone kept hidden.

"It's a bit of family history," Jonathon replied with an odd discomfort. "We're here on Denbury property, but property only known to a few, and accessed by none. I was grateful the carriage path was still somewhat navigable when I first retread it the other day, though I had to take a scythe to it to truly open it back up again. All of this dates back to my great-grandfather's time..."

"A lady was kept here," Lavinia stated, picking up dusty, fine lace doilies and distinctly ladies' accessories: a stray glove, a fan set onto the mantle of a marble fireplace, a vanity placed rather prominently in a room that wasn't a bedroom, but... "It all looks like one large ladies' boudoir," she added.

Nathaniel strode over to a set of lush, thick red velvet curtains and swept one back, revealing an enormous four-poster bed that was nestled into an alcove crowned by an elaborate trim. Or, it would seem it was a bedroom after all.

Jonathon cleared his throat. "Yes. Supposedly, my great-grandfather had quite a precious secret that he wanted to keep quite hidden indeed."

"On his own property?" Nathaniel said, seeming a bit more impressed than he should have been. If this was going where I thought it was, this was not something a *gentleman* should aspire to. "I suppose the secrets kept close to home are the most titillating..." he added, tossing a burning glance at Lavinia, who held his gaze and returned it.

I refrained from folding my arms and looking at Jonathon pointedly, though I truly wanted to make him squirm a bit. The sight of the bed had me blushing again, and I cursed my revelatory cheeks. Thankfully, there were other mysteries of the place to catch attention.

Turning away, I gestured to an immense, intriguing door, a massive wrought iron contraption beautifully decorated with floral and ivy patterns, and then gestured back to the smaller door we'd come in through, the one that led out to the little walled garden one might expect of an average cottage. "If *that* is the front door," I began, then gestured back to the ornate metal garden, "then where does *this* lead?"

Jonathon swung the door wide. A big black chasm was revealed, with stairs leading down into a dark corridor. The first few steps were white marble. Everything else was entirely in shadow.

"To the estate," Jonathon replied. He couldn't hold my gaze as I blinked at him.

"So what you're *saying* is that..." I said slowly, "you've brought us to the secret mistress cottage that is *connected* to your estate?" Now I felt justified in folding my arms and glowering. "That's...that's what's going on here?"

"Great-Grandfather's cottage, this wasn't like some family tradition," he clarified, clearly trying to justify this whole presentation as an extreme outlier. "He was an infamous rake, excessive, mad to the point of abject hedonism. My family has worked very hard to restore the Denbury reputation."

"But still, kidnapping and then bringing the *lady* you're *courting* to the *mistress's* cottage?" I countered. Again, I looked over to Lavinia for support in my indignation. I don't know why I bothered. She was staring rapturously at Nathaniel. I folded my arms, turning back to Jonathon. "Well, it doesn't strike the best tone."

"I realize that, but none of this is about you, Natalie," Jonathon said, bracing me as if that might be a shocking revelation. I scowled. He continued. "And none of this should be seen in the eyes of courtship but of necessity. Everything I have done is about getting into my estate, unseen, still keeping up the guise until I am absolutely certain I could have no possible trail on us in order to safely survey the situation. This is the perfect vantage point, to enter from a secret passage. There will be ways to spy and listen in without ever being seen. In addition, no one in the house—"

His face flashed with fury. "None of those fools who don't belong there as it is not *their* house could know about any of this, not the passages, anything." He gestured around him to this unusual setting. "This was a very well-kept secret only between my mother, father, and me. We told none of our staff. The knowledge was bequeathed to my father when his father passed. Since this was a good escape route or hiding place in any emergency, we felt there was no sense sealing it off."

A fleeting glimmer of sorrow passed over his beautiful face. I assumed thinking of his late parents caused a pang, and I wondered at his strength of confronting all this; a house and family were taken from him, and here he was poised to survey it as if it wasn't even his anymore. Well, it wasn't; it had been stolen. But justice would be done. In the end. It had to be. But there were no certainties for us. His resilience in the face of it all was truly astonishing.

Jonathon continued further. "You and Lavinia will be safe here while Nathaniel and I see if the house is occupied or indeed as abandoned as Brinkman indicated it might be from recent exterior surveillance."

"You mean to leave us here?" I clarified quietly.

"It would be for the best," Nathaniel stated.

"No, I am coming with you," I declared.

Jonathon shook his head. "I knew you'd say that, but, Natalie, my dear—"

"If we are about to be bait, as it were, I'd like to know what may be in store. I want to know where and what I might be—perhaps literally— dragged into. As you say, I don't need to be visible, but waiting here will be maddening—"

"Well, then, if you're so insistent about it, Miss Stewart," Nathaniel interrupted crisply, "then we should take every precaution. If we are discovered during this surveillance excursion, we'll need to play our parts." He reached into the pockets of his long black frock coat and plucked out the bindings he'd taken off Lavinia, unfurling them through his long fingers once more. He turned to Lavinia with smoldering attention.

Nathaniel grasped Lavinia's hand and brought it to his lips. "My lady. Would you permit me this little ruse once more? It's just a game," he purred.

Lavinia bit her lip, nodded, and if I wasn't mistaken, she swayed a bit as if her knees were suddenly weak.

I balled my fists, and that blushing flare of fury lit up over my body once more.

"It is *not* a game, Mister Veil. It never has been. Perhaps this all seems like a grand act to you, but please remember people have died in this game. Your dear friend and myself, included. Not to mention your Association, too, if they're not careful."

The imperious actor turned a sober look to me. "If we don't make it a game, Miss Stewart, pretend we're not frightened, how in God's name will we have the courage to do what must be done?" he countered earnestly. "I stared into the eyes of that so-called "Master" of it all, and the soullessness I saw there, the pit left behind once all humanity has been removed..." He shuddered. "It defies description. And I'm *very* good with words. Perhaps you think me just an arrogant, carefree player after all. But I thought I glimpsed understanding when we met. I thought you saw, as Jonathon has always seen, that I take the terror I choose to counter with levity *deathly* seriously."

I nodded, looking away, contrite. He took a step closer to me, waiting to meet my eyes again. When we did, he added, "But you're not wrong to make sure of it."

"Thank you," I murmured.

I felt the pressure of Jonathon's hand in mine. I smiled up at him weakly. "Lead on then, Lord Denbury," I said, holding out my hands for him to make me out to be the captive again.

He smiled at me gently and was just as gentle as he took the fabric from his breast pocket and wrapped up my wrists, making it look like an intense bind, but it did not chafe in the least. "Thank you for placing your trust in me, Natalie. I do not take it for granted."

"That makes two of us," Nathaniel said to Lavinia, running a finger down her blushing cheek.

"How can the devils beat such a blessed team?" I asked, returning his smile.

Oh, but how I knew they'd try.

I closed my eyes a moment as Jonathon did up my hands again, trying to block out thoughts of how the toxin had overtaken me, how I'd been tied down for fear of harming others. How embarrassing. This was not much better, this show of humiliation.

I tried not to think of the helpless position this put us in, how as women we were expected to be the "bait" for demons, as I'd chosen to be once before at the Metropolitan, to lure out evil so that I might best it with a countercurse. That we were constrained to do so was inescapably sickening to me. I was aware that society relegated us to second-class citizens, though I believed with all my heart women were equal creatures under the God that I knew. Human law and opinion just needed to catch up with the divine. Just because I could play the game of my world did not mean I was complicit to it otherwise. Jonathon must have read the struggle on my face; surely he could feel it, for what he offered was a salve:

"I take no pleasure in anything that would give you discomfort, Natalie. I would never subject you to something I didn't know you could handle with the most impressive aplomb."

"Thank you, dear," I replied, opening my eyes to take in his kind gaze. He'd always been as much of my champion as I was of myself. Bless him for that. "Thank you. For such a thing as this is not easy to stomach."

"For a girl like you, hardly," he said with a little laugh. "And I'd not have that any other way." He tied the knot of the bindings, loose in truth, but looking quite thorough to an outside eye. He kissed me fondly on the cheek and stepped away.

Jonathon took his carriage lantern, Nathaniel, too, and as he went down the marble steps ahead, he called back to us. "Wait one moment, ladies, while we light the torches on ahead."

A dank, dark corridor was revealed beyond the descending set of stairs. The fine trappings near the mouth of the corridor, presumably all that a lady ensconced in that private cottage would have seen, were enough of a courtesy. But the route to get to her was something else entirely.

Jonathon and Nathaniel darted back up the corridor and up the marble slab stairs to fetch us. They led us each by the elbows down into the corridor, taking care with our balance. None of us were in a rush, as everything had an oppressive weight of dread about it. Poor Jonathon, who should have been so excited to return home. Now home was enemy territory that had to be approached by subterfuge...

The connecting passage was like an endless tomb. Dirt-packed walls were reinforced by wood and stone beams. The soot of torches and lanterns smeared big black tongues up the slightly arched ceiling that was not far above our heads. An interminable length lay ahead of us. Jonathon and Nathaniel had only lit the periodic torches for a few paces on, but Jonathon held out a lit taper. I assumed there were more yet to light. I wasn't necessarily claustrophobic by nature—after all, I lived in New York City—but this would try anyone's sense of space.

None of us felt compelled to say anything. I had a thousand questions as to what to expect, but I doubted Jonathon could offer me any answers. We were playing this game entirely by ear. I tried not to think about any number of my nightmares where terrible things happened down long corridors where I was, for all intents and purposes, trapped... When Jonathon and Nathaniel lit the lamps, I just prayed they would stay lit for us and not be snuffed out by God knows what... Hadn't I promised myself I'd avoid corridors? I was the worst tempter of fate that ever lived.

I had no sense of time or length of passage other than a great deal of it. Finally the mouth of it seemed to widen as if we'd come to the estuary of a river. Before us lay another set of stairs. Out from the tunnel rose another large metal door. Jonathon ascended the set of stairs, fished for the same key in yet another impressive iron lock, and was very careful to turn the lock slowly so that the latch would not echo.

"Stay quiet until I can determine if we've any measure of cover or safety," Jonathon whispered.

He gestured us through the door and into a strange space beyond, a little landing, wooden panels all around us and a few strange pipes, levers, and meters and small vertical slots in the panels before us. He very slowly shifted a lever, and a slot opened. There was darkness beyond. A sliver of light could be seen far in the distance.

"What's on the other side?" Lavinia whispered.

"Our library." He peered into the dim vertical opening once more. "Obviously, no one is feeling literarily inclined at the moment," Jonathon replied, still in a whisper.

"What is all this?" I gestured around me to the other levers, which I assumed may be other peep holes, but that didn't explain the pipes or meter.

"When the house was fitted with gas fixtures," Jonathon began, still keeping his voice hushed, "my father became rather entranced with the secret passages and with their possible advantage. I always thought he was a bit paranoid, but now I wonder if he actually was on to something. He was so protective of Mother, all my life, terrified of losing her, that I thought he was going a bit mad over it. I wonder if some part of him foresaw their doom..." Jonathon looked at the wooden landing beneath our feet. "I know Mother had a suitor early in her life that had caused her trouble. She'd only mentioned it briefly, when she was instructing me how to be a proper gentleman. It would seem he'd proven the very opposite. I hope I wasn't blind, that there was something I should have seen, been forewarned—"

I placed my hand on his arm. "You mustn't think like that. There's nothing you could have done, truly. And you *have* become the good and proper gentleman she'd be so proud of..."

He offered me a strained smile before shaking his head as if casting off something he didn't wish to consider further. He continued. "Father had a device fitted here"—he gestured to a little open-faced dial with a needle—"that tells us if any of the gas lines have been turned anywhere in the house. The needle is down, so that indicates no lamps have been turned. And he had every room fitted, even the kitchens. Told no one but Mother and me about this little area, as we were the only ones to know about the passages themselves. I never dreamed I'd actually have cause to *use* them. So by the lamp theory, no one is here at this hour, as staff, if any were here to attend to anyone present, would always be awake at this time."

I nodded. I nearly offered the critique that demons could likely act in the darkness, but I wasn't sure if that would be helpful. My body seemed to know when they were present before my mind had any registry, and while I was tense, there were no telltale hairs rising on the back of my neck. Not yet.

"And now we listen," he added, gesturing to a small phonograph-like bell. "There is a pipe from each room to carry any noise. It's frighteningly sensitive. Father never made it a habit to hide here, he wasn't mad about it, but he did threaten me never to keep secrets, as he said he'd hear everything like the ear of God." He chuckled again, and this time didn't bother to blink back a tear.

The poor man still had never had time to grieve. There had been no proper funeral for his parents. There had been no closure. My heart seized with an ache and a love so pure and raw. He hadn't spoken of them much since we'd met. I could see now that was only because speaking of them was so fraught with melancholy and wistfulness for the time wrongfully stolen from their lives.

"Do keep quiet and your breathing shallow, friends," Jonathon bid, "and let's see if anything picks up."

We listened. Only the occasional creak of an old house. No stirring of any presence, no footsteps, no words, snores, no rustling or shifting. An uncanny blanket of quiet.

"It would seem we are indeed alone, but I still say we proceed with caution. If anyone finds us, we play our parts. However, I'm not sure the bindings will be necessary. I'd rather do without them," Jonathon said, and in a moment I was free once more.

"I'll hold it in case," I said, keeping the fabric clutched in one of my hands.

With my other hand, I pressed against the stays and laces of my corset and felt the ridge of the small, sharp scissors I'd been yearning for earlier. I undid one hook and eye of my bodice near my navel to allow for a quick plucking out of the blade. The small comforts were profound.

Nathaniel untied Lavinia's wrists, and I wasn't sure which of them lost control, but suddenly their lips were as locked as their arms were around one another. Perhaps the quiet tension simply had been too much for them. In unison, Jonathon and I turned away as if we didn't notice.

But I thought I saw Jonathon smirk as he took my hand and led me forward, pressing his hand into the darkness. With the drop of a clunking lever, a panel swung forward into the library we'd been scouting. We left the panel open for the entwined couple; they'd see to it as they would.

I looked around in wonder at the dim library, rectangular and tall, with floor to ceiling books, lit only by the moonlight streaming in from behind the arched French windows curtained in lavish fabric. But Jonathon didn't linger here. I think he was too concerned with getting to the heart of the estate to truly take stock, for he moved forward with specific intent. The library led into a grand corridor with chandeliers dropping down periodically throughout the length of it, sweeping out into an open area beyond, likely the main foyer.

Everything ahead was shadowed and glittering silver, all the finery, all the mirrored and crystalline surfaces, the golden frames around still lifes and landscape paintings and well-polished wood. It was the hallway of a palace, with arches marching forward, everything dim save for a wildly bright moon that sent light in at odd angles to bounce off any responsive surface and make the hall look as if it were enchanted. I was, certainly.

He looked back to me, to why I'd paused, and his furrowed brow eased. He bowed slightly and tried to hide the pain in his expression, but I was too accustomed to that beautiful face to miss it. "Allow me to welcome you to Rosecrest, my lady."

Chapter Twenty-Two

As he righted himself, I curtseyed deeply. "My esteemed Lord Denbury, it is an honor to be here," I replied with soft earnestness. He broke into a smile. A genuine smile like I'd not seen for some time, a flame of his pride returning, and it was as if one of the gas lamps had been lit in the room. But it was only his eyes. The moonlight did all the rest. "I love the name of it," I added eagerly. "*Rosecrest...*"

"Dates back in something of our lineage to the War of the Roses. I'm not sure what's fact and what's familial aggrandizing." He chuckled.

And at the mention of family, there again came the pain, like a veil being drawn over those seraphim features of his. He reached up to turn the key of a gas lamp before thinking better of it, keeping signs of activity at a minimum. There was moonlight enough.

We set to wandering the quiet, dark, enormous old house. To say it was eerie was perhaps the understatement of my life.

And yet it was so arrestingly exquisite. Eerie didn't bother me. Eerie was enticing, the kind of setting where a soul could give over to romance, a place for passionate whispers and stolen clutches in dark corners, surrounded by shadowed beauty on all sides. Frightening was a different story, a shade darker on the palette. At the moment, we were firmly in the color of eerie, and I was content to stay in its entrancing hue.

Rosecrest was the kind of grand, palatial manor that would be its own character in a famous tale. Old and mid-eighteenth-century Gothic, it was everything a Brontë would have written about and that in any other case or company, I'd have unabashedly swooned over.

But I didn't need to make a show of any of that here, as it would have been a bit much. For Lavinia soon caught up with us and took that particular helm, her black layers as slightly askew as her coiffure, Nathaniel looking a bit smug behind her. His long black coat swept the floor as he stalked into the main foyer, making him look like these surroundings were one of his stage sets.

As my far more theatrical compatriot, Lavinia did all the sighing and exclaiming over the manor for me. Nathaniel was quite used to the place but seemed to love seeing it through Lavinia's eyes, and their impassioned, nearly childlike wonder was so refreshing against the anxieties that had my shoulders so tensed.

Allowing for momentary curiosity, I watched them. After that furious kiss of theirs in the underground corridor, I wondered if Nathaniel Veil, the Gothic Don Juan, was growing to favor Lavinia in the ways that I hoped, as I wanted her to be his foremost paramour. She was too much of his kindred spirit not to be, and her unbridled rapture at the estate was endearing and contagious. After a particularly rhapsodic ode where Lavinia exclaimed about the moonlight through the massive, arching window that illuminated the grand wood and marble staircase to upper floors "as a portal into the night court of the realms of faerie," I did feel compelled to add my own compliments to her panoply.

"It *is* so very beautiful, Jonathon," I murmured. "Breathtaking. All of it. And it *is* yours. That must not be in doubt. I know everyone involved will make sure justice is served for you and for this wondrous place," I reassured with all the confidences I could muster. I was sobered by how hard this all had to be for him. I reached out and pressed his hand in mine as he took us through the length of the main foyer.

"Why would the Society just *abandon* this *treasure*?" Lavinia exclaimed.

"Oh, they haven't abandoned it, it was overtaken by a nouveau riche family that fancied themselves landed and titled—or at least are trying to be—in a home they had no right to buy as it was stolen not sold, though they changed our family crests anyway," Jonathon growled. "The Society acts as landlord. Per Brinkman's exterior surveillance, it would seem that both the family and Society persons do come and go, but no one here has kept any permanent staff on retainer," Jonathon replied. "Considering the Society's penchant for experimentation, we need to be prepared for any number of things to be taking up space in my estate." The grim resignation in his tone spoke again of his amazing resilience. I took his hand again, and this time I just didn't let go of it as we continued the tour.

Thankfully, there were no obvious vials of "The Cure." No apparent wires leading to reanimate corpses stowed away in any of the upstairs guest rooms, fine set after fine set as they were. It would seem the Society kept the grand home as it was, rather than using its great resources as another testing ground. At least we hoped. Jonathon and Nathaniel ran downstairs to the kitchens and cellars and came back up shrugging, the place empty. For Jonathon's sake, I was so glad, though it continually felt like a calm before a storm. Like we were missing something.

I grew utterly overwhelmed by the vastness of the place, two long wings of bedrooms, studies and sitting rooms interrupted by the occasional alcove or balcony that looked down over the main foyer or the elegant ballroom, the whole of the house done up in a synthesis of dark, carved wood, archways, and stained-glass accents.

Eventually, we descended to the west wing and swept into the dining room. It was lavish, immense, full of dark woods and sparkling crystal, hard to take in at once for all the details and finery.

But it was all the portraits lining the walls, hung above the wooden paneling in grand, gilt frames that caught my eye.

It was a family, a well-heeled gentleman of middle age, two youths standing as if they were already adults to his left, a boy and a girl, bookended by a wide-eyed woman in lavish gown that seemed to be trying a bit too hard. The whole presentation was a bit too ostentatious to be tasteful, a sign of the striving classes I'd learned from one of Maggie Hathorn's rambling monologues.

I blinked. And in that moment, my vision swam a bit, as everything went out of focus within the frames. My throat went dry.

"Oh no, Jonathon," I said, suddenly dizzy with the further descent of dread that pitched my stomach. "The house isn't empty."

I pointed to the paintings. All of which had changed when I blinked. Each stoic form had suddenly shifted. All of them reached out their hands, open palms, desperate. Reaching out to me. Souls reaching out for help. Just as Jonathon had done when he was imprisoned in canvas. So the

Society had brought its evil unto Rosecrest after all.

"This house isn't empty at all," I said in a choking whisper. "It's full of trapped souls."

The four of us, collectively, shuddered in that quiet, lavishly appointed dining room with those four tragic portraits.

"Is it...just me..." Lavinia began hesitantly, "or did the paintings..."

"Change," I replied. "Yes. They are alive. In a way. The souls of those persons are trapped inside the canvass. Perhaps that's the family that took over the estate?"

I asked Jonathon, but he had turned away, as if he couldn't bear to look.

"It's what happened to me," he murmured bitterly. "My soul was trapped within while my body was overtaken by a demon. The family that the Society sold this place to were mere vessels. Cursed into servitude to the Society's ungodly bidding."

"But, Jonathon, my love, we know the countercurse," I murmured, going to him, finding that looking away from the paintings was much better than looking at them. "Hope is not lost. The Society can't know the basic weapons we have."

"But we need their bodies," Jonathon said mournfully. "To throw the demons into the frame and rip the souls back where they belong..."

"Then let's be sure their demon-ridden selves are invited to our little dinner party," Nathaniel replied.

"I suppose that is the only option we have," Jonathon muttered. "Throw the counter-curses before the police make arrests. I just hope the spy Brinkman and my solicitor contact, Mr. Knowles, have evidence enough no matter what the devils may try."

Jonathon stalked away. I gestured with a look to Lavinia and Nathaniel that it might be best if I went after him alone.

"We'll be in the foyer," Lavinia whispered. "As being here is just too..." She stared up again at the imprisoned family with an expression of horrified pity and shuddered once more, darting out in an opposite direction from Jonathon, Nathaniel behind her.

I took the route Jonathon took, listening to his footfalls, ignoring how much the corridors of his estate reminded me of my dreams. Dreams where something was always coming after us or keeping us apart. But unlike my dreams, here I could move. Here I could be active. Bold. Cross distances, be they physical or emotional.

I finally found him at the end of the next hall, as the door was open and I could see his silhouette near the doorway, a lamp lit in a small but grand little room...a study...

The study.

This was the room that Jonathon had been painted in. The study whose likeness had been his prison.

I recognized every detail of the finely appointed room, the stately furniture, expensive Persian rugs, the desk with gold-plated implements, leather chair, towering bookcases, the mantel with fascinating instruments and treasures, the grand window looking out to the darkened lands beyond, I recognized every detail. He turned a lamp, and everything took on the hues I'd been accustomed to. So much... So much had happened in this place. In the *likeness* of this place... It was surreal to see it *real...*

He must have heard me approach as I hadn't tried to quiet my footfalls and spoke quietly: "I wasn't sure I wanted to see it again. But now that I do, it's all right."

He turned to me, his beautiful face increasingly haunted the more time he spent in this house, and I moved to his side, reaching up as if magnetized to caress his cheek with my fingertips, to try and erase those wearying lines and darkening circles below those arresting eyes.

"It is all right, Natalie," he insisted. "Because you're here and we're on the other side. I am reminded of what was always real. The demons can't take my love of this place away from me. I won't let them. Nothing can take my love away, be it this place or you..."

He dragged me into the room, to the center of it, the axis of where our love had blossomed.

And there he seized me and kissed me ravenously, hungrily, and I gave over to him, giving him my weight, letting him hold me, responsive to him in my sighs and in the way I let my mouth tease his, a conversation of the flesh.

This was so much better than my dream, in the throes of that storm. Here—he was right—I was reminded of what was real, and our passion was the most real thing I knew; it burned in me with a flame that could rival the fires of every fireplace in this grand estate. This desperate embrace was so much more vibrant and raw than when our souls had kissed, and I had been pressed up against the very bookshelf near us.

The situation we were in was so intense that it needed release, it needed love. Declarations of it. Displays of it. I understood what had driven Nathaniel and Lavinia to just such an explosion; it was far better than the alternative of fear and loneliness. I suddenly felt invincible, as there was nothing in the world but him and he wanted me as achingly as I did him.

And then suddenly he withdrew and I wobbled on my feet, having given over so wholly to his hold. He dropped to his knee, staring up at me, his previously haunted face now flushed with desire, given new life.

"Here. *Now*," Jonathon said, his breath between words coming in hitches. "You can't deny me, Natalie. I need to know that we face the horrors ahead together. Till death do us part. Marry me. Please."

He fished in his breast pocket and plucked out a beautiful rose-gold band set with a deep garnet in it, a gorgeous and elegant piece. I stared at it, at him, frozen in a sudden and overwhelming bliss, drinking in his glorious words as he continued: "I've kept this in my pocket every day, undaunted. Waiting for the right moment to make this right, to make *us* right. Heaven sent you to me, and I must have you. We'll be stronger for our union. On this day and for what lies ahead. I need you now to make a pact, together, here our love takes a stand against our enemies. Here in this haunted house, I need you to become my Lady Denbury—"

"Yes," I gasped. "I will." I dropped to my knees beside him, taking his trembling fingers up in mine and helping him slide the ring onto my finger where it fit perfectly as if he'd had it made for me. Perhaps he had. I stared into those beautiful eyes, and for the first time in a while, I smiled with sheer joy. "I do. My lord. My love. I *must* be your Lady Denbury..."

I kissed him with the kind of passion I'd only dreamed about, allowing everything within me to channel through my kiss. This kiss was a medium to call forth all the spirits of my adoration, hopes, dreams, desires, and needs.

We sunk from our knees onto the floor together, wrapped up in layers of fabric and tangling sleeves and locks of hair that caught on buttons and ribbons and latches and laces as our caresses and kisses travelled. This time I didn't need to dream the storm. *We* were the storm.

Eventually, he drew back, as there was a line we did not dare cross though our bodies betrayed our intentions in a way that was unmistakable. Not yet. Not here. Not on the floor of a study.

In the instant we both pulled away, knowing that if we didn't we'd pull away clothing instead, the rush of cold air in contrast to our built up heat sobered us. The slow, creeping dread of what we both knew lay ahead and the roles we had to play was like a ghost haunting us out of the corners of our eyes. I could see my own sentiments reflected upon Jonathon's lovely face. My poor heart had swung in sickening pendulum swoops, careening from frightened to exhilarated, lovesick to impassioned, panicked to joyous. My life as presented to me was one of extremes.

I glanced to the side, out the door of the study. That was the corridor of my nightmares. Precisely. I stood, attempting to smooth my dress, my hair, all my undone strings and clasps. As I did and Jonathon rose to stand beside me to do the same to his own rumpled layers and undone buttons, I stared down at my new treasure.

"Should I hide the ring?" I asked, biting my lip. I blushed with pride and excitement to see it there.

"No, it'll keep me strong, seeing it there, as I have to play the part of the wretch. It will remind me that you trust me. It will remind me why we've taken the fight to this house. Because you *will* be Lady Denbury. Because Mother would approve..." His voice cracked as he said it, but he stared at me with adoration that pierced through his still-fresh pain.

I dived in again to press my lips to his before stepping back once more to smile, radiant; no threat could take the purity of this love away from me. I would be Lady Denbury. I would fight for this love. This house. For what God had brought together, let no demon sunder.

Still, there were details to consider.

"What if one of the 'Majesties' sees or asks about the ring? How attune to detail are they? Will an affianced woman affect their 'ritual'..." I shuddered.

"I'll say it was a pretty bauble I gave to you in order to toy with you," he replied. I shuddered again.

"Do you have any idea what will be asked of me? As 'bait'?"

"Nathaniel and I will be theatrical, make suggestions to appease the Majesty and any who might come with him, but Brinkman will send in the brigade before anything is actually done. We'll keep things vague, I promise. It's your presence that I think he'll assume is done in good 'faith' as it were." He sounded very confident, but I wasn't sure if that was for my benefit or his own reassurance.

He continued: "Tonight we'll stay at the cottage. Tomorrow, I go into London, meet with the Majesty, and set a time for a party," he said with false cheer. "There we encourage others within his Society to attend, as the scope of the organization and its possible members has been impossible to track down or ascertain. Then, I meet with Brinkman and the helpful solicitor Mister Knowles to update them. Together we'll see if we've enough straight evidence to arrest more than one person. We're trying to drive as many roaches out with light as possible, but the stage theatrics might be necessary for the results to be more damning."

I nodded. It was as sound a plan as I could hope for. We would have friends on our side. And hopefully the police. But in matters such as this, where every belief was wholly tried, I wasn't sure I could count on traditional law enforcement to quite be the security force it should be. For an age so obsessed with death, with mourning and spirits and the sciences of the unexplained, when something actually defied what was known about the natural world, a majority of people turned interest into frightened rejection and clung to the normal over the paranormal.

But true believers knew the truth because the truth had happened to them. Undeniably. But the truth was oft stranger than fiction in cases such as ours.

I lamented that Mrs. Northe wasn't here. I always felt safer when I knew she was with us, on our side, my mentor and spiritual guardian. I no longer worshipped her as a god like I'd once done. I knew now that she couldn't solve every problem and that she wasn't perfect. But we'd truly abandoned her. And I felt certain that she actually wanted to be here. Surely she knew we were here, she knew us too well...

But at the same time I didn't know what she could have done to help, other than to be another frightened heart watching, wondering, waiting...

She needed to remain in New York, keeping an eye out on that front line of the Society's unnatural warfare. Jonathon left her with addresses to inspect. I was sure she was up to something productive. Father, on the other hand...

I couldn't think about Father. I just couldn't. I embraced Jonathon so he could not see the pain on my face. When I got through all this, because I had to get through all this, I'd never again scare my father like this. We all deserved better than we'd been dealt, and him as much as any. Though he never faced the horrors we did directly, I knew his pain and anguish over me was as rife as any, and his confusion far greater. Being left out was the worst thing in the world, I knew it, and I hated having done that to him. But he was not to be involved. He was never a part of the equation on the supernatural side. However, his love was a force to be reckoned with, yet another reason to fight for love to win over evil.

Jonathon hugged me back, fiercely, and it was as if he read my mind. "We will get through this, Natalie. My Lady Denbury. And then I promise you a life so full of light and so far from all this haunted pain..."

"Yes, my love. My lord. We shall see that day together, until then we fight, stronger for our union."

We kissed once more and reclaimed that study, the place that had been used as a prison, for the freedom of our love. I ignored the corridor of my nightmares that awaited just outside.

Chapter Twenty-Three

It would seem that my nightmares waited to strike. At least, during the course of our time within the estate, which was drawing to a close for the evening.

However, I refused to get too comfortable. My nightmares weren't to be dismissed so easily. The worst kind of terrors were those that lay in wait.

Jonathon and I returned to the dining room. With determination, I went up to the paintings and examined them. They did not change for me this time, but they were still beseeching in the same pose as before. That was problematic, as it indicated a presence had been in the house. The Society would realize some sort of unknown variable. They might not trust Jonathon's invitation. I glanced behind each frame.

"Runes?" Jonathon asked. "Carved into the frames?"

"Indeed." I replied. "It's all looking just the same as it was done for you, *to* you. I imagine that once the devils realize what worked in your case, they would not have deviated in others. It seems like the same pattern, perhaps the same poem driving the spell, I'm not sure. I can only hope the countercurse will still drive to the heart of the matter, no matter what the runes truly say. I wish I'd brought the translation book—"

"We'd not have the time even if you did. We'd best not stay here any longer and should not be caught here sleeping. Back to the cottage we go, and on to London in the morning."

I stared back at the paintings. I couldn't leave them like that. Jonathon watched me, sensed my thoughts or emotions, and took my hand.

"You can't help them right now," he murmured gently. "Not tonight."

Something occurred to me. "I know. But I think I can give them hope. And you know better than anyone how desperately their trapped souls need it. Paper and pencil. Can you get that for me, quickly?"

Jonathon didn't question me; he just darted off. And for that, that simple respect of my agency, for his trust in me and my wits, I was grateful.

When he returned with page and pencil, I wrote a note and held it up for interminable moments before each portrait. The note said: *Return to your positions. Help is on the way. Patience.*

Due to Jonathon's internment and my experience within his painted prison, I understood the basic principles of what the suspended lives of these subjects were like. Sight beyond the frame was somewhat hazy but possible. I patiently waited before each portrait until the bodies returned to their poses as originally painted. The children were the last to return to their stasis.

When they did, I scribbled. *Thank you. Keep patience and faith.*

And then I walked out without a second glance behind me, as I could not bear their pained eyes. Neither could Jonathon, even though they were the unwitting souls who had usurped his property. They had been duped. We'd all been victims. But I didn't want to relegate myself to that and neither did Jonathon. Neither did any of us fighting the good fight.

We found Lavinia and Nathaniel sitting on the wide window ledge of the downstairs foyer, bathed in a shaft of moonlight that made them look like they were in a stage photograph, all in grayscale and silver light. Their hands were clasped together. All I heard was Lavinia respond simply.

"You didn't drag me into this. Our Association was sought out."

"I dragged you into this," Jonathon declared. "All of you. Though I certainly didn't do so wittingly. I promise I will repay you however I can for all we've endured. Come, let us return to the cottage. A night here is..." He looked about. "Unwise. But, give me a moment. I've something by which to cheer us."

He darted off past the dining room, and I heard a door open, heard feet down stone stairs, and there was silence in the house for long, interminable moments before a slow tread up again, a door closing, and footsteps upon the wooden hall led Jonathon back to us once more.

He appeared in the moonlight of the foyer with a bottle in his hand. But he was ashen faced, changed in the silver shadows, a haunted look on his face I knew all too well. In his other hand, he'd drawn his pistol.

"What... What did you see, Jonathon?" I asked, dread in my tone. He gestured to keep voices down.

"We need to leave," he whispered. "Come on. Keep quiet." He gestured Nathaniel and Lavinia back in the direction of the library, and they quickly moved on ahead, impressively keeping the noise of footfalls at a minimum. I rushed with them, Jonathon at my side, back past the dining room once more where I refused to look even past the threshold.

"What is wrong?" I whispered again as he grabbed my hand and we darted back to the library. The maw of the door that was a bookcase opened on its side to reveal the secret passage stood before us; the dim golden torchlight of the underground corridor beckoned eerily from below. Jonathon shut the door behind all of us, gesturing for us to go on ahead, Nathaniel in the lead. We were many paces into the earthen and stone corridor before Jonathon answered.

"What we saw in Preston's office," he replied gravely. "That's what was down there."

"Oh God..." I swallowed hard. "They've a corpse below? One they're trying to reanimate?"

"No corpse. But everything else was there. The table. All the wiring and equipment. And small, suspicious boxes. Bottles of fluids, medical and funereal. The scent of decay. All in my bloody wine cellar," he said, spitting out the words like venom as we darted up the long corridor.

The scenes of Preston's basement hospital wing, yet another dread corridor, came back to me in the forceful way terrible memories resurfaced. Either they were preparing to reanimate a corpse and tether numerous spirits to its form to power the animate force of the thing, or they had already done so. And if they'd done so, the whereabouts of the creature were cause for great concern.

Finally, we resurfaced in the cottage. Jonathon bolted the iron door behind us. Next he checked the whole of the cottage, pistol drawn, then surveyed outside. Nathaniel joined him outside, going to check on his horses.

I sat down upon the dusty but plush velvet window seat of the bay window and looked through the glass, trying to appreciate just how beautiful the moon was.

Lavinia went searching about for something. I wasn't sure what, until I heard a "pop." And then the clink of glasses. She returned to me, two wineglasses filled with deep, dark red in her hands. She handed me one.

I had never been one for alcohol, save in communion at church, but this seemed the thing to do right now. One glass to calm the nerves. Some distraction. Some reminder that we were with friends and lovers. I was in a new country, something I'd never done before. I wanted to feel like there was some excitement. I was engaged to the man I loved. I smiled at Lavinia, feeling some of my tension ease before I'd even begun to sip the glass.

The gentlemen soon returned to us. Lavinia had poured for them, and they glided, as if magnetized, to two more crystalline goblets she filled upon the golden lacquered center table that she'd cleaned of its layer of dust, leaving the surface to glimmer in the candlelight.

"To sending devils back to hell," Jonathon said, lifting his glass and looking each of us in the eyes, mine last. We all toasted gladly to that. His eyes burned into me, and I felt the pledge of our engagement swell in my heart. I thought about telling Lavinia and Nathaniel about it in the moment but thought better of it. Somehow I knew it would sting Lavinia, and I couldn't have her feeling insecure when she was called upon to do something so brave.

"It's a good thing this bed is enormous," Jonathon stated nearly draining the glass in a few long drinks. "Because I'm not sleeping on the floor." He grabbed me around the waist and dragged me to the grand alcove where the vast four-poster bed was visible behind its open red curtains. I let him. He spoke over his shoulder to Nathaniel. "Come on, you two, there's room for all on here. *And* that will force us to behave ourselves."

"Normally I'd object and find some dark corner to drag this one off to," Nathaniel replied, grinning at Lavinia. "But I'm deathly tired. I'm sure we all are."

It was true. I was utterly exhausted, and I allowed myself to acknowledge it, finally, as I felt a modicum of security. The cottage did feel safe, an unused place the Society clearly hadn't gotten its hooks into, a piece of lost history, a secret put to good use as an encampment before an upcoming battle rather than a clandestine affair.

The temperature was nearly perfect, and so I didn't need to crawl under the velvet duvet. I simply allowed Jonathon to drag me onto one side of the bed, and I lay back in his arms. Sleep overtook me almost immediately. The ability to breathe deeply in a setting that didn't have all my hairs on edge, coupled with the glorious protection that was being in his arms, was enough to sweep me into much-needed rest.

Chapter Twenty-Four

I didn't demand to go with the gentlemen to the Majesty's office, but I did demand to go to London. What else would they have done with me? Lavinia had a dear friend she wished to visit, desperate to have something of normalcy. I had no plans, but I didn't dare miss *London*.

During our carriage ride, the gentlemen took turns driving. Jonathon was quiet and introspective when he rode with us, his hand entwined in mine. Lavinia stared at the new engagement ring with a wistful envy that she did not voice. As we'd readied in the morning, she noticed the piece, and I told her what had happened, my initial rejection of him, and the second chance in the study. She had embraced me and congratulated me. But I could feel the pang then and saw it now as she turned away from the garnet treasure upon my finger.

Nathaniel entertained us ladies with new material, blatantly overjoyed to have a captive audience. Thankfully, in this case, it was no trouble to be captive, as he was exquisite in his rendition of Shelley's *Ozymandias*. It was an interesting narrative, the epic poem, as epic London grew before us, beginning in modest outlying villages to clusters of greater population in a radius around the heart of the matter and unto the great, gargantuan golem of a city that was London...

Ah, *London*. What a beautiful mess. What a terrifying wonder and mystery. Did newcomers look at New York this way? Utterly overwhelmed?

Nothing could quite have prepared me for the scope of what I was seeing out the carriage windows. Manhattan, while vast, was an island, so simply its space had limits. London seemed an endless sprawl that was utterly confusing. There was no grid. No numbered streets. Everything was at twists and turns. And nearly all of it covered in soot. Though I wasn't sure what of that lens was made a shade darker by the gray, overcast sky.

The city grew narrower in brick alleys and confining arches over our carriage head and then expanded to grand lanes in dizzying instants, devastation like I'd seen in records of Manhattan's Lower East Side, but then palatial stretches much like our Fifth Avenue. They were sister cities in their own right, I supposed, centers of the world very much in many ways. But I was left with no idea where I was or how I could ever orient in such a tangle of streets and masses of people. It was vibrant and dark, grand and guttered. Impressive and terrifying. And it seemed without end.

The carriage made its rounds, Nathaniel first escorting Lavinia to a mutual friend, leaving me alone in the cab while Jonathon stayed with the horses. Next, I was taken to a friend of Mrs. Northe, Mr. Knowles, who would keep me until the gentlemen came back with news of their plans. We were in a business district; I could tell from the pristine streets and the lack of human bustle. If there were residents in the area, they kept their lamps trimmed low or were not yet home from being out and about on what had turned out to be a fine day with a brightly setting sun.

Nathaniel stayed with the horses, and Jonathon led me through an iron gate and up a stoop of a well-appointed building that had several names etched in gold upon the glass door. He plucked a key from his pocket and opened the office door.

"You've keys?" I asked, incredulous, as if all of London might be at Jonathon's disposal.

"Knowles and Brinkman have availed many resources to me," he explained. "As the Society is a sincere threat to crown and country, I've secret allies and places to hide."

"And yet you're confronting the Society directly, tomorrow," I said ruefully.

"Why can't all those secret allies and those threatened take over instead of us running blindly forward at this point?"

"Hiding in plain sight is often the best strategy," Jonathon replied with an impressive nonchalance. "Besides, prosecuting the Society's aims needs as much evidence as possible. So much of it is paranormal circumstance you and I could not prove in a court."

I nodded acquiescence as he led me into the first floor foyer and then moved ahead to a frosted-glass window that was lit from within. He knocked, was bid enter, and there was a conversation I couldn't hear for a moment before he poked his head back into the hall to gesture me into the room. I walked into a warmly lit office well appointed in leather and books. A vast desk with matching mahogany chairs faced a wing-backed leather chair prominent before a grand fireplace. The trappings were similar to the finery of the Denbury study, but in a business setting, not residential.

At the door stood an elegant, patrician fellow in a well-tailored suit, the splash of a russet ascot offsetting the gray of his entire person: silver hair, eyes, frock coat, waistcoat, and trousers all the color of the English sky.

"Mister Knowles, this is my fiancée, Miss Natalie Stewart," Jonathon said. As Knowles inclined his head to me, I smiled, for the first time hearing the word fiancée. The newness of it must have been evident in my blush, for Mr. Knowles's wise-looking eyes sparkled in a way that was quite familiar.

"You know Mrs. Northe," I said eagerly.

"That I do," he replied. He turned to Jonathon. "I know you must be off, feel free to leave the girl in my care. She is under careful protection here. An officer has been assigned to this building with the precinct on watch."

"Thank you, sir. I'll return with news." He reached out and grabbed my hands in his and kissed them, one then the other. "I won't be long, my brave girl."

I smiled at him with a look that spoke of trust and care and stood at the threshold of the office to watch him go, my heartstrings tugging along after him. He looked back at me at the front door and pursed his lips in a kiss. I blew one back.

He caught it and reached into his coat, placing it in his breast pocket, close to his heart. "For safekeeping," he said. "I'll need it."

And with that he vanished to go confront his enemy. "Be careful," I called as the door shut behind him. I clenched my fists and tried to set fierce worry aside, as it would do me no good. I took my place in Knowles office, sitting in one of the fine wooden chairs he proffered to me.

Knowles looked at me with a wistful smile as he set tea before me, gesturing me to a seat across his desk. "She was Evelyn Rutherford when I met her," Knowles began, "in her first 'season' in London, full of New York wit and vivacity, catching the eye of every available bachelor and married man alike. Who knew that quiet, unassuming Peter Northe would catch her in the end? Baffled everyone. But then again, aside from the man's money, he was simply kind. She always said a man's kindness was worth as much as his pocketbook. Thankfully, she earned double, then, while the lucky man lived."

I smiled back. I thought of my father. That's why she cared about him. A tear came to my eye.

Knowles pretended not to notice and instead leveled a gaze at me. "She's not happy you're gone, I'll have you know."

I chuckled and shook my head. "Oh, I'm sure she isn't."

"Not surprised, mind you, as not much surprises a woman as gifted as she. But she said if I ran into you, that there will be quite a talking-to that awaits you. Also"—his expression grew grave—"as you're not a child, I'll not treat you with kid gloves. But you should know that your friend Miss Hathorn has gone missing from Chicago."

I blinked at him. "When? Why?"

"Neither Mrs. Northe or Miss Hathorn's caretaker have any idea. But, obviously, if you in any way hear from her, do let Mrs. Northe know, she's sick to death about it. About the both of you."

I suddenly felt so guilty I hadn't written to Maggie sooner. Had she run away? Was she homesick and simply decided to make a run for it? Had something called to her and lured her back to the erring paths? She probably didn't even get my letter. A profound sadness hit me like a slap to my face. I was selfish. I wasn't the only one going through troubled times. She needed a peer, someone with whom to commiserate. I vowed to be that more strongly and presently for her if I possibly could.

"Don't keep Mrs. Northe in the dark," I replied. "I'm sure she knows where we went. She tried to stop us. But she went into a medium's trance, and we eluded her. The spirit she channeled guided us, warned us, Miss Kent and I. Feel free to write her about any of our goings-on if you feel they will arrive safe to her and not place her in any danger. Not having her at my side for this battle doesn't feel right, but I'd not dare try to involve her. I feel this is Jonathon and my fight to see through on our own."

"She told me you were a brave, dear girl. But no hero does his or her entire quest on their own."

I nodded, allowing myself to take that in as comfort. We shared more tea. He told me of his late wife who had died in childbirth, and of her ghost that haunted him still. Evidently, 'that was how he and Mrs. Northe had become close. Séances. He asked if I'd met Senator Bishop, and I promised I'd give the man my best whenever I saw him again at Mrs. Northe's house. If I ever returned to her house...

No. I couldn't think like that. Act like that. I couldn't possibly manifest that even as a possibility.

"I've my mother with me," I stated, invoking her as a ward and guardian to refuse thoughts of failure. "Much like your wife, I know she watches over me. I do know I'm not alone. And for that I rejoice. Loving souls are never truly alone, for those who have loved us are always connected. Even the death of a body cannot stop that tether."

"Spoken like a true Spiritualist," Knowles said with a fond smile.

"I've learned from the best," I replied, sharing the smile.

Jonathon returned within the hour. Nathaniel was with him. They entered the office, elegant black-coated figures shifting the quiet energy Mr. Knowles had cultivated into something alive and on edge. I jumped up, impetuously embracing him. I was his fiancée. I was allowed to do such things in the presence of others.

His tensed shoulders eased a bit as I snaked my hands around them and clasped my lace-gloved hands about his neck. "Well?" I murmured, noting that the look on his face was tired and haunted, but not defeated.

"I think the 'Majesty' continues to believe me," Jonathon said. "Nathaniel, too, but I believe the next step will be a test. Moriel is his name. He said he'd be delighted by a dinner party and would be sure a few of his ministers attend. We'll have our quarry. Let's make sure our trap is well set and in place. We must be able to draw out their strategy, and once they've confessed their plans to listening ears, we'll strike to the roots of their insidious tree and uproot it as best we possibly can."

"We have to take care in regards to the trapped souls in the dining room," I cautioned, turning to Mr. Knowles. "The family that took over the estate, their souls are separated from their bodies in a painted prison, likely the bodies possessed by demonic energies, as Jonathon's was. I do not know where the bodies are, I assume in the service of the Society, but the paintings, and the persons, cannot be harmed until body and soul are reunited. I cannot trust police to be delicate in those matters. That family will be collateral damage if we are not careful. We need to ensure the countercurse is landed before the police make the arrests."

"Very wise," Jonathon agreed, squeezing my hand. "See how sensible my lady is, Mr. Knowles? I am a blessed man."

"You have been a cursed man," Knowles said gently. "And so you deserve such blessings as she. It is only right and just."

I simply smiled, squeezing his hand back, tightly.

"Let's fetch Miss Kent and Mister Brinkman and ready the plan," Knowles said.

And we were off to the proverbial nightmarish races...

Chapter Twenty-Five

Evidently, the British agent Mister Brinkman was just across the street, awaiting a signal. I suddenly felt that, at any minute, any number of persons could descend upon us from unseen corners. The intimate, singular horrors that the Society had perpetrated upon Jonathon and me were now becoming a crowd sport.

Knowles palmed a small, hand-held lantern that had been sitting as a lit globe upon his desk. He moved to stand before the narrow, tall window to the side of his bookcases, putting a hand to block the orb's light and then removing it three times. A minute later, I heard a key turn down the hall, then the front door open and close quietly and then not a sound until an uncanny apparition was seen in the doorway: a distinct form in a black cape. The man set his hood back upon entering the room. Brinkman.

I wondered how intently the spy had been watching us. Reading lips through binoculars, perhaps, poised and on sharp alert to all tells and ticks? When he crossed the room in a few measured strides, his eyes went right to us as if he'd known our positions. He made me feel as nervous as he did safe. I watched Jonathon's face as he stared at the man, I assumed gauging his aura. As Jonathon remained cool and composed, the man's aura must have remained positive...or at least neutral to us. I took a moment to thank whatever magical offsets had granted Jonathon that ability, as it was one of the more useful supernatural traits our situation could have afforded.

Brinkman could see me examining his oddly handsome face, trying to get a read on him. So many years of mutism had made me uncannily adept at reading moods, bodies, intentions, and more, just by look and physicality. This man was a compelling, blank slate. He simply smiled enigmatically at me, giving nothing away but that he was a man not to be trifled with. A consummate spy. I was no less nervous. But I was just a little bit impressed.

"Miss Stewart," he said, bowing his head to me. I inclined mine in turn.

Knowles busied himself at a vast cherrywood credenza, making sure all the gentlemen had snifters of bourbon.

Brinkman turned to Jonathon. "From what you said upon our return ride from the Society office, it seems you laid the groundwork well, Lord Denbury. I'm hoping this little *party* will allow me to collar Moriel and his two top cronies. I'd like to cuff his whole cabal of six, but it would seem all the 'Majesties' are hardly ever in the same country, let alone the same room. Hopefully, the Society will fall out from under the top tier once we topple them."

"What brought the Society operatives together in the first place?" I asked.

"The only consistent factor is that they are very old aristocracy from three different country's traditions. Each of their line was at one point disgraced and remains relatively forgotten, with little money. However, they've gained traction in property."

"Making a deal with the devil for a return rise to importance?" Knowles asked, taking his place at his desk.

Brinkman shrugged. "That's the only thing I can figure about their aims."

I heard a key in the lock down the hall and then Lavinia's voice speaking in a pouting tone.

At the sound of movement at the door, Jonathon stalked out of the room and met them, lingering there at the mouth of the hall while Lavinia's voice continued, getting closer as she said: "You do realize how much I've given up, Nathaniel, back and forth with you across the pond. I truly needed just one *normal* evening with my lady friends. Must we strategize at this hour?"

"We'll address your sacrifices in time, dear," Nathaniel murmured as they neared Knowles's office door. "But that isn't for here and now, with lives on the line. Everyone is here. Please appear as sensible as I know you are capable of being."

Whatever Lavinia was feeling, she put on a calm and brave face when she entered Knowles's now-overcrowded office.

The solicitor gestured to a decanter of some sort of rose-colored cordial and raised an eyebrow at Lavinia and me. Lavinia set her jaw and pointed to the bourbon instead. Knowles grinned and despite the departure in custom, included us both in the gentleman's drink without question, a small courtesy that made us feel involved and respected. These were not times of common propriety. No one was looking to drown their sorrows in any substance; such behavior would not help our cause. But having something to hold and busy one's hands with was a tiny comfort to take the edge off the tension in the room.

"I never thought I'd be grateful for anything that has befallen me," Jonathon said as he reentered the room, stalking over to my chair and standing behind it to voice what I'd been thinking when he examined Brinkman. "However, the ability to see the lit aura, the incorporeal traces of any of my potential enemies is very useful. It would seem no one followed you here. I see no spark in the shadows outside."

"I told you I'd be careful," Nathaniel replied. Jonathon nodded at his friend.

"Friends," Jonathon began, addressing all of us. "Let's get to our points. The Society shall arrive at the estate at six tomorrow. I explained to Moriel that I would leave the proverbial 'bait,' the tokens, bound in the dining room." He squeezed my shoulder over the back of the chair. "Do forgive me, my love, for referring to you as such—"

"I understand, Jonathon. That's how they might refer to me. Not you. You will both have to play the part," I reassured, even while I shuddered at the thought.

"They seem to be interested in blood tokens," Jonathon said, clenching his jaw. "If you are bound at the table, my brave ladies, don't worry what will befall you. Nathaniel schooled me in some sleight of hand. I don't want you dreading anything that will be mere show, but please do react accordingly as though you've been affected."

Lavinia nodded. She was used to this sort of thing more than I; surely, one of Nathaniel's vampire bits on stage had her prepared for necessary theatrics. I swallowed hard and tried not to look ill.

Jonathon continued: "Nathaniel and I will meet the company at the door and lead them in, as it would be best they not find us all fraternizing in the dining room when they arrive. Tomorrow morning the Society said they'd return the staff to the premises to prepare the meal." Jonathon turned to Brinkman to explain in a bitter tone: "Moriel confirmed, laughingly, that the staff they retain are possessed bodies. The family that overtook the estate per the Society's coaxing is now enslaved to it. Moriel has taken those poor wretches on as his personal cook, footman, and the children as veritable slaves."

"And their poor souls are trapped in the dining room portraits," I added. "Before any arrests are made, we'll need to invoke a countercurse to return souls into bodies and trap the demons. It's not something I'd trust to leave to the average police officer. With all due respect."

Brinkman nodded and tried to act as if the directives were commonplace, but his halting speech revealed his discomfort. "If you say so. I trust, then, that... you'll handle the...countercurse?"

"We will, you must leave that to us," Jonathon replied. "Natalie, I'll trust you to later explain the principles of the countercurse to Nathaniel and Lavinia."

I nodded again. I sipped the bourbon, and its sting was a nice offset against nerves.

"I'll need a cue for my men to pounce," Brinkman stated. "I don't want it to come too early, but also not too late. I don't want these bastards to try anything."

"Or to let their magic build," I added. "We can't know just how many demonic forces they have, truly, at their disposal. Those we've seen have been embodied, but what about those awaiting a host?"

"We can't allow anything in," Jonathon murmured. "We don't know exactly where these demons *come* from. How they summon them. If you've ever had a faith, now is the time to hold to it. We must not give those wretched, soul-sucking entities any room for entry."

I nodded and thought of Maggie. I wondered what on earth could have happened to her. "Maggie's gone missing, Jonathon," I murmured. "No one knows where she's gone. Mrs. Northe wired Mr. Knowles here to tell us. If she or Karen has any clairvoyant indications about what went on, we don't know."

"Well, she let the beasts in, Natalie," he replied with a harshness I understood but didn't expect, "and allowed the forces that tried to kill us to grow stronger by her reverence and favor. We can't help her any more than we did. I can't worry what's become of her now. Not right now."

I looked at the edge of Mr. Knowles's fine desk and clenched my jaw, knowing Jonathon was right but still wishing there was something I could have done months ago to prevent her disappearance now. I said a prayer for her soul.

A slight movement of Nathaniel's hand caught my eye, and I saw him clutching a beaded length with a crucifix in his palm, something he'd wound around his wrist, perhaps a rosary. Anglican England still utilized Catholic-associated tokens as they were very similar in structure, just as Reverend Blessing owed a great deal to the Catholic Rite of Exorcism. Every denomination, at its root, directed back to the same governing principles. Symbols of faith were the touchstones of our own retaliatory magic. Ours was a different color and weight, but no less powerful than the breed the Society perpetuated. I had to believe we were as powerful as demons, so long as we stood up to them.

Brinkman's face was pinched; a slight crack in his facade indicated his own trepidation. I could empathize that a man like Brinkman didn't appreciate supernatural variables in a carefully calculated plan. "My men will be instructed to wait for my whistle," he stated, "but I can't cue immediately. Not until there's a bit of dirt under Moriel and company's nails, otherwise we may not have as flush and solid of a case as we need to ensure their downfall."

"If we're drawing out their plan," Jonathon piped in, "someone must be stationed to record what is said for evidence. If we place your men in my secret passages as we discussed, there is a pipe that's perfect for listening in."

"I'll be sure one of my best court recorders takes notes," Brinkman said eagerly. "If the paranormal aims of the Society are to be believed, we'll need as much in the form of a confessional as possible, the madness and desire for chaos expressly stated so that the threat to queen and country cannot possibly be denied."

"Jonathon," I murmured, a dreadful detail resurfacing. "What about the cellar?"

He swallowed hard.

"What about the cellar?" Brinkman queried, looking from one of us to the other. "I thought you said the estate was empty?"

Jonathon took a deep breath and spoke slowly. "There's also the possibility of a reanimate corpse as evidence. Be advised that the infernal magic the Society uses to reanimate the corpse makes the creatures very difficult to endure. There's a terrible mental strain, an inner sound of screaming, as if they creatures are built to rip apart the very fabric of sanity. A horde of ghosts is tethered to a body to make it come to life. The ghosts are the animate spark."

Brinkman's lips curled in disgust. "How horrid. Ghosts as Doctor Frankenstein's lightning?"

"I suppose. I've never seen anything like it before Doctor Preston's work in New York. I discovered all the same equipment we saw in New York down in my wine cellar. So I don't know what to expect."

"The unexpected is all we can count on, it would seem," Brinkman replied bitterly. "We'll all have to play it very safe, moment to moment, and very close to the vest." He bowed to us all and moved to the door, his tone allowing for a slight weariness. "Until morning, my motley battalion."

We stayed the night in London, one of Jonathon's finer carriages escorting the two couples to the Denbury flat, an exquisite set of gas-lit rooms in Knightsbridge. The place had a warm glow about it in all the golden flocked wallpapers, lighter woods, and gilt-accented furniture, a contrast to Rosecrest's deep, dark Gothic charm. The flat was that of more modern romantics, more fanciful in color and lush fabrics.

Nathaniel, being familiar with the flat, led Lavinia off somewhere. I wondered if they'd separate as propriety would dictate or if Lavinia would indeed come away from this a fallen woman. It wasn't my place to judge, she could make her own choices, and I hoped Nathaniel was man enough not to pressure her either way. Women were given little leverage in our world, and a girl's modesty was not something to be given or taken lightly, and men would do best to always keep that in mind.

As I sat upon one of the lavish divans in the main room, I had no idea how in the world I was going to sleep, but Jonathon seemed prepared for that, having stoked a small stove in a rear kitchen and returning to me with teacups in hand.

"Have some tea. It's... powerful tea," he said, handing me a warm cup and saucer.

"What's in it?" I asked, catching a whiff of a foreign scent.

"Some opiates and sedatives. I just took a draught myself. Else I'll never sleep. You and Lavinia can take the far room. Nathaniel is taking my room."

"You may have to untangle them—"

"I'm counting on Miss Kent to make an honest man out of Nat." Jonathon chuckled. "I don't let him play Don Juan in my home. I never have. He knows better."

"Where will you rest, darling?"

"On this very divan, dear. While the draught calmed my nerves, if I need to pace in the middle of the night, I'd best do it away from those I hold dear. You need your rest to be sharp."

"As do you..." I set down the cup and ran my fingers down the sleeve of his magnificent frock coat.

"When I was saving lives in my London clinic, sometimes my clearest decisions as a doctor came when I was truly exhausted and the drive of panic kicked in. Trust me, Natalie. I've faced many life and death battles. Just not necessarily my own. Not those most precious to me," he said, trailing a finger down my cheek, resting a fingertip upon my lips. I kissed his fingertip delicately, slowly, and he closed his eyes and let me see the shudder of sensual delight that coursed down his body.

"You're very brave," I murmured as he trailed the fingertip down my neck.

He set his own teacup beside mine before moving closer to press his lips to where his fingertip had been. After a slow, languorous kiss he murmured, "Didn't I tell you I learned bravery from the best?"

"You were brave long before me."

186 | LEANNA RENEE HIEBER

"But *together*..." He kissed me again.

Together is how our fates were determined. The course of my life, since the Denbury portrait had entered into it and I was granted a peculiar magic and agency to save this dear soul, was inextricable with his. Whether brilliant or doomed.

That night, in a lovely guest room done up in a soothing pale blue, grateful for a fresh dressing gown in which to sleep thanks to stores Lavinia brought for us, I tucked a bible under my pillow.

Lavinia, to my chagrin, had no trouble falling asleep across the room, not even bothering to change. She just curled up like a black-winged bird upon a lush velvet chaise and drifted off to some uncharted inner waters. I wonder if she'd been drugged harder. Or if Nathaniel had managed to distract her into bliss that powerfully.

I lay back and murmured what had been my mother's favorite psalm, number twenty-three, over and over again until the opiates finally took hold, first of my body, and then my racing mind.

Chapter Twenty-Six

The morning was spent in whatever preparations we could. Lavinia dressed herself, then me, in frilly white and cream lace gowns that she'd chosen, making us look as though we were either dressed for our weddings or our funerals. Which I supposed was sort of the point. Part of the theater of ritual. The gentlemen donned plain black frock coats and waistcoats with matching dark crimson undershirts with wide cuffs.

To Nathaniel and Lavinia, I explained the countercurse and the general properties of the magic as we knew it to be. Jonathon made sure the surveillance properties accessible from behind the library bookcase were in working order.

We tried knots and bindings that looked tighter and more restrictive than they were and set them in place. Jonathon explained any secret passages and their accesses. He and Nathaniel braved the cellar. It was still empty.

Time passed. We swallowed back dread. Jonathon ensconced Lavinia and me in a top servant room where a mirrored trap door offered a view of the downstairs foyer. At noon the family arrived; the four possessed bodies whose souls languished in the dining room paintings. The wife was a brown-haired woman who would have been pretty if she weren't so vacant and dark-eyed. The husband had prominent jowls and bushy eyebrows that accented the sunken quality of his own eyes, reflecting strangely as he and the wife gazed about, sniffing like animals, behaviors signatory of the possession. The children, a boy in breeches and a girl in a white pinafore stained on the edge with a red substance I shuddered to imagine, trailed behind them like animate dolls, and behind them, additional staff.

A few frightened-looking underclass women completed their entourage. I assumed the lot was there to help with the cooking and preparation. When the paths were clear enough to do so, Jonathon moved Lavinia and me into a secret dining room passage behind the walls that connected in a confining path down the great hall and into the library landing. We watched the staff prepare, moving in and out of the dining room to set place settings and down the servants' stairs to the kitchens, the pathway blocked by a large ornate screen the help would stand behind during dinner so as to be out of sight.

The possessed family that had inherited not an estate but a nightmare moved with a slight unnatural pattern that was impossible to look away from.

Just as Lavinia and I were about to be set into our places, thirteen officers filed silently into the passages, and as they passed I tried to bolster myself with the knowledge that the walls themselves were filled with support.

At five, Lavinia and I emerged in the library and were taken to our positions with a bit of a show and mock struggle. The gentlemen said nothing to us, other than the occasional order that we were to mind our place, lest the possessed bodies of the family tell tales of us that would not suit our plan.

We were placed across from one another at the midpoint of the grand dinner table, and our hands were gently bound behind our backs by our respective gentlemen.

"I am sorry to have to do this, beloved," Jonathon murmured in my ear. "Forgive me."

"I will," I whispered. He stared at me achingly and left the room.

The dining room table before us was set with white bone china and soft linen, a red runner bisecting the wooden length where three golden candelabras glittered with tall tapers that set off the crystals of the chandeliers dipping down from above, making the whole room glow and glitter. While places were set before us, we would not be able to partake unless someone saw fit to unbind us. Lavinia and I stared across the lit tapers at each other. I felt like I was a part of the upcoming courses, there as an appetizer for the demons. I kept reminding myself that the arrests would happen before any malevolent forces were summoned or allowed to wreak any havoc upon us.

The gentlemen took to the front foyer. In time, the summoners of hell arrived. Brinkman was with them. Whatever the Society had over Brinkman was evidently enough to make Moriel feel confident Brinkman was on his side. This leverage hardly bolstered my trust in Brinkman, but I had no choice. I heard voices engaged in a bit of pleasantries, the weather and such, all of it absurd considering the circumstances.

Jonathon, playing as though he remained possessed, a role he had done so well before, led the "Majesties" in, and I quelled my shudder.

A short, thin-haired, bulbous-nosed man I assumed was Moriel entered first. He was too ugly to be so terrifying, and yet there was an air about him of power and privilege that was as undeniable as he was unattractive. His eyes were small, dark and beady. His gaze flitted about and pinpointing his attention like a fastidious but jittery hawk. Everything about him reeked of unpredictable danger, like a pervasive cologne gone putrid.

Another man followed close behind. Together, they made two specimens that had awoken on the wrong side of the genealogical bed. The other Society operative was a taller, thinner, jaundiced-looking man with similarly limp hair. Both men were dressed in ostentatious suit coats and trousers of a loud red and gold, looking like a bizarre graft of king and a court jester from another century that had long since passed them by.

Brinkman and Nathaniel flanked behind. The Society heads immediately stared at Lavinia and me with an odd, unsettling hunger and smiled sharp, crooked-toothed smiles. Jonathon pulled out the Master's chair and then the second-in-command with a bit of exaggerated flourish. They sat.

"Welcome to what was once this body's home," Jonathon said with a little sick chuckle, taking the head of the table opposite Moriel. The vast dining room fireplace behind Jonathon yawned like a great marble mouth, a dark, unlit maw.

"Ah, these morsels will do nicely, Whitby," Moriel said, appraising Lavinia and me up and down. "Majesty Vincenzi is en route with a third course, a little fly that wandered right unto his web at the office this morning. Three does make a more magical number for sacrificial flow. I do hope you've drugged them, boy. Women can be feisty. Not worth all the trouble, if you leave them unadulterated."

"Ah, no, I've never had a trouble overcoming them, Majesty," Jonathon said, raising the stakes of the Majesty's perversion with an even uglier undercurrent.

"Nor I." Nathaniel matched Jonathon's tone as he moved to take a seat next to Lavinia, leering at her impressively.

"Ah, to be young and virile, then," the Majesty said with a chortle.

I slowly breathed in through my nostrils at this to keep calm. I knew I'd be offended when face-to-face with the "Majesty," and yet I remained impressed—and disturbed—by Jonathon's aptitude for playing the part. Nathaniel's theatrics had clearly rubbed off on his best friend.

I wondered what other poor girl would throw off our number and plan. This was not welcome information in the least. Brinkman surely felt it too, the frustration of another variable in our equation, but he remained visibly unruffled, simply standing to the side of Moriel as if he were a bodyguard, expressionless. Lavinia and I played our worried, scared-looking parts, which was truly not difficult. I tamped down upon my rage for the proper time.

"Come now, gentlemen," the second Majesty said, his voice gravely as if a vocal chord had been cut, reaching into a breast pocket to flourish a small, sharp knife. "Fresh and sweet, give us something to use." He made a piercing gesture that I tried not to jump at.

Jonathon nodded, snapping at Nathaniel. "Of course, Majesty Sansalme."

Both Jonathon and Nathaniel rose, plucking knifes out of their pockets, tucking at their coat sleeves, and came over to us, Jonathon to me, Nathaniel to Lavinia. They bent over us, loosening the bindings of the hands respectively nearest to the Majesties.

"The blood of the martyrs," Jonathon said, admirably trying on the demon's tone. My eyes fluttered shut at the memories of the terror that had breathed down my neck in his visage once before. With a sharp and sudden move, Jonathon drove the knife toward my hand, clutching it between both of his, and I screamed. Lavinia cried out in tandem.

The knife punctured something up Jonathon's sleeve and blood spurted onto my empty plate, and Jonathon moved our entwined hands over the glass goblet before me, filling a few ounces with dark red fluid. He dropped the bloody-tipped knife on the table, and Nathaniel did the same, with a flourish over another goblet. Their bodies slightly blocked us from the Majesty view. Jonathon was the first to rip the lace of my cuff, and he used it to bind up my hand as if stopping a wound. The choice of the gentlemen's crimson cuffs smartly hid whatever telltale droplets sourced the blood. It had to be blood—it looked and smelled of it—I was just wondering whose it was.

I'd been prepared to offer mine in part, within reason and safety. We'd have to see if that was yet further called for. Hoping this was the last of our "'sacrificial'" role, I couldn't help wondering at this impressive sleight of hand but doubted Nathaniel would give up his secrets were I to ask. Blood had been drawn from somewhere, perhaps predrawn, as neither of the gentlemen continued bleeding themselves, and though the source had come from them, they disguised it by tying off our hands, letting enough blood to drip around to make the whole thing seem more spontaneous and messy than it was. Jonathon and Nathaniel presented their glasses to the Majesties like an offering.

I thought at first Moriel—and his counterpart Sansalme—were going to drink the glasses and the blood therein. But neither did.

Instead, Moriel gestured for Sansalme to rise. Brandishing the knife, the associate moved to the wall behind the Majesty's chair and drove the blade into the fine paper and the plaster behind it. He serrated the blade down the wall in a line, continuing unto the wood-paneled lower wall. He shifted a few paces, the length of a door threshold, and struck another line into the wall from above his head down to the floor. He then took one glass and tipped it at the top of one of the lines, blood pouring downward in a messy rivulet to pool at the baseboard. Next, he lifted the second glass and poured another bloody line. I heard him murmuring something unintelligible at the wall. The hairs on my arm nearest to that wall began to slowly stand on end.

"One should never *waste* blood," murmured Moriel in a hungry tone. "It is too precious of a resource. But *that* is what your kind thrives upon, does it not, Whitby? Forgive me if I do not call you by a more ancient name.

You have taken a body in this time, and that is how I shall refer to you, everything and everyone in their place."

"Call me what you wish, but I hesitate at your making assumptions of me. What do you presume I thrive upon?"

"Waste, wantonness, disregard for life." Moriel gestured to the spilled blood behind him. "See how we honor the desires of creatures such as you?"

"Ah. Yes. You have honored my kind perfectly, Majesties."

"And it is how we reach out and call to you," Moriel said with a deadly little smile. He rose. With a scuff of his boot, he kicked back a length of fine Persian carpeting beneath the dinner table, revealing the wooden floor. "Now you see how we built bridges unto you in the first place."

I glanced down to see that the floor beneath the long, thick rug was covered in symbols of varying kinds, runes and numbers, a mess of different religions and traditions, symbols of faith inverted and perverted, some of the floor carved, some covered with chalky powder, some drippings of wax, some patches painted in tar-like substances and burn marks, some washed in an iron-red stain that was surely blood... A deal of it I recognized as being similar to what Maggie had hellishly fashioned inside her empty closet when she was recreating the demon's likeness out of the scraps of Jonathon's damaged portrait.

It was a mess of ritualistic offerings and evocations to bring terrible things to life... The pooling blood behind Moriel's throne of a dining room chair began to dribble toward those grooves and carvings, soaking deeper into the damaged wood as if it were parched earth.

I shuddered. Why didn't we think to look under the surface of things?

Jonathon pretended not to notice, as if everything was perfectly normal, if not boring. Whatever he had done to steel himself to such revelations was the most impressive thing I could imagine.

Brinkman was a statue at Moriel's side. I wondered what was going through both of their minds. Whatever was carved, painted, and bled onto those floorboards was yet another spell to break, and I tried not to panic, as I only knew one countercurse, and that had to do with the poor prisoners on the wall who had, thankfully, remained in their painted positions.

"Before we get to our meal, let's talk a little business, shall we, Majesty Moriel?" Jonathon posited. "Your plans. I need to know what all is unfolding both here and in New York. You've courted us here, to walk the earth, summoned by your dark dealings, lured by your promises. My kind seeks our utopia. I do hope you're getting closer to providing it. I want to know how you'll be doing so, beyond your various tenuous experiments that have suffered as many failures as successes."

Moriel and Sansalme looked like beady-eyed vultures, staring at Jonathon with a strange, collective expression that shifted discomfortingly between starvation and caution. Moriel smiled again, revealing more of his jagged, yellowing teeth. Sansalme reached into the briefcase he'd set to the side of his chair and threw something heavy upon the table with a resounding thud. It was a ledger.

"Before we do that, Whitby," Moriel replied in a singsong tone. "I'd like to summon more of your kind to the dinner table." His eyes swept to Lavinia, then me. "Since you've provided such fare..." He checked his pocket-watch. "And Vincenzi should be here any moment to provide the lintel."

I turned away so that he could not see my fear at being called "fare." The blood offering was not enough, clearly. I did not wish to appear complicit, as that would be too convenient, but I would not let him have the pleasure of my discomfort. Lavinia did the same, and I could feel her eyes boring into me for strength like pulling water from a well.

Lintel, Moriel said. The top part of a door... That's what the two carved and now bloodied lines were upon the wall. The sides of a door... No... I could feel my bruised and punctured hand begin to shake. We had to move forward, quicker, before they opened something to only God could know what...

Moriel gestured for Sansalme to bring the ledger forward, toward me.

"If God writes your name in the book of *life*," Moriel began in a grand tone, curling his hand in a slow flourish, "so shall your names herein be written in the book of death. The power of the name is vast, as we know. And the more names rent asunder in our cause, the more powerful our book of *death*."

The long, leather rectangular ledger was black, tipped in red. The lackey flipped it open and shoved it under my nose. The ledger bore names inked down one column.

Lord and Lady Denbury

There was an underline beneath their name that carried over to the X like a smear.

Jonathon Whitby, Lord Denbury III

Another X crossed out Jonathon, as his soul was still presumed dead...

Mister Crenfall
Doctor Neuman
Doctor Preston
Doctor Stevens
The Winsome Family

The top three names were blotted with an X. Crenfall was useless. Preston was dead. Was Samuel, Doctor Neuman, Jonathon's friend in Minnesota, dead too then? Likely presumed so. The last doctor, the one who had been working on the chemicals in New York, did not have his name crossed off. For now. The Winsomes I assumed were in the portraits, though I couldn't be sure.

There was another host of names listed under "parts." All the names were smeared. *Parts.* I swallowed back bile. Perhaps whatever corpse had been built in the Denbury cellars, these were the names of the poor souls who could never find rest, not while a part of their bodies were sewn up into such unnatural horror. Wondering where that corpse was threatened to undo any false calm I managed. I was frightened it would turn up at any moment, around any corner...

Each name in the book was written in a dark red substance that was surely blood. Whose, only the devil could know. But there was an X and several blank lines...

"Go on, write yourself down, girl," Moriel said to me with a brilliant, nauseating smile. "Just...sign on the line..." Moriel looked toward the ornate screen for the servants to stand behind. "Come here, little Barty Winsome, come when I call you," Moriel cooed.

The little Winsome boy, who looked like such a cherubic little gentleman in his portrait, such a contrast from the hollowed, sickly child before me, shuffled out from behind the staff screen and toward me. Moriel slid his ceremonial knife down the silk runner and with a preternatural motion, Barty stopped it.

I felt rough hands that were not those of a child fumble and pull at the bindings of the hand that hadn't been "cut."Fingers chafing and bruising me with clumsy force, a knife sliced through the fabric around my wrists. Once my right hand was free the possessed boy seized it, brought it around over the book, and punctured my index finger with the tip. I cried out. He forced my finger onto the line of the ledger. "Sign," the boy said in a gravelly voice that was incongruous with his body. I made a feeble, wavy line that in my mind was not putting down my name but instead a scream. In my mind I declared, with that blood: *I renounce thee...*

There was a slight breeze in response, ruffling the pages of the book. Moriel sneered, as if my blood were in his power. I liked to think it was the direct opposite.

Curiosity seized me, and I rifled through the book before me. The child made a move to stop me, but the Majesty clucked his tongue.

"No, no, let her look..."

The page numbers were not in order but in that reverse of the golden ratio, and each page bore names and plans, some sketches, chemistry, and theory, all madness. The Society's disparate wings of experimentation, horrible upon horrible. A deal of it matched the wretched sprawling scrawls upon the estate floor.

"Are our plans not beautiful, little girl?" the Majesty cooed, drinking in my disgusted expression. "We will rebuild the natural world with unnatural evolution. In doing so, restore natural order, with infernal lineage."

I stared at the ugly man in horror. All of their work was in defiance of divine patterns, of the laws of life. The Society wished to rewrite the very building blocks of all that was good and beautiful upon this earth, withering the sacred, making heaven's natural order unnatural chaos. The theorists and doctors of the day may argue that God could come down to numbers and mathematics. If that were true, then maybe so too could hell be summed up in equations. It was a mad book of possibility, but all of it was most certainly quantifiable.

There was a rustle of noise in the hall, and a figure appeared in the doorway of the dining room. One that caused my heart to tumble deep into my chest.

Margaret Hathorn stood framed by shadow in a lovely pale blue dress the color of a bright New York sky...

A hulking, awkward, bug-eyed man loomed behind her, surely the third "Majesty." They all looked as though they were the worst of what blue-blooded inbreeding had done to elder generations. And then there was beautiful little Maggie among us, a jewel, a wide-eyed lost lamb offsetting such ugliness.

Maggie's gaze swept the room blankly. As if she didn't know any of us. Her gaze lingered on Jonathon. "Hello, Lord Denbury..." she said slowly, as if she were determining something. I doubted there was anything left of her mind, by the look of her.

I managed to hold back tears. If she would not acknowledge us, I could not act like we knew her. For all the Majesties knew, we were all strangers. That might play to our advantage. A flicker of confusion passed across Brinkman's eyes, but it was soon lost again inside the walls of his cool facade.

Jonathon only stared at Maggie and offered one of the trademark leers the demon had been so good at, and he purred: "*Hello, pretty...*"

I could not hold back a revolted shudder at that. At those exact words the demon had once used upon me. Jonathon had heard and seen it all from his painted prison, and for a moment I feared that whatever magic was in this house was reverting him back into what his body had become... No... I had to trust him. Even though everything felt like it was sliding against us... There were officers in these very walls... We couldn't lose, surely...

"Majesty Vincenzi," Moriel said, gesturing to the lumbering, black-and-gray-haired man with sallow olive skin. "How good of you to come." Vincenzi moved forward to kiss Moriel's hand before pulling out a seat for Maggie, two seats away from me, each of us spaced out around the table with a chair between us.

"Before you clutter this home with more of my ilk," Jonathon demanded with a stern tone, "answer my questions." In the end, the demons seemed quite sure that the humans who wished to use them, in fact, answered to them. The Majesties were playing with the most terrible kind of fire, one they couldn't safely control. "Tell me your plans going forward, so that I may approve of them or set you on a new course."

Moriel furrowed his thick, graying brows. "Why, we play for the hearts and minds of the nations that have turned from our power. We seek to take our magic right to the core. The very crux of the matter." Moriel smiled eerily, his milky eyes lit. "You know, Whibty, this isn't a casual association, our being in the Denbury estate today. We're not just here because it's a lovely property we got hold of. One could call my being here a vendetta. Though my perspective was one of a slow-burning flame rather than a constant war. I wanted to be sure that when I went after what I'd always wanted, it would be unquestionably mine. When you resurrect the dead, they are unquestionably yours."

Jonathon, in playing his part, bowed his head as if he understood. But I knew this was a new and unexpected wrinkle. Something flashed in his eyes. Perhaps his father was right and there had been something to be paranoid about after all, something in the Whitby past to be concerned about. Moriel gestured Brinkman over toward Jonathon.

"Mister Bank, do take up my knife there and use it to keep an eye on Whitby. I'm interested in putting his body to the test." Moriel's sick little smile curved his thin lips. He gestured to Sansalme to his right, who withdrew his dagger again and held it very obviously in front of Nathaniel. Perhaps our valiant gentlemen were not trusted as Society associates after all.

"Majesty Vincenzi," Moriel said sweetly. "Did you bring my lady along as I bid you?"

"Of course, Your Highness," Vincenzi replied in a thickly accented voice I assumed was Italian.

"Very good."

Moriel reached again into his pocket, and this time withdrew a small silver bell. He rang it long and hard, a sharp, high-pitched ringing that went reverberate through the house.

"We've still one more guest to seat," Moriel explained grandly, winking at Jonathon. There was a tense silence. Then a thud from the foyer. And another thud. And a scrape.

Footsteps.

Inelegant, clumsy footsteps. Outside in the hall, the gas lamps that lit the corridor were dimming. One by one. Shuffle by shuffle. Lumbering footstep by lumbering step...

Whatever was coming was taking all the light with it...

"Say hello to Mummy, Johnny..."

Oh, God. Horror of horrors.

Lady Denbury.

At the threshold.

She was the body. She was the amalgam of "parts." *She* was the reanimate terror. The final, desecrating insult to the Denbury legacy...

A yellowed corpse with matted, dark hair that was tousled in what had once surely been a very lovely funereal coiffure now stood as the next parading terror at the dining room door. She was swathed in black robes synched by a golden belt, the flowing fabric hiding the somewhat disjointed and uneven height of her, as her body would have been pieced together from myriad bodies. This was done so that the unnatural creation would tether as many ghosts to the reanimate body as possible, one ghost per harvested body part, harnessing the most amount of life force possible to make the corpse active.

And then the corpse opened its mouth. Everything in the air screamed in response. This was just like it had been for us in Doctor Preston's hospital before; the unnatural tie of spirits that powered the body, the tenor of the dark magic carved into dead flesh, made the very fabric of the air shriek in a pitch specifically designed to undo the sanity of anyone within earshot. As the unseen ghosts that made the room drastically chill by their presence were worked up into spiritual frenzy in the hellish siren wail, plates and silverware lifted off the fine linen upon which they'd been laid. The poltergeist phenomena of the attendant spirits was now made active. One reanimate form created myriad paranormal problems in its wake.

Lavinia and I winced, shrinking from the noise; Nathaniel clapped hands over his ears, unprepared for this turn. Brinkman closed his eyes and remained calm.

Jonathon stared in horror at the openmouthed creature that bore some slight resemblance to his face. This time, this was not something Jonathon could endure without reaction. He stood and pounded his fists upon the marble-topped table, causing all silverware airborne by spirits' affectation to clatter back down onto the marble. "Enough!" he shouted.

Moriel rose and went to the standing, swaying corpse, taking its yellowed hands in his. "That's enough, dear. You heard him." The corpse shut its mouth and turned to Jonathon expectantly. It just stood there like a terrible statue as Jonathon's knuckles went white when he clutched the back of his chair.

"You will not dishonor the late Lady Denbury so," Jonathon growled. "It is an insult to this house!"

"Well played, Lord Denbury III," Moriel laughed, applauding Jonathon. "You did originally have me convinced. You'll *have* to tell me how you managed to get yourself out of the painting, I simply *must* know!" he said eagerly. "And *also*, what you did, then, to one of my demons! If he is not within you, whatever happened to him? He'd have wanted a new place to stay..."

Maggie piped up with a distant, airy voice. Amid the latest horror, I'd almost forgotten about her sitting a seat away from me. "The demon left Lord Denbury because he wanted to be with *me*. I kept him... I loved him! He became mine!" She swiveled her head to Moriel, her eyes glassy, her lips dry and cracked. I wondered if they'd sedated her with something, or if her mind had simply gone, all the work in Chicago for nothing.

"Ah, did he then?" Moriel asked Maggie gamesomely.

"He did!" she insisted.

"Then you do have your uses, little poppet." Moriel laughed. "Delightful, all of this! What discoveries we make! Sansalme, make a note of all this in the book!" The second-in-command pulled out a fountain pen from his pocket and loomed over me, flipping to a blank ledger page and taking notes in deep, iron-red ink...

Maggie swiveled her head back and looked directly into my eyes. Something hardened there. She pursed her lips. She knew me. A fire flickered there. What was she up to...?

Majesty Moriel looked at the dead Lady Denbury and back to Jonathon with a sick smile. "I knew resurrecting Mumsy would put you to the true test, son. I assume your friend here and your baits, then, are plants." Moriel leered at me, then Lavinia. "But good that you brought them. They're pretty, they'll do." Then he whipped his gaze back to Maggie with an altogether darker intent. "Don't you think, Miss Hathorn? You're very pretty, you've done nicely thus far, to trap a demon for your very own?"

Maggie just nodded primly and regained that airy voice that did not sound inhabited as her own. "Thank you, Your Majesty. All for the greater purpose."

"You see," Moriel said to all of us. "You'll all come around to Miss Hathorn's way of thinking. You'll see it is the *only* way." He looked over his shoulder. "Isn't that right, Mister Brinkman?" Brinkman nodded. I gritted my teeth.

"Do secure Mister Veil there," Moriel instructed of Brinkman before turning to Jonathon. "It was good you tied up your girls, Denbury. Less we have to do." Brinkman pulled a leather strap from his pocket and secured Nathaniel's hands behind his back. Nathaniel started to struggle, but Moriel whipped out a second knife from another pocket, cautioning: "Careful, Mister Veil. I spend my spare hours testing throwing knives on peasant flesh. I doubt your redhead there would look improved with a blade jutting from her gullet, now would she? Let Mister Brinkman do his work."

As Nathaniel quieted and Brinkman obeyed, I questioned the operative's loyalty. I felt everything begin to spin out of control. We weren't going to make it out alive. The fear I'd kept in check threatened to undo me. I tried to hold back tears, but one escaped.

The Majesty turned to the yellowed corpse hovering beside him and instructed: "Go and tie up your son, my love. I don't want him getting rowdy, but I'd like him to see all this. If he's a good boy, I might even deign to adopt him as my own. He should've been mine all along."

Jonathon spit at the wretched man. If looks could kill, Jonathon's expression would have ripped the Majesty limb from limb, slowly and agonizingly.

The hideous form of what was supposed to represent Lady Denbury lurched over and bound Jonathon's hands behind the back of the beautifully carved chair. He would not look up at the thing as it tied him. I did not blame him. I stared at Jonathon, willing him strength and if he could read minds, telling him how much I loved him. Suddenly, for him, I felt invincible, despite these harrowing turns. God had to be on our side. Heaven *had* to be watching and waiting for us to make our move... For no one should be meant to endure such hell.

Once finished, the effigy of Lady Denbury shuffled back to stand against the wall, leaning against the marble of the mantel, slightly in shadow, as if it needed the corner to prop itself up. Its milky, cataract eyes were unfocused as it stood awaiting its next orders and purpose.

I wanted to look at Brinkman, to demand, with one glance alone, why he wasn't saying or doing anything. Surely, this was all punishable to the death. The Majesties had damned themselves enough, hadn't they? But no, our rule still stood. We hadn't yet done the countercurse and that *had* to be done to restore the Winsome souls to their bodies, lest that hapless family be caught up in collateral damage. We had to limit the circumference of this ever-expanding circle of woe.

"Now, dinner! Sit and watch your betters eat," Moriel said to the gathered company gleefully. "That's how it should be. How it should always have been. *Always* should be!"

The family came in to serve the three Majesties dinner, moving in a daze, their possessed bodies less animate and more unwieldy than when the demon had overtaken Jonathon. Aprons were slung over their fine clothes that had begun to tear and fray. I found I couldn't look at the two children. It was too painful. But I couldn't look at the representation of Lady Denbury, either; she was too horrid. So I stared at my empty plate and prayed for our lives. I struggled to keep focused and not give over to panic and futility.

Food was laid before us. Not that I had any appetite. Not that we were free to eat. The laying out of food seemed symbolic, a representative trapping. The Majesties didn't eat, either; they merely drank a dark wine—if even wine at all, something thick and pitch black like tar—in crystal goblets. I didn't want to know what it was. It seemed too viscous and dark to be blood. It left a black stain upon their yellowing teeth. I imagined all this lavish food going uneaten spoke to the Majesty's desire for wastefulness, greed, for lavish loss at the expense of others. I could see them just leaving this whole table to rot. But not while I had breath in my lungs would I be that passive.

I had been given a second chance at my voice. I was not about to lose that power now.

Bound or no, we all still had our voices. Leveling the countercurse would set things in motion as planned. We couldn't have figured the equation changing so horridly with the corpse of Lady Denbury, but we couldn't let that derail us. It was up to the rest of us to stay strong when Jonathon was doing everything in his power to maintain his sanity. He couldn't look at the creature, either. I didn't blame him. He'd never properly mourned. I longed for the moment he could and put all these nightmares at last to bed, with my help.

"The lintel, please, Vincenzi," Moriel said, some of the dark substance dribbling down the side of his paunchy face.

Vincenzi leaned over toward Maggie, and I saw the flash of a silver knife and blood spurted onto the marble table as Maggie shrieked, her finger dripping scarlet in the instant. He grabbed her hand and squeezed it into the goblet before him. "You could have warned me," she pouted to the large man. He sneered at her. She didn't fight him as he clamped her hand tighter, swirling the blood in the glass. I had to remind myself she had somehow come here of her own volition.

The third Majesty rose with the last offering. With the bloody-tipped knife, he carved a horizontal line meeting the two vertical lines in a tall rectangle. He poured the contents of the glass across the line, scarlet blood dripping down the fine wallpaper in dark, garish streaks. I felt the ground tremble a bit. Vincenzi was murmuring to the wall like his counterpart had done. As I blinked my eyes, it seemed the wall itself rippled. Moriel and Sansalme took up murmuring too. Numbers, in a sequence. It was what Crenfall had been murmuring in his madhouse cell. The golden ratio, but the divine pattern uttered in reverse. It was writ on the floor in tar and blood and now murmured actively on their lips.

The first course was being cleared around us. Soon the possessed bodies of the wretched Winsome family would either be downstairs or hidden again. I tried to catch Jonathon's eye. We couldn't delay. We needed to level the countercurse *now*, while all four of them were in the room. Even though Jonathon hadn't managed to lure out the Society plan for the recorder in the wings as Brinkman had demanded, if what that carving of the wall meant what I thought it might, we couldn't afford a *portal*... Whatever was being called or loosed in this room... The police couldn't arrest *that*... A mouth to hell...

But I couldn't do the countercurse on my own, not with four souls and bodies to reunite. We all needed to do our part and all in one concerted effort. I kept trying to get Jonathon to look at me, but he was transfixed at what was becoming manifest behind Moriel.

A dark rectangular shadow opened up, like a door swinging open. Where there was a wall, there was now a corridor. Inside, just like the girding behind the walls of a home, was the framework between life and death. It was an awesome and terrible sight that was impossible to truly comprehend, even when staring into its abyss.

I recognized this from one of my dreams, a corridor between life and death, between forces for light and those for the dark. Wavering threads hovered inside, weaving and moving like a busy New York street. The fabric of the very universe was laid bare before us, something we shouldn't be privy to, but as the Society was tampering with the very tapestry of the world and tearing at its threads, sticking wrenches into gears, the divine skeleton was visible beneath the flesh.

Five black, vaguely human forms peeled out from the ether and into our world, crossing the threshold with horrible murmurs rising in the air like the cresting of a storm. They were like shadows without bodies, and they whipped about the dining room like careening ghosts.

They were visible, black holes, obliterating chandelier light, firelight, and candlelight as they passed by it. Fomented misery, they made the air not only frigid, but bitter and malevolent. The taste of unadulterated evil. As Moriel laughed the forms flew faster, dizzying in their movement. These were what possessed bodies. These were the host demons. The sweat of panic dripped down my temples.

The corpse of Lady Denbury began to groan again; at any moment I expected another full-fledged wail. The silverware rattled and lifted, hovering a few inches above the table once more. I wished I could, through force of will, like I had seen spirits do once before, shift all the knives and forks and any pointed object. I wished I could drive everything straight into Moriel's chest.

"Come, come," Moriel cried to the shadowy forms. "I am here to give you life. Soon we'll outnumber our enemies. Life by life, blood by blood. Come! *Take...*"

"Yes, come!" Maggie cried suddenly, pushing back her chair, rising to her feet. "Come unto me, demons! Fill me! All of you!" Maggie cried. "I want you..."

The shadows pacing the room suddenly turned as if dogs catching a scent.

"No..." I murmured, wresting in my chair. My words fumbled in my throat, my old disability threatening to halt my words as anxiety tended to do. "No...don't...do that..."

"I want you," Maggie continued. There was a horrific and unnatural shudder of her body as the shadows all pounced at once, disappearing into her. The Majesties gazed on with a sick, eroticized hunger.

"I want you"—a sudden, fierce fire leaped into her eyes as she retaliated with a scream—"to *go to hell!*"

From the pocket of the prim pinafore she'd worn, she withdrew a glass bottle with an ornate cross upon it, clear liquid inside.

I realized dimly she was not cursing us to hell. She meant the demons. The demons that had overtaken her. Or, maybe...that she had just entrapped...

Seizing the bottle of what I realized must be holy water—why else would there be the cross upon it?—she drank it down swiftly, emptying the whole bottle, choking but drinking still. Her face contorted in agony. She crumpled forward in a jerking movement. A wretched gurgle sounded in her throat.

"No!" Majesty Moriel cried, his look of ecstasy suddenly turning to rage. "Traitorous little bitch, what do you think you—"

Brinkman suddenly punched Moriel in the face, and he slumped face first into a bowl of pudding. As the other Majesties on either side rose to fight, Brinkman whipped two pistols from his pocket, one trained on either of the Majesties. My heart buoyed. The man was our side after all.

Thank God. He waited long enough to prove it. No. Brinkman was smart, the souls weren't yet back in the painting, and him playing their side had bought him more leverage, to be standing so close to the wretches, able to escape being bound like the rest of us.

Just as I swelled with hope, Maggie started screaming.

There was smoke curling up in wisps from her bodice. Something had ignited upon her, perhaps within her... I struggled with my bindings, lifting the chair up behind me, managing a heavy step nearer to Maggie, but she shoved my shoulder with preternatural strength and I nearly hit my head on one of the table's sturdy candelabrum, a wisp of my hair catching in a candle flame.

It was a cross that burst into fire right at her sternum. A large crucifix had been hidden beneath her bodice, and it burned free of the layers, a solid metal pendant the size of my palm. As the cross ignited and sizzled her flesh so did it seem the demons burned within her, broiling from the holy water.

Jonathon jumped to his feet in the chaos. He hadn't been tied to the chair, only bound with wrists behind his back. He turned his back to the table and lifted his wrists over the candles on his side of the table, burning his hands and his cuffs. I could smell these terrible separate stenches of burning flesh and fabric. But in doing so, he burned his bindings too. Brave man, he suffered melting flesh on the side of his palm but snapped his wrists free. He too bounded toward Maggie, but she tossed him off as if he were a rag doll and his body came perilously close to the still-open portal where forces hung suspended in this precarious battleground.

Jonathon reeled to regain his balance and rushed back over to me. As the side of his palm wept blood and peeling skin, he undid my bindings.

It was not only Maggie's scream that filled the room but a magnified and horrible sound, many screams, burning from the inside out as the blessed liquid doused the demons within. Demons who were surely killing her from inside, as blood began pouring from her ears, dribbling from her lips, tears of blood rolling down her cheeks.

Her still-standing body went rigid, shuddering and shaking, the blood pouring faster. It was the most horrible sight I could have imagined. This was after having witnessed the sallow flesh of the dead come to life. But to see the *living* tortured so...

"Maggie!" I screamed amid the screams. She staggered to the side, to me, into my arms, and I sunk with her to the floor. I held her tight. And because I spoke now for someone else's life, somehow my disability was no match for this fight. My tongue and speech were free.

"Maggie, listen, say with me, say to the devils," I cried in a choking, desperate gasp, tears streaming from my eyes as the blood wept from hers. "*I renounce thee... I renounce thee...*" Her body shuddered and shook, her blood seeped all over my skirts and sleeves.

Margaret Hathorn looked up at me and smiled weakly, causing another river of blood to pour forth from her lips, and there was an aura of great white light about her, an angelic halo that took my breath away with heavenly beauty. She seemed as though she wanted to say something.

But then she died in my arms.

I screamed a wailing sob. I closed her eyelids immediately. Her dead, open stare would undo my mind. I held her close, her body and blood still warm.

But there was no time to mourn. For then, another cascade of events happened all at once. It was everything I could do to keep up.

The other two Majesties started up with the counting and the chanting again, which made the demonic threshold active, rippling open once more, but their incantation was stopped by Brinkman cocking the pistols. Nathaniel had managed somehow to wrestle one of the throwing knifes into his palm and was cutting loose his bindings and Lavinia's in turn.

Jonathon picked up a pitcher of water and threw them at the portal, directly toward the lintel and sides, trying to wash away the blood and ash that had activated it. Nathaniel did the same with a second pitcher. Lavinia took up a tureen of soup and poured it over the floor, falling to her knees and scrubbing free all the terrible things that had made this room such a magnet for the demons. All this action against the portal caused the rectangle to flicker. The heavy dread of the room lifted slightly. A scale sliding more toward our victory.

But the corpse of Jonathon's mother started screaming again. Items lifted off the table again and all of us winced, clapping our hands to our ears. I lunged for the terrible ledger book of the Master's Society, searching for clues in its terrible pages. We had to calm the spirits tied to the effigy of Lady Denbury. The names of the "parts" had to be addressed and sent to rest.

I dimly heard running footsteps in the hall coming closer. Was it the police officers at last? But Brinkman hadn't blown the whistle... Who else...

Yet more familiar faces ran into the room, one dark and one fair, both looking alarmed. Reverend Blessing and Mrs. Northe! Blessing dressed in his clerical suit and collar, Evelyn Northe in an elegant but unadorned riding habit.

Exactly where they'd come from, I couldn't know. They likely had traveled as soon as they could. Mrs. Northe wielded a pistol, the reverend, a cross. My heart soared, but as Brinkman trained a gun toward them, Jonathon, Lavinia, and I all lurched forward and shouted some variant of:

"No, they're on our side!"

Moriel, who had roused again from the punch, was aghast at the sight of the reverend's dark skin, for he snorted: "Oh, and you *dare* bring a *blackamoor* into my sight to soil the very air around us? Your species really is—"

Another punch from Brinkman sent Moriel back into the pudding again, causing Blessing almost to smile, but his gaze was soon focused directly on the more pressing matter of the reanimate corpse, and he moved near it, knowing exactly what to do as he had done in Doctor Preston's hospital wing. Mrs. Northe took a moment to consider the wavering, open portal but swept the room to meet our gazes first.

"My friends," Mrs. Northe cried. "Are you all—" That's when she saw that Maggie was in my arms. Alongside the siren-like wail of the reanimate body, she shrieked, falling to her knees at my side. I stared at her helplessly.

"She took them *into* her," I cried. "Demons. From the portal. Five of them. We couldn't stop her, we didn't know—"

"It should have been me," Mrs. Northe insisted, tears splashing onto Maggie's scorched bodice. "It should always have been me, bearing the brunt, my poor girl, no, it should have been *me*—"

208 | LEANNA RENEE HIEBER

"Right before Maggie acted," I explained, "she looked at me, with stern resolution, as if this was the only thing she could do." I spoke as if somehow an explanation could ease the pain. It didn't.

In the background I heard Blessing begin an exorcism rite to untie and set to rest the collective of unseen spirits that by our experience we knew were attached to the embodiment of Lady Denbury. The other two Majesties were laughing and taunting the black man, calling him derogatory names, the Society clearly based on the falsehood of racial superiority along specific bloodlines.

But Blessing was unruffled by the racist slurs. He remained focused on spiritual matters at hand. The Denbury body was one thing, but the retinue of spirits, they were further unwanted company. We could all feel the chill the ghosts carried in their wake.

"Reverend Blessing, the names of the dead are writ here," I declared, sliding the ledger book across the dining room table toward him, fighting to be heard against the din of spiritual unrest.

He nodded and began addressing the spirits the Society used in their methods to power reanimate bodies. He called them by the names listed in the book. He bid them leave the dead flesh and promised that their remains would be put in sacred ground. The poltergeist effects the spirits were wreaking in the room began to settle a bit. Mrs. Northe echoed all of Blessings words, acting as his assisting minister in the exorcism rite, though she reiterated and enforced his scripture while still rooted to the ground near Maggie's cooling body.

The two conscious Majesties started up with insidious chanting again, in a tongue indiscernible to me, and as they did, the open portal wavered, dark shadows drew closer to the threshold, as if another wave of monsters were about to seep over. Brinkman nodded at Nathaniel and spat in one of the Majesty's faces. Sansalme just sneered up at him. Nathaniel moved to gag both the men on either side of the still unconscious Moriel.

"This is just the beginning," Sansalme said in a slight accent I thought might be French. "You've really no idea." He dabbed Brinkman's spit out of his eye with a silk handkerchief.

"Well, I'm sure you'll be telling us all about it in a court of law," Brinkman growled.

"No..." Sansalme replied, seemingly unconcerned. This terrified me as much as the portal. What could threaten these wretches? I shook myself away from staring at them in disgust.

"We need to get the 'help,' the family, together," I cried to Jonathon, to Mrs. Northe, to Nathaniel and Lavinia, who were still trying to repair and erase the various dark magic effects upon the room. "That's the cue for the arrests!"

We had to settle the room, lest the police turn against the unwitting victims, as the officers could hardly be sure who or what was doing the damage. This was the type of horrific chaos the Society wished to wreak, where no one could effect change and keep faith, where no one knew who was friend or foe. Where everyone turned against one another. But the Society couldn't know what a wonderful team we had among us.

I stared down at Maggie's corpse. My despair would not help the dead woman in my arms who had been so brave. It was my turn to show that kind of strength and willingness of sacrifice. I had the knowledge to wield a countercurse, and I needed to wield it now. I shifted Maggie off my lap, and Mrs. Northe took her into her arms instead. Her blood had soaked through my dress, was all over my hands. I couldn't worry about that.

I darted to the elaborate screen that traditionally hid the staff during the meal and closed off the door that led to the kitchen stairs. And there the family stood, dazed, just behind the wooden panels. Glassy eyed, they stood slightly swaying, waiting to be summoned. The sight of all four of them triggered my immediate shout as I dragged the children forward first. As soon as I moved, Jonathon was with me in the instant, following with the wife and Nathaniel with the husband.

"*Ego transporto animus ren per ianua*, Beelzebub the Devil!" I cried, and Jonathon echoed me.

The adults struggled against us, the demons within sensing that we were at war. Jonathon dodged a punch; I nearly had my hands bitten by the red-eyed children. Lavinia, Blessing, and Mrs. Northe all rushed to lend hands while still spouting scripture. The forces which sought to harm us recoiled. Together we took up the same shout, shoving the disoriented, confused bodies toward their respective paintings.

We said the countercurse again and again: "'sending the soul through the door...'" This had been Jonathon and my puzzle to sort through together when we met. The words were roughly translated from Latin, but with an Egyptian word for "soul-door" put in for an extra complication, as the portrait frames were literally a door for the soul to be deposited into. It had been a hard-fought mystery to solve but the countercurse had worked for restoring Jonathon.

Jonathon, Nathaniel, and Lavinia, all of us took up the countercurse together, utilizing variants on the Devil, Satan, the damned, any possible name for what was supposed to be the penultimate of evil, the prince of darkness itself. We tried to encompass all that these foul energies wished to be, and in doing so, trap them by the title they aspired to. The power of the name, we'd learned, was one of the eldest powers of all, and it was one the Society seemed to take very seriously. We had our faith. They had theirs. And now we had to play ours against theirs with everything we had.

Mrs. Northe, seeing that we had the family well in hand, turned her attention to the wavering wall portal, staring at it with concern. She began murmuring another iteration of numbers, but this time, from what I could guess, it was a sequence in the proper golden ratio, as high as she could think of and starting back again at a low number. Reclaiming the divine patterns, wresting a semblance of peace from the grip of malevolence. The edges of the carved wall, now cleansed of the blood tokens, flickered back into becoming a wall once more.

I stayed focused on the shifting paintings and the struggling possessed bodies, though I wanted to see the look of surprise on the faces of the two conscious leaders. None of them could have possibly known we could directly reverse one of their most consistent magics. I deserved a self-congratulatory moment of pride, but I didn't dare take my eyes off my targets.

Nathaniel rose to grab the little girl, even as a shot rang out. There was a scream and a clatter of a gun. One of the Majesties was clutching a bleeding forearm, blood all over the white tablecloth. It would seem Vincenzi had tried to fire a weapon, trying to take advantage of the chaos of wind, still-hovering objects, and the maddening whispers that summoning demons produced in the air, but Brinkman got to him before he could fire, a wisp of smoke floating up from Brinkman's own pistol.

Vincenzi was too late. The countercurse worked its magic.

There was a crackle of fire, and a fresh new screaming in the air added to the ongoing wail of Lady Denbury's ghostly retinue. In a huge, roaring pop, the paintings all came off their hinges and slid to the floor, leaving tracks of greasy, bloody paint along the wall as they descended; the canvasses were wet with indeterminate moisture. Trapped now in the frames leaning at odd angles against the wall were horrid forms, twisted and nearly gargoyle-like. Indistinct, demonic heads topped the fine clothes that were warped and dripping. Only the most ugly ephemera remained; an evil imprint, oily and greasy, a sheen of bloody perspiration bubbled up on sulfuric canvasses.

So too did the bodies fall, slumping to the floor as if marionette strings had been cut. We knelt with the families as they began to rouse, terrified, but as Jonathon did, having some sense.

Brinkman took one look at the horrid exhibition against the wall and blew his whistle loud and several times, until the room crawled with officers. He instructed them to get the Winsome family to safety and explained in no uncertain terms who was friend and who was foe. The family was all too happy to exit the premises. The little girl threw her arms around me. The husband scooped up his son in his arms and seemed too ashamed to look at any of us who had helped him. The mother collected her daughter and murmured to me as an officer ushered her out: "I don't understand, but thank you..."

Above the din of the police, Reverend Blessing continued the exorcism rite, and this seemed to give comfort to the pallid officers, coming into the scene with no idea what to expect, but seemingly glad for some kind of spiritual offset. If the officers were uncomfortable taking blessings from a man of color, they didn't show it. I think they knew, seeing this scene, what was right to fear and who was a mere brother in humankind.

Blessing clutched the Society's insidious "'book of death,'" and between scriptural declamations he continued to read off names within, bidding that the souls mauled by the claws of the Society find their deserved rest.

"Spirits who weep here, heed me," Blessing bellowed into the foul air, his deep, rich voice captivating and compelling. "These men seek to gain power through methods of torturous unrest. Be their downfall by granting your own souls the peace God wants for you."

There was still a wavering line where the portal had gaped wide. Mrs. Northe was facing it, her arms out, her body fierce and taut, proclaiming scripture at the portal to try to shut it at last. Wrestling against the closing of the door, a black form darted out from the portal and careened into the hall. A demon on the loose.

"No!" Jonathon cried and ran after the wretched thing in the instant.

"No!" I cried and ran after him. I didn't think twice any more than he did. I just pursued.

Dimly, I realized the force was headed for the study, snuffing the lights out down the hall as it passed. Light by light, the vile force plunged our surroundings into darkness. We pursued it into the study where one gas-lamp chandelier remained dimly lit, casting the room into an eerie glow.

But the moment we both crossed the threshold, the door slammed shut behind us of its own accord and the gas lamp guttered into a pale, sickly blue pilot. Now it was just us in the dark. And a raw, untethered demon.

Jonathon went to the desk and turned a lamp, which illuminated for us that the black form stood in front of the window where beyond, the night was cool and dark, but the demon was blacker than the black night, its form not richly beautiful in night shadow, but empty and void of all life.

Jonathon and I stared at one another helplessly, and in the instant we both started crying scripture at its chasm-like form. Jonathon threw himself in front of me as the form floated closer. I struggled to put myself in front of him instead, but he kept me behind him. If such a thing inhabited Jonathon again, my mind would crack under the strain.

I withdrew the sharp scissor point from my bodice. But what a blade would do against an incorporeal force was laughable.

A wave of anger and despair washed over me, perhaps the effect the presence had upon us. Suddenly I wanted to shove Jonathon away from me. To be anywhere but near him. Ugly sounds gurgled in both of our throats. Snarling, animalistic noises. It would turn us against each other. In a locked room. While chaos still reigned in the rest of the house.

Down the hall I could hear that the wailing had resumed. This time, it had more voices.

The siren that was dead Lady Denbury had all the officers screaming too. It was, in the end, too much for us.

The spirits animating the corpse, the open portal, the lingering dark magic, all the amassed horrors the Society had brought upon this house, down into the floorboards and mortar, it was in the end too much for a few stalwart souls to close up and shut down. We needed an army of those as experienced as Blessing and Mrs. Northe. The rest of us were too beaten down, our reserves tapped by so many facets of this unexpected war. We'd fought a good fight. But now...

Our shoulders sagged as Jonathon and I both choked and shook. We were paralyzed by the dread and horror that was the core of the demonic presence. I felt a hand clamp around my neck. It wasn't Jonathon's. It was my own, the terrible force eating us inward, turning our own tired selves against us. We sunk to our knees, both of us gasping and snarling. I tried to rally, to reject the presence. A choking "I renounce thee..." afforded me one deep breath before the suffocating darkness threatened to overwhelm me once more.

I clutched the small scissors in my hand. Whispers careened around my ears. They urged me to drive the blade into my own flesh. To just give up. To let them in. To give them room. The point of the very sharp scissor point pierced my wrist, by my own doing. A drop of blood welled up. I remembered the runes that the magic had carved into my flesh, and I found myself making a line up my wrist, searing, burning pain sharpening every sensation.

"Natalie," Jonathon choked. A tendril of black shadow sweeping out from the demon's wake was wound around his neck, manifest evil taking shape and wielding violence.

I stared at the line of blood seeping from my wrist, my heart racing from the burning pain of it. I couldn't give up like this. This incorporeal beast before me was just that: incorporeal. It needed to be shot down with a bullet of light, faith, hope, and determination.

I pulled upon everything that had brought me to this point in one final shrugging off. I thought of all the sacrifices, Maggie's lovely, bloodstained face flashing before my eyes as if I were praying to a saint. She was a saint here today, and I was stronger than this. If she could take in five of the beasts, I could take on one. The worst wretches of the corporeal and incorporeal world always underestimated determined young women.

I remembered the cross that burned upon her, and with one even slice of the open scissor blade, I intersected the bleeding line up my wrist with another one, to make a cross. I lifted up my wrist, blood pooling in the lace at my cuffs. "I renounce thee!" I cried as the black silhouette of the demon advanced upon me, hovering.

I flung myself back, giving myself space from the beast as I plucked the cross I wore beneath my layers out into the open. It was a small, elegant cross my mother had given me after I'd gone through my confirmation classes at Immanuel Lutheran. I thought of Mother, of Father, of the beautiful fiancé before me, and suddenly I felt like Joan of Arc must have felt before going off to war, surrounded by saints.

But like Joan, I needed more armor. I looked around wildly for something else. I picked up the inkwell on Jonathon's desk, and I plunged my finger into it, making the sign of the cross upon my forehead as if it were Ash Wednesday. From dust we were made and unto dust we would return. But not today.

"I renounce thee!" I shrieked again. Jonathon was trying to close the distance between us, and I fell to my knees before him, using the inkwell to paint a messy cross over his brow. "We renounce thee!" Our rejection caused a tremor in the room. Books rattled on their shelves. The expensive trinkets from around the world shuddered on the marble fireplace mantel. The window panes shivered.

Jonathon shook his head, as if tossing off a terrible dream. He narrowed his eyes at the hesitating, pulsing dark form. "Upon the graves of our beloved mothers," Jonathon bellowed, "we renounce thee!"

A sudden burst of light had us blinking and wincing, and suddenly between us and the horrid, silhouetted form of congealed evil, floated the bright white forms of two beautiful women. Angels called down to the fight. I recognized one of the angels as my own. And the second one looked a great deal more like Jonathon than that thing wailing down the hall did.

"You leave our children alone," the spirit of my mother said to the vacuous silhouette in a venomous tone. "This is the end. Your kind has failed. You cannot win against such wondrous love as this." She turned her beaming, beautiful face upon us, and tears of amazement rolled down my cheeks.

"Did you hear that?" said the second spirit, a beautiful woman in a lavish gown, in a vicious hiss In the name of God the Father, of the Son, of the Holy Ghost. In the name of all the saints, the host of angels, and *everything* that is *holy, get out of my house!*" shrieked the spirit of Lady Denbury.

Lady Denbury was not tied to that body in the dining room at all but instead tied to her beloved son. Her spirit was resilient and made new again in the fight. The bright, transparent form of Lady Denbury lifted an elegant hand into the air and sharply backhanded the inelegant, tar-black form before her, and it splintered into a spattering mess, wet ashes upon the fine rug, nothing but ugly residue.

Jonathon seized me and stepped back so that none of the demonic muck could land upon me, all the while staring up at the ghost of the mother he'd never had time to grieve. The two ghostly women looked down at their embracing children.

"Don't go, Mother," Jonathon gasped, his tears flowing as freely as mine. "I never got to say good-bye, I—"

"I love you too, my darling, perfect boy," Lady Denbury said with a dazzling smile. "And you needn't say good-bye. I'll always be with you."

"I am so sorry, Mum," Jonathon said in gasping breaths. "I should've done more, I should've saved you—" He tried to reach out and touch her, hold her.

"You've done everything you can," Lady Denbury replied. "Look at all you've done. You've done more than you even know, my darling. I am so proud of you."

"Both of you," my mother added. "Don't they make a perfect couple, Lady Denbury?"

"Indeed. *She's* Lady Denbury now." Jonathon's mother smiled at me. "And I couldn't rest happier."

"Be well, darlings," my mother said as she and her friend in heaven began to fade. "We're never far, we live within you, and in any darknesses, we are with you. Never forget. Live in the light."

"I love you," both Jonathon and I blurted to our mothers simultaneously before they faded entirely. We swayed on our feet, breathing heavily.

The study door swung open again of its own accord. There was no more screaming anywhere. Just the murmur of activity. Of cleanup. Of a battlefield victorious.

Somewhere I could hear Moriel raving as he was being led away, leveling threats and decrying the undeserving underclass. There was another loud smacking thud, and I suspected Brinkman had knocked him out again. It was admirable Brinkman hadn't killed Moriel, really. I'm sure the government would have given him leave to do so; however, whatever secret Moriel held had something to do with someone Brinkman loved. Human beings could do amazing, nearly inhuman things for love. This was something the Society seemed keen on subverting though they seemed unable to understand it. It was not something they could overpower. That was their ultimate hubris.

I heard Mrs. Northe calling for us.

"In here," I called into the hall with the last of my energy, allowing Jonathon to gather me up into his arms, sinking with me again onto the floor, our backs against his beautiful bookcase.

We were bloody and drenched in sweat, ink, and water, our clothes torn and besmirched. Bruised, battered, alive. Grieving. Joyous. Relieved. Exhausted. *Alive.* Jonathon tore his black silk cravat and made a bandage for my wrist.

Suddenly there were shouts and screams once more. Did I rejoice too soon? I smelled smoke. And burning flesh.

The dining room was on fire.

Brinkman popped a sweaty, smeared face into the study, standing wide-eyed at the threshold. "The corpse. The corpse of Lady Denbury... It..."

"Went up in flames," I finished. "The spirits will have their revenge. Let them combust the body. It's part of resolution..."

"My men are instituting a bucket brigade from your rear well, Lord Denbury," Brinkman said. "We'll do what we can to save the building. You've a haven at a safe distance, yes? We should evacuate you and your friends from the estate at last."

Jonathon nodded. "Up the earthen corridor behind the library. A cottage."

"Go on then, quickly." Brinkman shooed all of us into the hall and toward the library. I saw my four friends going on ahead, with Reverend Blessing carrying Maggie's corpse in his strong arms. The sight made tears spring forth again. Nathaniel and Lavinia directed them toward the library, and they disappeared into the next rooms.

"Do hurry," Brinkman insisted. "After all we've been through, I'd hate for a lowly fire to take you down. I'll join you once I see to it the men are at work with the well."

"Thank you, Mister Brinkman, for everything," Jonathon called. Brinkman batted a hand in the air and ran off.

Jonathon Whitby, Lord Denbury, III, paused in the middle of his corridor, watching flames licking out into the hall from Rosecrest's lovely dining room. Jonathon stared at the flames of destruction. "Sometimes," he murmured in a haunted, sad voice that was elder than his years, "some things are best left to burn."

He grabbed me by the arm, and we darted toward safety.

Chapter Twenty-Seven

Jonathon and I jogged up the earthen corridor, coughing. The increasing smoke would present a problem indeed if we didn't keep moving.

My whole body ached as we finally climbed the stairs into the cottage. The rest of our compatriots had all found places to collapse ahead of us, draped on the edges of the bed or leaning bent against fine furniture that our sooty, bloody, bedraggled forms looked so at odds with.

Someone had opened the front door to the night, to the forest. Everything outside was still, save for the night sounds of insects and birds. So quiet. Peaceful. We did not turn on more than the one lamp at the entrance. We did not want to see the sharp details of what the night had done to any of us. What it had taken from us.

Jonathon brought a wet towel moistened from an outside water basin over to me and washed the inked cross from my forehead and then his own.

Reverend Blessing had laid out Maggie's body upon the bay window where the moonlight upon her face made her lovely face even lovelier and turned the garish pools of blood all over her dress into grayscale. Mrs. Northe had Maggie's head in her lap, at work in the moonlight, removing the blood from her face, neck, arms, and hands with silken kerchiefs.

I knelt upon the divan, and Jonathon drew close. As he sat I collapsed onto his lap, resting my head in his gentle hands that were shaking so hard. But he stroked my hair anyway. Wherever we landed, we wept. Silently. For a long time.

Finally, Mrs. Northe stirred, gesturing Reverend Blessing over to her side. "Reverend, I'd like to pray with you here, over my niece, if you would be so kind." I'd never heard her speech so gentle, so tired, so grieved.

I rose and moved with him; kneeling before the bay window bier, we prayed over her, said thanks for her, her bravery, and sacrifice. We asked for forgiveness of all of our sins that led to her death, Mrs. Northe having a most difficult time with the guilt of it.

I simply took Evelyn's hand, and she held it. I was well aware it could have easily been me upon those cushions with hands folded over my still breast. I might have done the same, trying to buy us time, but I'd never have thought to do what she did, not so boldly. With great sadness I realized she probably hadn't gotten my letter. I was a fool not to have sent it sooner.

Death brings such guilt to the living, illuminating all the things undone and unsaid. It wasn't fair. She didn't deserve such a death. And yet we didn't deserve such a sacrifice. But if she hadn't done what she did, likely casualties would have been higher. She may have had no choice.

I wondered what had happened in Chicago right before she left. I wondered if she had dreams like I did. She'd shared with me, once, that the demon had visited her dreams. What if she knew it was all as inevitable as I had known? Somehow that gave me comfort, as her actions seemed far too calculated to have been inspiration in the moment.

Mrs. Northe had promised there would be death. But even the most clairvoyant, if too close to the truth, couldn't see it. Not precisely.

"I should have known, I should have seen. It should have been me." Those words she kept repeating numbly in different variations. I shook my head at her.

"That does no good, Evelyn," Blessing murmured. "Accept the facts as they lie. As you live, give thanks for her life. Pray for her undying soul, that will be rewarded in heaven for such selfless acts."

Mrs. Northe nodded and just kept stroking Maggie's hair. That was a comfort, the idea of her reward. I hoped in heaven, for Maggie, there would be lots of balls and pretty dresses and exquisite company, that she'd have no need for gossip or intrigue, merely be loved and cherished by heavenly hosts until I'd see her again in some future day and thank her soul myself. I moved back to rest in Jonathon's arms.

After some time, Brinkman banged upon the iron door from the other side, making us all jump. He called out to us to let him in.

"Most of the wing was saved," Brinkman said as he entered, mopping a sweaty brow. "Thank goodness for stone frames between wings. But you'll need a new dining room, Lord Denbury. I'm off to Scotland Yard, friends," Brinkman said, crossing the cottage in a few stern strides. "I'll fill out the reports and keep your further involvement to a minimum. I'll push for an immediate trial."

"Shouldn't you rest, Mister Brinkman?" I asked.

"Not until I have my satisfaction," he said gravely. "Those wicked bastards have my son. My child. My only joy in this goddamn world. I'd rip out all their throats with my bare hands if I thought I could still find him without their knowledge."

There was a terrible silence in the room at this still unfinished business.

"Let us know how we can help," Mrs. Northe said gently.

"Thank you," Brinkman said, burying his pain. He glanced at Maggie's body. "I take it you knew her. I'm sorry for your loss."

"We'll be praying for your son," I offered. Brinkman managed a slight smile.

"Thank you. Ladies, you were very brave. I doubt the men hidden in those walls waiting for the signal could've done all you did. If it were up to me, I'd have the queen award you a medal, but I doubt we'll be allowed to talk much about this, if any of it, ever again," he said with bitterness. "I'll follow up with Knowles about the properties to make sure any lands and assets seized by the Society are returned to proper owners. This is your estate. You've a grateful family who have been ferried off to the station that would like to return Rosecrest to you."

Jonathon nodded. Brinkman bowed slightly and stormed off. I heard a cry urging on a fast horse. Hoofbeats pounded off and faded into silence. For poor Brinkman, this was just one ongoing nightmare. Suddenly I felt very lucky. I had my joy in this room with me. Maggie's body notwithstanding.

I glanced from Mrs. Northe to Jonathon, to the tall form across the room of Reverend Blessing, dark skin gleaming in the moonlight as he remained in prayerful watch over Maggie's eternal rest, to the brave entwined couple of Nathaniel and Lavinia who had risen to the ultimate challenge. Lavinia was already fast asleep on Nathaniel's shoulder.

I had everyone I needed right here, except Father. Mother lived on in my heart, having always shown herself when I needed her most. Love was like that, taking the form of angels when faced with devils.

As the cottage had neither amenities nor staff, it was not a place we could weather the night. The appetite we'd all lost during the battle returned with painful awareness. But we couldn't be seen like we were. Nathaniel gently roused Lavinia, and we each did as best we could to put ourselves together. We hid our bloodstained clothes under cloaks and rode into Greenwich proper in Nathaniel's fine carriage. All of us were able to fit as Lavinia chose to ride up above with Nathaniel driving. At the back of the carriage, laid out upon clean boards and swathed in thick layers of black fabric, Margaret Hathorn's corpse made the journey back with us.

We went to the nearest inn, a modest establishment, and took over a shadowed corner of the public rooms and ate everything they could lay out for us. Something about the looks on our faces did not invite any comment. It was late, after all. And we were a bedraggled, strange set of compatriots that thankfully no one took exception to. Surely we looked as haunted and as at the precipice of death as we felt.

The gentlemen took turns driving back to London, all of us dozing in and out. That night, in Jonathon's flat, the whole motley crew remained gathered. None of us could bear to be alone or separated because our collective trauma made us stronger.

I cried myself nearly sick. Nothing else would do. The anguish I felt was only matched by a wave of hatred for myself, guilt threatening to drag me under into a mental state that I wondered if I could recover from after the progressive stages of grief. I'd been stronger when I had been trying to soothe Mrs. Northe. Now that reality was truly setting in, I was coming undone.

Someone dying in your arms is something no one can prepare you for.

It is the most terrible thing in the world.

It is the most incredible thing in the world.

Because never are you so aware of your own fragility, of that precarious moment between life and death. One moment here. The next, gone. A fleeting, breathless moment gives over to no breath ever again.

It was eerie, it didn't feel real, it felt like a thousand knives in my heart and in my eyes, replaying her final moment. Her fine, amazing, brave, incredible final moments. Here I thought I was brave and she was weak. I was a fool, and she was a savior.

I threw up everything that was in my stomach and cried every tear that could be cried and still they came. Jonathon just continued to bring me water and hold me tighter. But he couldn't hold this away. Sometimes we cried together, for my tears granted permission for his.

Seeing his reanimate mother had to have been one of the worst possible sights a person could ever see. The fact he retained his sanity was a miracle. I was grateful I'd encountered my dead mother again as a ghost, a beautiful spirit helping me from the beyond. Poor Jonathon had been first confronted with his mother's desecration, and I would do anything to have taken that sight away. At least her spirit had won out and helped us, managing to redeem that dreadful blasphemy into a transcendent truth.

Our pain was so severe and so specific, we just held on to each other, knowing we were all we had, companions who had been through every level of personal hell, together, miraculously still alive to speak of it. Though I wondered if we'd ever speak of it again. I wanted to forget everything but the feel of his arms holding me as the sensation made life bearable.

Jonathon just held me until it was inappropriate for him to be in the same room with me any longer. It was only a mere hour or so before dawn. Lavinia and Nathaniel were curled up somewhere, recovering on their own time and terms.

At some point sleep claimed me until I was roused by something bright and cold hovering at the foot of the guest room bed.

Maggie floated before me.

I couldn't be sure if it was real or a dream, but I was very glad to see her spirit, in whatever way it wished to see me.

"Hello, my friend," I whispered. The tears came again. "I don't deserve you."

"Me?" Maggie scoffed. "The friend that almost had you killed back in

New York? Of course you did. You *do*. This was my penance, Natalie."

"No, Maggie—"

"It was, Natalie. It was foretold. Your mother has been very kind to me. She's been showing me the ways of this place, this in-between area where I'm still watching the world but above it. The Angel Walk, she calls it, as she fancies herself your guardian angel."

"She is," I stammered through my tears.

"There are two walks," Maggie's ghost said excitedly. "The angels walk a path. And so do the devils. That's the path the Society was trying to carve open. From here you can see where things have come and where things may go. One life to the next, one body, one soul to the next... So many possibilities." Her voice was filled with a beautiful wonderment. "When you and I meet again someday, I'd like to think we will be better friends."

"We will be," I said through renewed tears. She was staring at me with such calm, such care, such love, the sort of warmth I always imagined an angel or Jesus might look upon me with, a look that knew of terrible suffering, temptation, and pain but chose to stare lovingly instead. "I promise you. If whatever or whoever I am is too blind to see the woman you're capable of being, shake me out of it."

"I think you'll know, next time," Maggie said. "If there's such a thing as past lives, well, we will have learned in the next one."

"We are imperfect creatures down here, Maggie. I'm sure things look so much different up there."

"Perspective." She said, bobbing slightly in the air. "Don't lose yours. There may be storms yet ahead, who knows. You have people who need you."

"We all needed you."

Her grayscale form smiled. "It was nice to be needed for once."

"You were never not needed, we—"

Maggie held up a ghostly hand to shut me up. "Stay safe, Natalie Stewart. Take care of that lord of yours."

"I promise I will. If you can visit again... I hope you will."

Maggie shrugged. "I don't know... I've a lot of exploring to do."

"Evelyn will want to see you. Your aunt is devastated."

224 | LEANNA RENEE HIEBER

"In time." Maggie shrugged. "When she's ready, she'll see me. We see what we need to see when we can best handle it, whether it feels like it or not. I've a letter for you, back in New York. It will explain everything."

"Thank you." I reached out to the chill air before me. "Truly. I owe you so much more than that, but—"

"You're welcome," Maggie said, waving a ghostly hand as if it were nothing. When it had been everything. "Truly." And she vanished.

Chapter Twenty-Eight

It was only when Mrs. Northe handed me a ticket for the steamer in the morning—leaving in a mere few hours—that my future flashed before my eyes.

What about Jonathon? Would he come with us? He had left early in the morning, saying he'd return, but what was our plan? Was I to live at Rosecrest? Could we face it? What about Father? I'd agreed to marry Jonathon, I was at his command, no longer Father's... But I wasn't sure I could just up and leave New York behind. I reeled.

I had assumed we'd live in Manhattan, but it was stupid of me to make such assumptions. I wanted to cry all over again. I couldn't ask Jonathon to leave his homeland any more than I wanted to leave mine. I liked London, and Rosecrest was beautiful, but wouldn't it be too haunted? This London flat of the family was plenty, lovely, really. With the Denbury resources, I could visit home often... I felt torn, raw. I wanted to look forward to our wedding, our home, our life, but I could hardly move, think, feel...

Mrs. Northe was watching me, likely making clairvoyant notes about my mood, but she said nothing. I noted the dark circles under her eyes, and I wondered if she too had wept the night through. I debated about telling her about Maggie's spirit, but Jonathon interrupted us before I opened my mouth. Nathaniel and Lavinia were standing close behind him.

"Three o'clock?" he asked Mrs. Northe, coming close to kiss me upon the head. She nodded.

"Will you be seeing me off or coming with me?" I asked quietly, trying not to let the desperation I felt edge into my tone.

The idea of taking another trip without him, the idea of being parted as we'd been several times during our ordeals was too much for me to bear at present. Yet I had to allow for him to deal with whatever business he had to arrange and manage. But for my part, I could not leave my father in such an emotional lurch as I had left him. I owed him my return and reassurances of my love.

Jonathon wound his arms around me as he sat next to me on the divan. "New York has captured my heart, because New York's prettiest, bravest girl has agreed to become my lady. Wherever we can remain furthest from the dark magic, there is where we should be. Though I would be anywhere. Provided I am at your side."

"So New York?" I asked hopefully. "With seasonal trips to London, of course," I added.

"A home in Greenwich, New York, to match mine in England. Rosecrest must remain in the Denbury name, and its wing shall be rebuilt, but I can't bear beginning our life and family there..." He shuddered. "Too haunted."

I nodded and kissed him my agreement, all my worries fading into excitement for our future.

The steamer trip was pleasant and blessedly uneventful. And very quiet. None of us dared speak much. None dared try to encapsulate what had happened. The scope and depth was too vast to digest, too overwrought and unbelievable, even for those of us who had experienced the Society's madnesses before. The fact that none of us had been carted away to England's infamous Bedlam was as impressive as coming out of it alive.

For most of the journey, we sat on the main deck, in a line of reclining chairs, and watched the water. A line of fine funereal clothes one after the other, our deck chair procession afforded us quiet and space from other passengers. The unchanging expanse of water allowed our tired bodies and minds to rest whenever rest claimed us. Otherwise we exchanged fond looks, held hands, and let tears come as they would.

I couldn't shake the knowledge that Maggie was there with us too, down below in the cargo hold. Her body crossing the great ocean with us. I hoped the great beyond was treating her beautifully. I was grateful Mrs. Northe took the lead on the transfer of her body once we docked in New York, Lavinia stepping up to assist. Those kinds of logistics I simply couldn't face.

We collectively returned to Mrs. Northe's home and fell into respective tasks. Our group reverie was broken by the crazed bustle of the city that intruded upon contemplation. Lavinia and Nathaniel went their separate ways, needing to check in with various friends and family members who were nearly hysterical about their disappearances.

I knew my duty at hand was to reach out to Father, but I wanted Mrs. Northe's advice and protection as I was unsure what sort of anger I might be facing. Jonathon kissed me softly before going off to first open a New York bank account and then talk to a broker about a home. He wanted to keep busy.

I was left alone for a moment in the parlor while Mrs. Northe checked in with her staff about the goings-on during her absence. I took a long, deep breath and tried to stop myself from pacing a hole in her parlor carpeting.

"Keep yourself together, Natalie," I demanded. "It's over. It's all over, and you have to let go or you won't actually have won…"

My eyes fell upon a letter that the maid had left sitting out at Mrs. Northe's writing desk. It was in familiar handwriting. It was addressed to her and to me. And the moment I saw it, tears sprang to my eyes.

I found Mrs. Northe midconversation with one of her newer staff. The look on my face had her immediately escorting me by the elbow back to the parlor.

I lifted up the note in a shaking hand. I saw Mrs. Northe swallow hard. We sunk together onto the golden velvet settee, and I opened Margaret Hathorn's last letter.

Dear Natalie and Aunt Evelyn,

By the time you read this, I am likely dead. Writing that phrase has finally driven home to me the reality of what is about to occur. I can't say exactly what will happen or how it will. All I know is that I am slated, scheduled, and prophesied to die.

I wish I knew how to prepare for this inevitability. Karen has envisioned it, in two different ways. I have dreamed of it with a sort of surety. Auntie, you'd call it prophecy. And it was very clear, from

Karen's visions and from my own dreams, that I could either be tortured by the Society and used as a sacrificial lamb, or I could try to take down the devil with me.

I was never very brave, you both know that, but I was always curious. Look at me, talking about myself in the past tense already. Perhaps that's for the best. I do hope you'll make sure I'm wearing an exquisite dress when I am laid out for mourning. And you'd both better mourn bitterly. If I can, I'll be watching. I don't exactly know how much control I'll have over being a ghost. Haunting you might be terribly fun.

Karen has been giving me laudanum so that I can sleep, as I've been having such fits, and I must say the effects are most pleasant. I can understand how so many women of our station are a little too fond of the stuff. It manages to deaden the abject panic that facing death creates in a girl.

Dear, dead Amelia—who I now know for certain was Karen's lover (ghosts don't care much about keeping proper secrets. Still, scandal! But the scriptures say judge not so I'd best not be judging before I'll soon be judged)—has come to visit. Amelia is what you'd call my spirit guide. She promises she'll be with me when the event happens and will help ease any discomfort, fear, and pain. She'll help me let go.

There's a great deal of bloodletting and various violations if the Society is left to kill me. I think, if our plan of holy water does the trick and I take the initiative, the pain will be less. At least, that's what I fear the most. Pain.

Here I thought I'd fear a season without suitors. A poorly made dress. A betrothal to a hideous old man I hated. Unjust gossip. Being thrown from society—well, I've already faced that fear. After dreaming of a bloody, gruesome death night after night, suddenly millinery and couture all seem very faint and somewhat laughable.

What you mustn't do is blame yourself. I know you will. I can't know if anything would have been different. We can't know that. All I know is that something is about to come to a head in England, and I am supposed to be there for it. As part of the grand finale. The Society craves a coming out party, a debutante ball. I would like to make sure it is instead their final curtain call.

I knew what I'd been doing wasn't right. Now I'll pay for it. Magic has consequences. Courting evil can't be undone. But, I confess, it was delicious at first. You know I always did love a good delicious secret, a hint of scandal, something seductive and grand. The demon and the vein-like net of its powers certainly knew that. What an easy fly I was for that web. I'm embarrassed. I'd crave a good old, normal deflowering by a handsome stable boy over all this shame and guilt.

At first I didn't understand what I was dealing with. I knew I'd gotten in too deep, that I was under the influence of dark magic too far to ever be truly free of it. I let it nearly take my life and that of Natalie. I don't remember much about that; all of it feels like a terrible, distant dream. Being in Chicago has helped me regain perspective, and I no longer see through such veiled eyes. It was smart of you, Auntie, to send me away from the hazy fog and into clearer skies.

What I had once exoticized and romanticized I now abhor, thanks to Karen and ghostly Amelia's efforts. They have withheld nothing from me in terms of spiritual realms and gifts. I see now just how backward the Society is from anything useful and fair in the world. An enemy to all things holy, they are the direct inversion of corporeal and spiritual progress.

Amelia promises me I'll walk with the angels for my sacrifice, lifted up as we send demons to their depths. When you read this, and I hope you both remain alive to pray for my spirit, for you'll know how it all turned out. Spare fond thoughts for me.

None of us can be exactly sure if a past life will return into a new life, but at least I'll have done right by this body, in the end, after having done wrong. I hope I return female. I know we don't have the rights and the votes that you want us to have, Auntie, but think of all the beautiful dresses... 'That'll be the hardest thing to leave behind. Maybe God will be very kind and bring me back as landed aristocracy! That's only fair...

Be well. Live well. Every day, be sure to steer clear of that which dragged me under and which will be the death of me no matter what I do.

With love, prayerfully and sincerely,

Maggie

I looked at Mrs. Northe, and we just watched each other's tears roll down our faces for a moment before I managed to choke out a few words. "She...did. She visited," I finally murmured. "Her spirit."

Before Mrs. Northe could answer, my father was shown in to the parlor. My face went red. I ran to him and threw my arms around him. My head hurt violently from all the crying.

"I'm so sorry," I gasped. "I'll never disappear again."

"I don't understand it," Father replied, clutching me tightly. "But your mother came to me and said it had to be done, that you had to go to England and face the enemy. I always trusted her. And I see so much of her in you. And thank God you're alive for me to see that."

I pulled back and lifted up my finger to show Father the ring. "Before we saved each other's life, again, we got engaged! He's a good man, Jonathon. Please don't let any of this damage your opinion of him."

Father smiled weakly. "I don't really think I have a choice about accepting him into our life. But at least he's an honest man. A haunted, but honest, man."

"The haunting is over, Gareth," Mrs. Northe assured. "Terrible tolls were paid. But the haunting is over. Justice is being served. There's still mess to clean, but Lord Denbury's part in all of it, and thusly Natalie's, has come to a blessed conclusion. And he truly loves your daughter. That is abundantly clear."

Father breathed a sigh of relief as Mrs. Northe continued. "Now please, Gareth, I insist you stay for dinner." She turned to me with a sparkle in her weary eyes, her body straightening to fully inhabit the beautiful blue dress she wore. "Finally, that engagement supper I've been wanting to throw you!"

Chapter Twenty-Nine

We had the loveliest dinner we'd perhaps ever had. Mrs. Northe sent word to Lavinia and Nathaniel, Reverend Blessing too, even the enigmatic Senator Bishop. Everyone was in a festive mood, so glad to have a fine dinner in a lavish setting without fear of demonic arrival and bloodletting between courses.

A huge weight collectively lifted from our shoulders. Maggie's letter had given both Mrs. Northe and me a much-needed closure and perspective to our grief and guilt. The weekend would bring Maggie's funeral. In the meantime, there was life to live and love to celebrate. When Jonathon returned to the Northe townhouse to tell me he'd found some lovely options of townhouses and flats for us to consider and warmly greeting my father as if he were greeting his own, I refused to let go of his hand.

Mrs. Northe opened the finest champagnes and toasted to us many times. The bubbles went delightedly to my head. We talked about utterly meaningless things. Senator Bishop told a few scandalous jokes that Reverend Blessing laughed the loudest at.

Not one of us said one word about blood, magic, death, or demons, and I couldn't have been more delighted.

At one point, having eaten so much rich delicious food and imbibed a bit too much champagne, I laid my head on Jonathon's shoulder. When I woke up, I was terribly disoriented. I was again in Mrs. Northe's guest room. My father was asleep in a chair. When I sat up, a ray of sunlight hit me directly on my aching forehead. I woke Father with my subsequent groan.

"It isn't that I didn't want to bring you home," my father rushed to explain as he rubbed his eyes, "and I wasn't about to leave you here, but Mrs. Northe said the dark magic…"

"Carries traces with it. Yes. We'll have to slough all of it off, day by day, prayer by prayer," I murmured. Father fetched me a glass of water, and I downed it eagerly.

"I have to go to work. Will you be all right? Jonathon is out on business again, he wanted me to tell you. Evidently he's buying you things," he said with a slight grin.

"I promise I'll be all right," I said, rising to throw my arms around him. Smoothing the dinner gown I'd borrowed from Mrs. Northe—I would have to do some shopping to believably be seen in the world as Lady Denbury—I escorted Father down and out the door.

Mrs. Northe was sitting in the parlor in a saffron day gown, smiling at me.

"Champagne," I said, making a face, rubbing my temple.

"The drug of the angels." She chuckled. "I bet you slept soundly, though, did you not?"

"Indeed. No dreams. No nightmares. Since I've been so vividly living the nightmares, thankfully none have come to collect their tolls for a little while."

"Go on back upstairs and pick something else out of the guest room boudoir. I *cannot* be seen with you if you're in an evening gown before noon."

I smiled and did what I was told. At some point Mrs. Northe must have had a few dresses tailored for me, because she was too tall for me to fit into them naturally. I glanced down at the hems that had been taken up, and my heart swelled at how amazingly I had been provided for by this worthy second mother who did so many things without any acclaim or fanfare, just quiet, subtle, thorough, thoughtful care.

Just as I put the final clasp on a lovely green tea gown that stirringly evoked the emerald of my eyes, there was a knock at the downstairs door, and as I descended to the parlor, I heard a brief discussion with the maid who answered and then soon came into the parlor, bobbing to us as she did so.

"A Sergeant Patt to see you, ma'am. Shall I send him in or would you prefer to see him another day? He was rather insistent. And very contrite…"

Mrs. Northe pursed her lips. "Oh, is he? Well. Send him in."

After a moment, in walked a tall, burly, mustachioed man with thinning blonde hair who didn't fit well into his tweed suit. He looked at Mrs. Northe and blushed.

"I've an apology to make, Mrs. Northe. And a request." The man then turned to me, noticing I was in the room. He cocked his head a bit, as if trying to place me. "I don't suppose you're a Miss Natalie Stewart, are you?"

"For the moment, I am," I replied. "I'll be married soon. Why do you ask?"

"Well, my sincere congratulations." He cleared his throat. "I have something that belongs to you, miss." He looked up again at Mrs. Northe. "I don't suppose you'd have a moment to come to the station?"

"Why?" Mrs. Northe said coolly. "Have you finally taken initiative upon my advice?"

"I've seen some mighty strange things these days," Patt said wearily. "Things I never thought I'd believe. Things I *can't* believe."

"And yet, we wake up the very next day needing to live a life we can make sense of, do we not, Mister Patt?" Mrs. Northe said gently, smiling, rising and gesturing for me to do the same.

"That we do, madame. That we do." Somehow that simple platitude seemed to mean a lot to him, as if he was forgiven his doubt, and he seemed grateful for Mrs. Northe's gentleness in the face of having being ignored.

"To your precinct, sergeant?" she said brightly.

"If you don't mind. And then, also if you don't mind, there's something else I'd like you to see."

A few blocks walk, we moved in silence, as the sergeant's awkwardness around women was rather painful, and there wasn't any small talk to fix that. I assumed this was heightened by the fact he didn't seem to like apologizing to women, either. I had to keep myself from grinning. Mrs. Northe had gone to the police, was not believed, and now, the truth would out, unbelievable as it was.

We first went up the stoop to the precinct front door, but he gestured next door, where there were a few men in police uniforms blocking the entrance of a simple Federal-style building and speaking in frightened, hushed tones.

"That's next," Patt said. But first he led us into a modest office with a deal of file cabinets, chairs, and a few ceramic mugs that had been left on worn desks. The mug nearest me had dark fluid of indiscernible contents. Likely crude coffee. Perhaps dashed with alcohol.

Patt withdrew sets of deeds from a wooden file cabinet. He handed them to Mrs. Northe.

"These are the addresses you suggested," he stated. "All along Park Avenue, down to Grand Central depot. Every one of them belonging to a company. I assume you recognize the seal."

I saw the red and gold crest of dragons, the seal of the Master's Society. But only now did I truly see the great irony of the crest.

I had thought upon first glance that the dragon's tails were entwined in a show of strength. But upon a closer look, I noticed the sharp point of each dragon's tail was piercing the other in the heart. It was, simply, a crest of powerful beings killing one another. It was a hopeless crest. Somehow in hopelessness Moriel saw power. And in that moment, all I could do was pity him, even after all he'd put us through. For I simply couldn't understand the lack of conscience, of empathy, of humanity. The vacant and cruel look in his eyes was indeed the most horrible thing, even despite all the bloodshed and victims. I couldn't bear the idea of such an unconscionable look spreading. I would rest better at night once that pit of despair had been executed so that such an example could never more be set.

Patt then reached into a drawer and pulled out something thick that was covered by a yellow file folder. He plucked a leather-bound journal out of the folder, a few pieces of paper bordering the book. A book I knew quite well indeed. I bit my lip.

"I believe this belongs to you, Miss Stewart."

He handed me my diary; the pages that had chronicled the whole of meeting Jonathon, falling in love with him, and saving his life. Pages that spoke of befriending Maggie and her first descent into the madness she so bravely sacrificed herself to make up for.

Tears came to my eyes as I took it and held it close. "Thank you."

"I'd like to show you one of the addresses, right out the door," Patt said, gesturing us out again. "My men found relatively the same thing in each of the apartments or offices along the avenue." The tone of his voice indicated he was still shaken by what he'd seen. "How...large is this 'Society' network, do you believe?" he asked quietly.

"We have no idea," Mrs. Northe replied. "Lord Denbury and his associates tried to trap as many of the leaders in England as possible, but that was only three. They are in custody and will be awaiting trial. Those I spoke with there hope to flush out as many conspirators as possible. They do have operatives here, clearly, to do something of this scale, though I think all the financing began in England."

"There are international ties," I added. "At least, I know one of the "Majesties" was foreign, possibly Italian. Another French. Old, forgotten aristocratic lines."

"The financing has its fingers here, too, to have pulled off these kinds of buried leads and various payoffs," Patt stated. "And those frequenting Wall Street have increasingly big pockets, our recent depression notwithstanding. The rich still seem to stay rich even in decline. We will be keeping an eye on any connections."

"Good," Mrs. Northe replied. "Very good."

"Are there any other operative names you can give us from your experiences?" he asked, taking out a notebook to write down anything she mentioned.

"Doctor Preston was killed by his own reanimate creation," Mrs. Northe began, speaking nonchalantly. "Mister Crenfall, the original broker of the Denbury portrait, lost his mind. Though an eye should be kept on him as it was his numerics that gave us these addresses. The mentally ill still have plenty to offer the world in information and perspective. And then, of course, there are the demon-possessed lackeys and servants. They've a certain look about them. Glassy and animal-like around the eyes. Their movement is often a bit stilted."

"Right," he said, writing down words haltingly in the pad, as if trying to make that seem like a normal detail of a normal case.

"If I see any, I'll be sure to alert you," Mrs. Northe assured. "Though

I do think we've struck to the heart of the matter. If you have further concerns, as I am hoping our *personal* involvement in these matters is at a blessed end"—she included me in her gaze, and I nodded agreement—"please contact Senator Bishop. The senator has a...particular investment in investigating any sorts of occurrence that is...out of the ordinary."

"Indeed, I've already spoken with him. His clerk, oh, pardon me, his... *Chief Inspector*"—he said that with a grimace, as if the word didn't quite fit, almost as if it were blasphemous—"Miss Templeton is already down the block, seeing for herself."

Ah, yes, of course. A *chief* most certainly couldn't be female. Were the police actually employing women? I'd heard of a matron in one of the precincts; that was a sensation in and of itself. Women had always served in one way or another, but to be at the head of anything was unprecedented indeed. Exciting. It must be a very special branch.

"Oh, good." Mrs. Northe beamed. "I've not seen *nearly* enough of Clara these days."

"You two know each—of course you'd know each other..." Patt grumbled.

Sergeant Patt led us up the nearby stairs of what appeared to be—or have been—a law office. He waved the uniformed patrolmen at the door to the side of the landing.

"*More* ladies?" one officer murmured to another at the door. "What does the sarge think he's doing? Ladies shouldn't be exposed to this sort of devilry."

Mrs. Northe turned and smiled, making the officer blush under his cap for having been overheard. "But when we *are* exposed to such horrors, as the devil plagues men and women alike and equally, it's then up to us to help prevent it from spreading. Don't shelter us, officers. Listen to us. Respect our knowledge and expertise, which is why we are here. If you did so without judgment, your force would be far better informed."

They simply bowed their head, and I held back a smile of triumph as we entered the building. My smile soon was wiped from my face as I beheld the devil's laboratory.

One of the large rugs was pulled back to reveal a sprawling mess of symbols and quotes painted upon the floor in a dark, brownish-red, thick substance. Blood. Some in thick tar. There were the familiar runes as used to carve into the flesh of possessed bodies and of the reanimate dead. There were the numbers in their reversed golden ratio. There were quotes from arcane black lore that did not sound like books anyone, lady or gentleman, should read. Symbols of all faiths were inverted and turned on their side, shifted, askew, repurposed for the inverse of love and guidance, instead fostering misery and misleading woe.

It was all very similar to the floorboards of the Rosecrest dining room. This was the ground work for a portal to one of the "'devils' walks'" the Society opened in Rosecrest.

What I didn't see at first, due to the pocket doors having been closed in the entryway, was perhaps the most actively alarming thing of all. The evidence of an all-out strategic attack...

The sergeant returned us to the front of the building, to a main office with a lovely bay window which was closed, facing the busy Park Avenue. By the window was a device that looked like a propeller, attached to a bellows that was then fitted to a steam pipe that went to another area of the building. Before the propeller was set a metal trough filled with dark red powder. The chemical horror. What the Society so sickly called "The Cure."

Next to the device stood an elegant woman, older than me but younger than Mrs. Northe, in a matching linen jacket and dress trimmed in elaborate black detailing, a white lace blouse with a large cameo at her throat and full skirt; the full ensemble of dark green accented bright, nearly yellow eyes framed with dark blonde curls kept neatly beneath a green felt hat with a bit of a black veil. She was scribbling with a golden fountain pen into a notebook cupped in her palm.

"Miss Templeton," Patt said quietly. She looked up, and her pretty face lit. She greeted Mrs. Northe with a dazzling smile and kisses on both cheeks.

"Hello, Evelyn, it's so good to see you! Though I wish under better circumstances. Rupert told me you were instrumental in bringing this "Society" to the attention of the authorities. Thank you. I know the city will never appreciate you as it should, but I always do." She turned to me. "And you are, young lady?"

"Miss Natalie Stewart," I replied. "Pleasure to meet you, Miss Templeton. I've met Senator Bishop at dinner. He seems very wise and kind."

Her golden eyes sparkled. "Oh, yes. He is. And oh, yes, I've heard of you."

I furrowed my brow. "I'm not sure if I should be flattered or worried."

Miss Templeton winked at me.

"Scenes just like this, ladies," Patt interrupted, irritated by ladies' niceties, "were found at all the addresses I shared with you. Similar disturbing things scrawled on the floors and walls with only God knows what as paint. Generally a body starting to stink somewhere under the floorboards. Don't know if the bodies were sacrifices or just someone in the way at the time, we're trying to determine the links. Maybe they were storing them for that...reanimation you were talking about. Hell if I know." He grimaced and gestured to the contraption before us. "And *all* of the properties were fitted with a device poised to blow that powder out unto the New York City streets."

"You'd have had endless riots on your hands," Mrs. Northe said in a horrified murmur. "Any further holdings must be brought to light, though I do fear what's already fled underground. I am glad to hear you put Stevens in custody. If you hadn't? I have a feeling these fans would have started to blow and you'd have a volatile mess. All the way downtown."

"The city in chaos," Patt agreed, his round face ashen. "So I suppose that's what the Society wanted?"

Mrs. Northe nodded. "And in that chaos, gain assets, seize properties, make new disciples, and begin to influence leaders. That's my belief, though someone would have to ask the devils directly for confirmation."

"That seems to follow," I murmured. Miss Templeton said nothing but scribbled with impressive speed, all without taking her eyes off us.

"I'm not sure who was poised to give the order to strike," Patt said. "But thank goodness no one did."

"Possibly Stevens, possibly the "Majesty" in England. I wonder if we'll ever know the time frame they targeted. Do be careful disposing of that, sergeant," Mrs. Northe said, gesturing to the powder.

"Oh, we will." Patt assured. "Already had to subdue and sedate several officers who first came in contact with it. Then I remembered the articles." His round face flushed red again. "And I remembered what you said to me. And I'm sorry for not having taken it more seriously, sooner," Patt said quietly, looking at me in the apology and then back toward the interior of the office, bewildered. "I just don't understand how people could be so elaborately diabolical."

"Some people, a few. Not sane ones," Mrs. Northe reassured the sergeant. "Unhinged creatures urged on by the negative spirits of all that is horrific about humankind. Demons aren't corporeal unless imbued with the power to affect human will and conscience. The Master's Society tried to harness raw evil, congealed it, and sent it unto the world. Those working for them were simply under the influence. And not powerful enough to shirk off the yoke." Mrs. Northe spoke so eloquently and sensibly she made everything, even the most trying theories, make sense.

Patt furrowed his brow, having difficulty accepting something so vague, so gray in the areas of good and evil, so diffuse. However, to his credit he did not argue.

"Cleaning crews are painstakingly taking care of every site. Is there anything you think we might be missing?" Patt asked, genuinely asking for advice. Miss Templeton seemed just as interested in the recommendation.

"An exorcist. And a medium," Mrs. Northe replied brightly. "The most important part of the cleaning is all the things you can't see with *average* sight." At this, Patt looked very worried. Mrs. Northe smiled. "Never fear, sergeant, I'll send our friends to you. Reverend Blessing and Miss Horowitz. Now the reverend is a black man, and the medium is a Jewish woman. Both of them are the finest at their trade that I have ever met. So if you or any of your men give them any trouble or various intolerant slurs, I assure you you'll find trouble again on your doorstep—"

"Understood, Mrs. Northe. I will see to it he is denied nothing and escorted by my finest and most trustworthy."

"That better be a sound promise. We live in uncomfortably intolerant times, Sergeant Patt."

"And I'd rather not promote intolerance further, Mrs. Northe, truly," Patt said with weary earnestness. I remembered some of Father's scholarly friends discussing the fight for being considered human that most Irish immigrants had faced when arriving upon New York shores. Maybe the cruelty of human bigotry was something he could understand. The ruddy-faced sergeant shook his head. "An exorcist. And a medium. Heaven help us."

"Heaven most certainly did," I replied, beaming at the mention of Blessing and my dear friend Rachel who I would be so thrilled to see again, after she'd lent her aid in Chicago. Though I'd not be coming along on any of this reported cleanup. My time with all this was at its blessed end.

"Do keep me apprised, sergeant," Mrs. Northe said. "And I appreciate your showing us this. The Society has put us all through quite the trial. None so much as our brave Miss Stewart here. If you're going to finally deign to thank me, she deserves far more thanks than I."

The sergeant bowed to me. "I can't say I believe everything I read, Miss Stewart, not at all, but I do believe you must be a very brave young woman, and that's to be commended."

I blushed, clutching my diary tighter under my arm, wondering just how many persons had read all my kissing bits. I'd written rather rhapsodically about Jonathon and our first explorations of passions. I hadn't had time to redact them before the diary had found its way into Father's hands...

"I'd love to interview you, Miss Stewart, about all you've been through," Miss Templeton said quietly. "I truly value your insight. It would be such a gift."

I nodded. Something about the woman made me want to trust and confide in her. She was like a younger Mrs. Northe, and I liked the idea of having elegant, elder friends.

"After she becomes Lady Denbury, Clara," Mrs. Northe said with a chuckle. "Let the poor girl and her poor lord alone for a bit."

Miss Templeton beamed. "But of course."

"Dinner, soon, Clara. I don't know *where* you've been keeping yourself of late, but you'd better not forget about us. Rupert's just not the same when you're not around. You know I hate it when grown men pout."

Another engaging sparkle flashed like a flare of flame across her catlike eyes, and she nodded with a prim smile. "Dinner soon, Evelyn. I promise."

The sergeant walked us out and scowled at his men. No one made any further comments to us. He thanked us again and returned to his precinct offices, darting up the stoop at a clip amusing for his large comportment. I'm quite sure he was glad to be rid of us, even though he was grateful for the information provided. I didn't blame him. This was bitter medicine to swallow. I knew that better than anyone.

Mrs. Northe and I decided to walk a route through Central Park upon our return. The day was gorgeous; the people strolling under parasols and in top hats were marvelous, the light through the dappled trees that grew taller and fuller every year was resplendent, the park ever a work in progress, represented promise and life. It was the perfect contrast to the sobering threat of the Society we'd bested.

There was a look on Mrs. Northe's face that didn't really match with the situation we'd left behind. It was engaged, almost playful. "What?" I asked.

"Miss Templeton. She's hiding something. She's good at hiding from minds like mine," Mrs. Northe said, tapping her temple. "Maybe a lover. Hmm. That would be interesting. I wonder how Rupert will take that."

"The senator?"

"Yes. I've always wondered about them. She's old enough for emancipation, no longer his ward, exactly, though he's pledged his life to her it would seem. Yet she hasn't gone out and gotten a husband..." She stopped short, blushing. "Forgive me, Natalie. I must not gossip. It is unchristian to do so. However, gossiping about people I care for is infinitely more amenable to my mind than all the troubles and grief..."

I knew Maggie would've loved the gossip. We were likely thinking the same thing but didn't dare mention her name. Instead, I turned the tables on Mrs. Northe and dared use a name I'd not yet felt comfortable using. But it was well past time.

"So. Evelyn. Tell me. Are you and Father..."

"We are. We will. Provided you are comfortable. We want to see you through your wedding first."

"I'm comfortable," I agreed.

"You called me Evelyn." She beamed. "That's a start."

I tucked my arm in hers and squeezed tight. "I love you," I murmured.

She took my hand and clutched it in both of hers, tucking it toward her heart. I felt a tear splash onto the back of it.

"And I you. From the moment I first met you, I wanted you as my daughter. I knew it had to be. I...I saw this moment. Right here. Walking through the park, my long-lost daughter and me, on a perfect New York afternoon..." She turned away to dab her eyes with a handkerchief. I thought my heart would burst.

"I am the luckiest girl in the whole of this great city," I murmured. I looked up at the beautiful blue sky and thanked all the forces of light that had gotten me this far by stubborn faith and more blessings than I knew what to do with.

We took the longer route back, arm in arm, me and my mentor and second mother, a bond that had saved my life. I'd like to think I'd saved hers too. At least her heart.

Lavinia came over for tea, sweeping into the Northe parlor in something just as black and dramatic as usual. Something about our earlier bout of gossip and talk of love and lovers made me bold, and so I asked:

"When is Nathaniel going to stop running from the obvious and marry you?"

Lavinia shrugged wistfully. "I've no idea. I can't force him. He is his own beast. A wild creature that will only stop pacing when he wishes. I know he loves me. But I'm not sure what that means to him."

"With your parents still having cut you off...what will you do?"

"I've found work for her," Mrs. Northe said with a smile.

"Via Senator Bishop," Lavinia continued excitedly. "He's associated with an office that quietly looks into paranormal goings-on in the city. They're selective and *very* secretive. Evidently they had only men as doorkeepers at their office for quite some time. But they all kept falling for the woman in charge, the senator's ward—"

"Miss Templeton? I just met her."

"Indeed," Mrs. Northe added. "It would seem the senator finally got tired of intimidating all the gentlemen doorkeepers, so Lavinia will be a great addition to their little cadre."

"Especially considering the experiences we've had," Lavinia added. "If you'd like work, I'm sure he'd like to talk to you, although the idea of

'Lady Denbury' taking a *job* doesn't sound quite right," she said with a wink and a smile.

"Miss Templeton did seem quite interested in talking to me," I replied. "But I'd prefer not to work in any field we barely survived... After all we've been through, I'm surprised you'd want anything to do with anything paranormal."

She smiled. "Has your time with our club, Her Majesty's Association of Melancholy Bastards, taught you nothing? We court this sort of intrigue!" She laughed. "No, truly, think about it, my friend. My name is *Lavinia*. A Shakespearean character who, in *Titus Andronicus*, was raped, her tongue cut out, and her hands cut off. No matter that it was a "family name," I made it my mission in my life that I would not let my name damn me. That I would live loudly and fully. That I would live as dramatically as I please, with no men making decisions for me that I would not make on my own as best I could. To take a job, a position, for a secret office? Something empowering and fascinating? Why, it takes that Shakespearean tragedy and makes it something glorious."

"Well played, Miss Kent." Mrs. Northe applauded.

"Indeed, I think it's lovely, Lavinia. While I go off to be a titled lady," I said with a grin, "we'll all have the best of adventures together. Safely away from any demons, haunted paintings, or reanimate corpses."

"Huzzah to that, my lady. No more of that indeed," came a familiar British accent lilting off lips I longed to kiss. Jonathon swept into the room with a bouquet of red roses for me. "Come, come, Lady Denbury, shall we house hunt? It's my favorite kind of quarry, lavish lodgings that can't run away from my title. Fit for a very pretty girl who can't run from it, either."

"As if she'd ever want to," I murmured, lifting my face so that he'd bend over the settee to kiss me. He did. I jumped to my feet, sliding my arm in his, holding the roses very princess-like in the crook of my other arm. "If you'll excuse us, ladies..."

Lavinia and Evelyn grinned, shooing us to the door.

As Jonathon and I descended onto Fifth Avenue, the bustle and swarm of New York before us, I had never felt so vibrant. So full of all the possibilities I could make manifest. The life and family I would lead and create. Mother's causes I would soon take up. All the art I would buy for Father's beloved Metropolitan Museum. The clinics I would help Jonathon open.

For all that the "Majesties" had wanted to take from society, we would do all the more to lift it up and serve the world with love. With the second chances we'd been given. With the lives we were lucky enough to still live.

I stared out at my beloved city and promised I would live to the fullest all that our infinite blessings dictated. For all that my beloved Jonathon and I had seen of tragedy, of darkness, of the double life of solid and shade, we were all the better equipped to shine, throughout this life and unto the paths that angels would tread.

Epilogue

From the Desk of Miss Clara Templeton
Internal Director, Eterna Commission, established 1865

Notes:

Senator Bishop gave me the case of Lord Denbury and Miss Natalie Stewart and the various issues that befell them for consideration.

Though I am not sure what it may have to do with issues of immortality that the Eterna Commission has been charged with examining, I find everything about the Master's Society to be fascinating. Harrowing, but fascinating. I do not envy all those two young lovers underwent.

I spent quite some time in the sergeant's office, examining the deeds in the sequence as the inimitable Evelyn suggested. Her clairvoyance never ceases to impress me, and I confess I am envious of the gift.

I believe my office could benefit from similar experiences of the teamwork displayed by the friends drawn into the Society's sinister web. Though I doubt Miss Stewart or her lord would wish what they lived through upon anyone.

The police, when it comes to many spiritual or inexplicable matters, seem more than happy to let women handle them. While the paranormal does not favor a gender, I do find that more women of this gilded age of ours remain open-minded about the inexplicable, and perhaps in some ways that may make us more vulnerable. We are, after all, the founders and purveyors of Spiritualism.

It was all very personal, in the end, this Mister Moriel's targeting of the Denbury family. To reanimate the corpse of the woman who rejected him?

How tasteless. But wars are waged over trivial matters.

People live and die over personal matters, not global ones.

And that's perhaps why Miss Stewart and Lord Denbury won, in the end. They too made it personal. Faith is personal. Resilience is personal. And the pasts, the energies, the ghosts and the angels we carry with us. Those are very personal indeed.

I have asked to interview Miss Stewart—once she's Lady Denbury— and glean from her a specialized wisdom this sort of trauma creates. I've been considered gifted for so long, I need to be challenged, else I'll become a bore to myself.

I need to make everything personal. That's the only way forward in all that I seek.

I have enclosed a letter from Lady Denbury responding to my request for a further interview, along with a package that I am humbled to have received. And I'm certainly up for this challenge.

Dear Miss Templeton,

I received your request for an interview along with the gift of the silver platter Senator Bishop sent as a wedding present. It's lovely and very generous of you both.

I have just returned from honeymooning in Paris, which was transcendently romantic. If you've never been, I insist everyone should go there with someone they love.

I'd rather not, at the moment, talk about what I've been through. Jonathon and I are determined to live our lives out from those dread shadows. We were so relieved to hear, just as we began moving into our Greenwich Village townhouse, that the wretch Moriel has been sentenced to death. The Society operatives have been rounded up and may face the same. Their radical madness is ended at last.

I wish we had received confirmation from Mr. Brinkman that his son has been returned to him. However, as he is a government operative, I am sure the man's details will forever be withheld from us. I must content myself with the surety that they are reunited. However, I would encourage persons in such an office as yours to keep vigilant.

Since I have refused an interview, I will grant you something more comprehensive, in the interest of making sure no one ever has to go through the sorts of things we have gone through. I have enclosed my diary for your perusal. These pages detail my first encounters with Societal magic and what we did to save my husband's soul.

However, as you are a lady, I ask you, please skip past all the kissing bits. And please return it to me as soon as you're finished. I never intended for the diary to become a novel for others to read, but it would seem it has become one. Let it be a lesson to keep faith and believe in love above all else.

Sincerely,

Natalie Stewart Whitby, Lady Denbury

The End

OF THE MAGIC MOST FOUL SAGA

More of Clara Templeton, Senator Bishop,
Mister Brinkman, and British Counterparts,
featuring appearances from Magic Most Foul
and Strangely Beautiful characters, in:

THE ETERNA FILES
Summer 2014 from Tor / Macmillan

&

The award-winning, nationally bestselling, acclaimed
STRANGELY BEAUTIFUL SAGA:
New, revised editions, coming 2014 from Tor / Macmillan

Acknowledgments

Thanks to Marcos and to the Hieber family for unconditional support of me and my work. Thanks to the readers who donated to the serialization of this project along the way, I cannot thank you enough for helping to sustain the venture. Thank you Perseus and Draco LePage for sharing my work so constantly and generously, that's only one of the ways in which you are Angels, Treasures and Family. Thank you to my fabulous editor Haleigh Rucinski for coming on board with this whole madness and being such a help and a dear along the way, I couldn't have done this without you. Thank you to my critique partner Cassandra Johnstone for fielding some of this half-cooked madness. With wine. Thank you Stephen Segal for the amazing cover and your services, you are a hero. Thank you to Melissa Singer, my upcoming Tor editor, for encouraging me to serialize this novel, it's been an amazing and fulfilling experiment and I cannot wait for our next adventures.

To my readers, you are why I do this. To God and the Angels, I promise to do my best in your honour.

CPSIA information can be obtained at www.ICGtesting.com
Printed in the USA
LVOW07s2320140916

504678LV00005B/150/P